THE HUNGRY DARK

MICHAEL COOLWOOD

COOLWOOD BOOKS

Chapter One

The night before the humans attacked, I went to meet the Hungry Dark.

On that cool night, the first of the Month of Falling, I felt as if my illness was crushing me. I needed to find beauty somewhere, anywhere and the dark was the only option I had left.

I slipped out of Mrs Noyer's restaurant as soon as my shift was over. Both moons shone down, picking my village out in indigo and silver. The serenity of the scene should have been breath-taking, but my illness had twisted the sight one too many times.

Even with my heart bound tight, my legs aching, and my thoughts shrouded in fog, I still felt a dull pain in my chest at the thought of choosing the dark over Ekzilo. Nevertheless, I strode towards the northern gate.

We're all outcasts in Ekzilo. We're wasters, deviants, foreigners and disabled. We're changelings, shapeshifters, and witches. There are even a fair few humans living about the place, but no-one would ever stoop so low as to call them that. My friend Teya is human, biologically speaking, but she's not *human*: she's one of us.

I passed Ekzilo's priestess, lighting lanterns with a brass-tipped pole. Green and blue lamps twisted away into the night like stars, guiding me onwards past fields, workshops and out through the hulking wooden gates at Ekzilo's northern border.

My breath hissed between my teeth as I descended the thirteen slippery steps to the cave entrance. Tension tightened my stomach as I approached the great iron door – all that protected the outside world from the dark inside. I'd never opened the door without Teya.

Wheels connected the bottom of the door to an iron track, meaning I'd be able to roll the door aside without Teya's help. I could just roll the door open and fill my night with more beauty than the preceding twelve, but, were she here, Teya would advise caution.

I squatted down and swept away a snaggle of fallen leaves, twigs, and hawcorn shells which threatened to jam up the wheels riveted to the door's lower edge. One time, I'd neglected to make sure the wheels and their track were clear and so, when Teya and I had needed to leave the dark in a bit of a hurry, the door had jammed open, leaving us vulnerable to fallen. One way or another, that's the sort of mistake you only make once.

My hands shook as I rolled the door aside. Stepping forwards, I smiled to the darkness. "It's just you and me, this time. I know you probably wanted to see Teya as well, but I'm sure we'll have fun together. Do you have anything interesting for me tonight? I bet you do." The Hungry Dark wasn't known for listening to those that ventured inside, but I didn't like to be impolite. Such respect was proper for my ancient enemy and revered friend.

Thick tendrils of shadow oozed out of the cave, creeping around my ankles. The dark wouldn't get far, not on a cloudless night with both moons beaming down. But it could still snatch at me if it wanted to.

I reached for the bracelet of teeth hanging at my wrist, and twisted one free. I popped it into my mouth and swallowed it whole, feeling its power radiate out from my stomach, a tingling, tangling sensation which made me shiver. I exhaled, and allowed power to shine out of my skin. Deep blue light poured from me, forcing the malevolent darkness back, and back, and back, until the chamber was safe to enter.

The chamber walls were a soft bone colour, now tinted blue by my light. Many years ago, the chamber had been small, the size of a bedroom, with a narrow fissure in the back wall that led to the rest of the cave system. Now, the cavern was house-sized, and the fissure had been shattered, leaving an enormous passageway in its place. No one knew why or how this had happened. Teya and I had concluded that something truly massive must have burrowed its way into the cave system. Or maybe it had broken out.

I strode into the chamber, tiny cyan flashes dancing in the light around me. Just over my head, a shadow tendril wriggled, seeking a way past my light to the mundane darkness at my back. My light sliced a path ahead, turning the cave from a wall of impenetrable midnight, to a roiling, seething darkness, to two deep pools of shadow. One more step, and the shadows fled, revealing two passageways forking away to the left and right.

The smaller passageway to the right led to the other ground level caves. The left passageway, nearly four times the size of its counterpart, led down to the dead city of Tenebro. If it was risky being alone in the caves, it was unthinkably dangerous to go solo into Tenebro, but the steps, the trap and the city beyond, soaked in the dark were calling to me. It would be rude not to answer.

The dark flowed around me as I strode down the left tunnel. A stream flowing around a stone. I brushed my fingers against the tunnel wall as I walked. The rock was smooth but curved in and out, with peaks and troughs that made it feel as though I was strolling down a creature's throat.

The edges of my vision fizzed. I tried to concentrate on the sensation of air moving in through my nose, down my throat and into my lungs. My breath felt ragged and thin. I tried to keep a grip on the flow of my magic, but it slipped away from me, flaring, illuminating far more of the path ahead than I needed.

My uncontrolled flare turned out to be fortunate. It meant that, when I reached the cavernous stairway that led down to Tenebro, there was still plenty of dead space in between me and the creature that was climbing up the stairs.

Its bulk completely filled the tunnel and was shaped roughly like a humanoid face, glowing a clear, cold blue in my light. Two black holes occupied the space where I'd expect eyes to be, but otherwise the face was unbroken. Smooth, like porcelain.

I should have retreated, but I didn't. I should have run, screaming, but I didn't. Instead, I let out a breath that had the suggestion of a shiver at the edges. I'd come into the dark looking for something to make me feel that life was worth living, and here it was. The weight in my chest had been dragging at me. No more. The fog in my head had made me feel as if I was drowning in wet clay. No more.

"Please, don't run." A low, moaning foghorn of a voice. Had it come from the creature?

I wavered, not knowing quite what to do. Pinpricks of darkness fluttered in my vision. My magic flooded from me, leaving nicks of pain as it burrowed out of my skin.

I stared at the face, took in two quick breaths, and then started to descend the steps towards the face. "I wouldn't dream of running. I'm pleased to meet you. My name is Melita Eklumigi."

"I am very pleased to meet you, Melita Eklumigi. Call me Vakua."

My light was fraying slightly at the edges, and the blue colour was beginning to dim. I slipped another tooth into my mouth and swallowed. I held my hands behind my back so the creature wouldn't see them clenching and unclenching all by themselves.

"What brings you to Tenebro's grand staircase on this particular night, Vakua?"

Vakua remained motionless. "I was just going to visit a village on the surface some call Ekzilo. Do you know it?"

"Oh... a little." My voice cracked on the last word. I clenched my fists tight behind my back. This was what I'd wanted. I needed to be calm. This was exactly what I'd wanted.

Vakua paused. "You're scared of me," she said, finally. "You think I want to eat you."

I took another step towards her. "You don't have a mouth..."

"It's possible that my mask is a living substance and, if a person were to get close enough, they would be absorbed through the surface and their life force would be subsumed to my will."

My mouth had dried to a husk. Vakua was entirely still. Three steps separated us, then two. I stopped on the final step and reached out. I brushed her cheek with my fingertips – cold, like stone. My flow of magic shifted, a thread slipping into my hand, up my finger and to my fingertip. A moment's hesitation stalled the thread, before the halting sensation fell away, and the thread flowed into Vakua.

Vakua's porcelain skin lost the dead cyan tint I'd been bathing her in. A glow bloomed in its place. Fresh bluebells from the first days of spring. The tunnel around us shimmered, truly radiant for the first time in maybe two hundred years. My power flowed into a truly perfect moment.

My stomach clenched, a dreadful emptiness opening within me. I was using far too much power. I withdrew my fingers from Vakua's cheek, letting the perfect moment fall away.

Vakua sighed. "You've been so kind to talk with me for so long. I wonder... but no. I can't ask any more of you."

"What would you ask?" I tried to keep my voice flat. I had a serious backlog of debts, and I yearned to offset some of them... But would helping this creature be a good thing? Would it balance out some of my debt – or make it worse?

"I can't tell you. Not here. You are a cave raider, yes? Come and see me some time. I live in the castle on level two of Tenebro."

"I've never been down that far."

"Is it too dangerous for you?"

"That would be putting it mildly."

The face nodded carefully. Perhaps she was avoiding sudden movements, given I was standing this close. It felt as if she was treating me like an easily startled hare. "Well then, how about I offer you a little something that will help you get down to level two? If you find it useful, it's yours to keep. Otherwise, you can return it to me when I see you next."

I couldn't accept any more help; I just couldn't. I opened my mouth to reply, but Vakua spoke first. "Wait, I recognise that expression. You are worried to be in my debt. Believe me, I am indebted to *you* for this conversation. It has meant more to me than you can know. Cave raiders never want to talk to someone who looks like this." The face towered over me. Blank; monolithic. "If I were to gift you a little something, it would merely be a token of my thanks for your kindness."

Her words warmed me. "Very well, I would be honoured to accept your token."

"I do not have it with me at present. I will leave it for you just inside the entrance to the... caves..." The blackness where Vakua's eyes should have been seemed to shift. "Something's coming."

"What? What's coming?"

"Stumbling feet. Shallow breathing. One of the fallen. You'd better go. Keep your weapons handy."

My hand strayed to where the sling containing my collapsible spear conspicuously wasn't. I'd left the house without any equipment. The world around me swayed, and I had to close my eyes for a moment. "I don't have any weapons." A snarl echoed out of the dark, followed by scraping, shuffling footsteps.

"What? Why would you come down here without any weapons? No, no, no! The first person to talk to me in years isn't going to die to one of the fallen. Not today. What can we do?"

Ignoring her panic, I sprinted back up the steps. In the tunnel that led back to Ekzilo, a figure skulked into view. It was the size and shape of an adult human, but its movements were sharp and uncontrolled. I wasn't close enough to see its face, but I knew its eyes would be milky and its teeth splintered. It was too late to back away – it had already seen me, glowing like a blue star. The creature howled ... and charged.

The tunnel was wide and smooth with no other exits. With the steps behind me blocked by Vakua I had no way to retreat, and I couldn't fight without weapons. My heart pounded, and my fingers tightened into fists.

I backed away towards the top of the stairs, thinking fast. The steps leading down to Vakua were made from huge unbroken slabs of marble, bordered by banks of loose stones which might once have been beds for subterranean plants. I dashed to the nearest bank and grabbed the three biggest rocks I could find.

"What are you doing?" Vakua called from below. "It's coming. It's coming. It's coming."

No time to reply. I turned, threw a rock at the fallen's head, and missed. My guts twisted. I hurled my second rock, grazing the mindless monster and leaving a crimson gash above its left eye. The fallen howled in rage, put its head down and sped up. I dropped my third rock and released the hold I'd been keeping on my power. My bubble of cyan exploded, tiny bellflower bird shapes burst from my skin and fluttered away.

The fallen rasped, but didn't slow down. If anything, the light seemed to have enraged it further. I waited for one more teeth-grinding second before diving to the side, out of the creature's path.

It hurtled past me and met the top of the steps; unable to stop, it tumbled at bone crunching speed down towards Vakua. The sound of flesh on stone made me wince.

"Ah," came Vakua's voice, deep and faint, almost completely obscured by the crashing and thrashing of the fallen. "You know, I'm actually a little impressed. Better hurry up, Melita Eklumigi. That little hornet won't be slowed down for long."

The fallen lay prone, struggling to get to its feet. "Unless," Vakua said, "unless you would like me to snuff its little life out? I could do that for you. All you'd need to do is ask."

"No! I'll be fine. Thank you." I shouted in alarm. My pacifist principles might be a little more flexible down in the dark but they didn't stretch to killing something when I could just as easily escape. The fallen weren't sentient, but they were still alive and all life was precious.

Vakua nodded, slowly. "As you wish. See you soon."

I turned and ran, her words ringing in my head.

Chapter Two

My feet pounded against the dirt floor of the tunnel, my steps a drumbeat for my flight. A howl echoed out of the darkness behind me and my light was fading. I'd used up too much power whilst luring the mindless monster over the edge of the stairs. I could try to snatch a new tooth from my bracelet but there was no time to stop.

I hesitated at the final turn, realising that it wasn't going to be enough just to get out of the caves. The fallen could follow me into the mundane darkness if it wanted – out into the world. I would need to shut it in. It was impossible to know from the screams how far ahead of the creature I was.

I careened through the final passageway and skidded past the cave door into glorious moonlight. The fresh air was sweet and fragrant. I drew in two heaving breaths, then grabbed the handle of the massive iron door and strained.

Wheels screamed in their tracks as I finally got the door moving. The Hungry Dark snapped at me from inside the cave, but its looming maw grew smaller and smaller as I slid the door shut across its jaws. Then, my light picked out movement, and a snarl of triumph ripped towards me out of the darkness. I gritted my teeth and tried to haul the door across the last half-metre. The rusting metal of the handle scraped at my fingers; my feet slipped and slid in the rain-softened dirt. Only a sliver of dark was still visible, I was so close.

The fallen snarled, and surged forward, ramming its arm through the tiny gap between the iron door and the cave wall. The door crunched into the fallen's arm with a *snapping* sound which turned my stomach. The monster's hand scrabbled and clawed at the air. I dodged away and punched the arm as hard as I could, but that only made the thing angrier.

I snatched up a fist-sized stone and smashed at the arm. I struck it once, twice, three times. It screamed. It scrabbled for me. I lost myself, screaming in harmony with the fallen as I hit the thing again and again and again. The limb kept flailing as though possessed, until eventually something snapped. The thing inside hissed and drew its arm back into the cave. I grabbed the handle of the door and hauled it shut.

I collapsed to the ground, exhausted, and convinced I was having a heart attack. I breathed, rolling onto my back, my vision spotty, my chest heaving. I breathed.

Once I was sure my heart wasn't about to explode, I picked myself up, dusted myself off and started walking back towards Ekzilo. My legs began aching as I climbed the thirteen steps, and I couldn't get a good handle on what my mood was doing. Part of me was thrilled to still be here after my brush with death. More familiar parts of me wanted to curl up into a ball and cry. But at the very least I'd be exhausted enough to sleep tonight.

Vakua's final 'see you soon' lingered in my mind. I'd have to tell Teya about her. A creature that uncanny, that could also talk – that had a *name* – would definitely be something Teya would want to know about.

The lamps of Ekzilo glittered as I reached the gates. On my bad days, I thought the buildings in my village all looked the same. When I was feeling better, or at least not terrible, details shone out at me. Here, on Tolis' general store, the rafters had been carved with prayers for good fortune and blessings for those that passed through the doors. Graf's Whiskey Bar's windows were surrounded by lamps, and their light caught the wooden statues of tricksters and minor daemons outside the marshal's home, making them flicker with uncanny life.

The lights seemed to fade as I approached Mrs Noyer's restaurant. I was terribly grateful for her both housing and employing me. I owed her more debts than nearly anyone else in the village. It was... it was just I had spent a long time living with her, and that was a long time for the misery that leaked out of me to seep into the timbers.

I crept to my room, not wanting to wake anyone up. My legs burned, and I knew I only had moments before my fatigue would overwhelm me. I stripped off the sweatiest of my clothes, gathered up the drift of Kyrene's notebooks that lay spread across my bed and dumped them next to a pile of artefacts Teya and I had recovered from the dark, but not yet got around to selling.

My head still fizzed even as I climbed into bed. After work tomorrow, I'd find Teya and tell her about Vakua.

The next morning, I woke to find an iron weight had been surgically inserted into my chest. My legs felt weak and I could barely think. I tried to concentrate on what I needed to do in order to get ready for work. I couldn't let the Kaskado Disorder beat me. I needed to push through. I needed to get up. I needed to push through. I needed to get up. I needed to push through. I needed to get up.

Those two sentences rolled around my head, back and forth, to and fro. My limbs felt numb and useless. I was lying on my side, my right arm trapped underneath my body. Pain spiked down the arm as I lay on it but I still just lay there, unable to move.

'Move', I thought to myself, 'why can't you just *move*?'

I tried instructing myself, begging with myself, screaming internally. It took a full hour and a half to reach a point where I'd gathered enough energy to sit up, and then stagger to my feet. My legs felt heavy, and my head had been stuffed with cotton wool by someone with a warped sense of humour. I raked my nails across the underside of my left arm to try to wake myself up a bit. I had to run a hand along the wall as I walked to the bathroom to steady myself. Bathing, dressing and grabbing breakfast took another forty-five minutes, by which time I was definitely, definitely late for work. I always did this. I always let people down.

The stairs down to the restaurant creaked as I descended. Dozens of people sat at tables chatting happily; their noise wormed its way into my ears and burrowed me empty. I wanted to run back upstairs. Unfortunately, two people sitting cross legged at a low table had already noticed me, so I couldn't run away without lowering my status in the village even further.

I concentrated on the familiar smells of cabbage and fish broth, took in two deep breaths, and tried to focus on why I was here. I picked my way between the tables and approached the counter, where Mrs Noyer was industriously chopping vegetables, her greying hair scraped back into a ponytail under a cloth knotted around her head. Behind her, Mr Noyer, a slight man who was a little younger than his wife, was washing dishes.

"Welcome!" Mrs Noyer cried, before looking up and realising it was me. Her face only fell a little. "Hello, Melita, could you take over the cleaning from Thadeus?"

I bowed, took a cloth from Mr Noyer's outstretched hand, and got to work.

In Talvik, breakfast is traditionally a meal to be enjoyed by the whole family, but there aren't many traditional families in Ekzilo. We've generally been chased away from other places. Because of this, breakfast is more communal, and places like Mrs Noyer's restaurant are vital to that.

It was hard to concentrate on my cleaning at first, but I got into the swing of it. The dishes kept coming and I kept washing. I concentrated on the textures of smooth wooden soup bowls, the delicate grain of ceramic plates and the unpredictable notches in steel cutlery. For two hours I was kept gloriously busy whilst people came and went. I cleaned, I fried eggs for omelettes, I greeted customers. I lost myself in the work.

I was beginning to flag as the final customers left. I wanted to collapse into a chair and appease my aching legs, but there was still plenty to do. I had to push through. I started wiping tables down. After around five minutes, Mrs Noyer joined me.

"Your friend," she said, scrubbing at a stain, "is she okay?"

There was only one person she could be referring to. "This time of year is tricky for her."

"The family she lives with… they're worried."

My guts twisted. If things were that bad for Teya, I should have known. I'd been with her for the anniversary but if things had stayed that bad… "I'll talk to her," I promised.

"Thank you, Melita."

The door to the restaurant slid open, which was odd. Most people were out and about working by now. Three women entered the restaurant – strangers, dressed in rugged trousers and tunics made from thick, worn cloth. Farmers, perhaps.

I bowed to them. "Welcome. Please come this way."

I ushered the three women to a freshly wiped table, noticing that their sandals were clean; if they were farmers, then they clearly hadn't started work yet today. Were they newly arrived refugees from another village?

One had a scar on her cheek, another was bald and the third wore a cloth face mask. They had no missing limbs. They didn't have horns or eyes that leaked smoke. They kept eye contact with each other without difficulty. They looked like perfectly ordinary humans.

"Would you like anything to eat or drink?" I asked, a slight tremor in my voice.

The woman with the cheek-scar glared up at me, "Hey. Bring me some tea, would you? What do you two want?"

"Soup," said the bald woman.

"Yeah, soup," said the woman with the face mask.

I bowed. "I'll be just one moment."

I approached the counter and relayed the orders to Mrs Noyer. She waved her knife at the sink. I took the hint and walked behind the counter to finish the washing up.

I tried to concentrate on my work, but couldn't help sneaking glances at the women. Two of them had shoved their chairs away from the table so they were facing the windows that looked out over the street, their legs spread wide. The third's left leg was jiggling in short, jerky motions.

The people of Ekzilo are united by many things, but one of the key ones is the fact that every foul act that caused us to wind up here was committed by humans. My human parents exiled me fifteen years ago when they discovered I'd been gifted with magic and cursed with Kaskado Disorder. Humans shunned Mrs Noyer after the accident that scarred her face. Humans found Teya and her wife Kyrene starving and destitute, and rather than feeding and sheltering the pair, they marched them out of town. Supposedly in Talvik's great cities, humans still believed in the principles of tolerance and pacifism. To the humans in villages near Ekzilo, those principles were worryingly flexible.

"Melita?" said Mrs Noyer. She'd finished preparing the humans' orders.

I ferried the soups and tea over to the humans. Two of them glared up at me, but said nothing. I kept my breathing even and returned to the counter. Halfway there I realised I was clutching the tray against my chest.

"I can take care of the rest if you like," I said.

My landlady shook her head, slowly, but didn't look up from polishing the already well-polished counter. "You see that?" she said, so quietly I could barely hear her.

For a moment I had no idea what she was talking about. Then one of the women shifted in her chair, leaning back like a magistrate considering a distasteful opinion. Her tunic gaped open to reveal a knife in her belt. To see a knife carried so casually outside of a workshop was chilling.

Mrs Noyer leaned towards her husband. "Thadeus," she said, her voice low and urgent. "Go out the back and spread the word we've got a breach of the peace waiting to happen in here."

I kept watching the women, who in their turn were watching the street. Mr Noyer slipped out of the back door and slid it shut behind him. An idea struck me. "Should I try talking to them?"

"What about?"

"The great war. The reason why we stopped doing what they're thinking about doing."

"What are you muttering about back there?" one of the women shouted.

"Oh, nothing!" I said, my voice bright.

"Think we're not good enough to eat here?" growled the woman with the scar, rising from her chair.

"No, no!" I said, walking out from behind the counter, my arms spread wide. "I'm deeply sorry. Please, let me—"

The punch came out of nowhere. One moment, Scar was glaring at me. The next, pain crunched into my cheek and I staggered back, my eyes watering. I stumbled, but steadied myself on a table.

Baldy and Face Mask stood. For a moment, I let myself hope they were coming to help me. Then, one by one, the three humans drew curved, notched knives.

Chapter Three

The three women fanned out across the restaurant. Mrs Noyer edged towards the back door. She caught my gaze, her eyes wide, her lips parted. I shook my head and nodded to the exit. She dipped her head and slipped out the back door. She was safe. Time to run.

"Hey," said Scar, rapping her knife against a table. "Pay attention."

I could lose the thugs easily once I was out in the open. The trick would be getting past them. If I were human, I'd consider giving one of them a shove, kicking another between the legs and making a break for it, but these creatures weren't like the fallen, they were sentient. I couldn't hurt them.

Scar swaggered towards me, "We're done having wasters like you around, you hear?"

Baldy circled to my right, waving her knife in lazy arcs. That knife strengthened my resolve. Fighting wouldn't just go against my principles, as well as those of my nation, it would also be dangerously stupid.

Baldy grinned, sizing me up, but suddenly froze. "Grace! This freak is a witch. Check out its wrist."

My right hand darted to my left, covering my bracelet of teeth from view. My stomach growled.

"Show me your wrist, freak," sneered Scar.

I had an idea, but would it work? I didn't want to stoop to their level, or break principle, but that knife was pinning me to the spot. Gently, slowly, I slipped a tooth out of my bracelet and hid it in the palm of my right hand.

Scar flourished her knife. "Looks like you were right, Ada. Only one reason to have a bracelet of bones. It's a predator." She took a step forward.

"Please, no…" I shuffled back and held my hands to my face, trying to look small and helpless. At the same time, I slipped the tooth into my mouth.

Three things happened at once:

First, Face Mask said, "Grace, watch out, she might have…"

Second, Scar lunged forward to grab my wrist.

Third, I swallowed the tooth, reaching out to my power.

Magic sparked in my stomach. I called it up and I called it out. I was used to directing power to a certain part of my body and letting it emerge however it wanted. But this situation was different. I concentrated.

Power exploded out of my skin in a blinding strobe of green light. It ripped along my arms, up my neck and around my forehead. I staggered, half collapsing onto a table.

The humans screamed and threw their hands up. Scar and Baldy collapsed backwards, crashing into tables. Face Mask sank to her knees. My vision swam, but I dodged past Scar. I nearly tripped over Baldy, who'd tangled herself in a chair and was writhing around, making mewling noises.

Stumbling out into the street, I found the main road through the village deserted. It looked as if Mr Noyer had spread the word and everyone was hiding, hoping the humans would go away. There was no real procedure for responding to humans starting trouble, so I had no idea what to expect. One time, the entire village had lined up in front of the invaders and knelt to them, showing unity but refusing to be cowed. Resisting the invaders, but not fighting them. Never fighting. It was one of the ways we, exiles at the edge of the world, were able to feel like a real part of our nation, despite what our neighbours thought.

I darted across the road, making for the overgrown space between Ms Graf's bar and the noodle joint next door. I threw myself into the long grass, hoping the frilly white fronds would camouflage me from the road. I eased a few stalks aside, delicate foliage tickling my fingers, and stared at the door to the restaurant, barely breathing.

Face Mask stalked out into the street. She still carried her knife in one hand but was rubbing her head with the other. This made my stomach tighten into a knot. I'd hurt the humans. I'd only meant to distract them. By hurting them, I'd probably only made them angrier. I'd escalated the situation.

Face Mask yelled something back into the restaurant, then Scar and Baldy joined her on the street. They glared around; knives clutched in their meaty hands. Then they each snarled at each other – it looked, from this distance, like a blazing row.

I watched the humans as a naturalist would watch a brown bear prowling her territory. They were unthinkably dangerous, but fascinating in their own way. They strode towards my hiding spot, still bickering. They might be searching for new prey or they might have decided to leave. Staying low, I shuffled backwards, putting more grass between myself and the humans. The sawing, chirping songs of cicadas grew louder as I nestled deeper into the grass.

Only then did I hear footsteps approaching from the other side of the village, and a child's voice crying, "Dad?"

I turned and peered out through the other side of the field to see the Vidals' kid wandering down the road. The Vidals were new to the village and the kid really wasn't coping with exile well. He tottered along in that way small children do: arms thrust out a little way from his sides, head looking left and right. His face was screwed up in a mask of misery. "Dad?" he cried again.

Running feet in the distance - the kid's dad sprinted from the doctor's office, where he'd obviously been sheltering. He scooped up the kid and wheeled round without stopping, back to the doctor's. The humans roared, and gave chase. Mr Vidal made it into the doctor's office and slid the door shut behind him. I held my breath. My mouth was dry, my heart pounding.

Two of the humans ran right past my hiding spot. "Did you see where they went?" rasped Baldy.

"Yeah, in that building!" said Face Mask, struggling to keep up. They were still holding their knives. Surely they wouldn't do anything to a kid? But maybe...

I'd slipped up. I'd hurt them. I'd escalated with my magic to the point where they were now chasing a kid. I had to put a stop to this now. I wouldn't fight them, I wouldn't betray the spirit of pacifism, but I could divert their attention. I leapt out of my hiding spot. "I'm sorry!"

The humans swung around to face me, leers of delight splitting their faces. I knelt, the rough gravel pressing into my knees through my trousers. I lowered my hands to the ground and bowed. "I hurt you. I didn't mean to, but still, I'm sorry."

Scar walked towards me. She reached down, grabbed my shirt collar and hauled me up so that we were standing nose to nose. "You didn't hurt me, alright?" she said. "I was just surprised, that's all. Takes more than a little light show to hurt me." She held her knife up and pressed it to my cheek. The searing pain forced my eyes shut.

"Fight back, you little coward," spat Scar, her breath hot on my face.

For a moment I was tempted to obey. Principles were principles, but if Scar decided to put that knife to work... If she decided to put the knife to work I was dead anyway. I could die upholding the principle that had led to two hundred years of peace in our nation, or I could escalate the situation even further, have it spin out of control, abandon everything I believed in, and then die anyway. That wasn't a choice. I opened my eyes. "I'm sorry," I said. "But I won't fight you."

Scar dropped me. "We used to be a nation of warriors! Look at you! Pathetic."

I touched my cheek and my hand came away bloody. I knelt again and bowed. My voice shook as I said, "I'm very sorry." The air was thick and sluggish, only the cicadas song felt real.

Footsteps circled around to my right, then a wrecking ball drove into my side, knocking the breath from me. I yelled and sprawled onto the gravel. Boots kicked at my chest, my back, my legs. I wrapped my arms around my head and curled up into a ball, praying for it to stop.

A human spat, and something wet landed in my hair. "Pathetic."

Another set of footsteps approached and I curled up tighter. My side and my ribs burned with bright, fresh pain. I had just one thought in my head: 'Please, please let no-one come and help me.' I could take this by myself. I was used to pain. I deserved the pain. I was taking this for the village. For everyone I loved. I was making up for all the help they'd given me. I was finally, finally, doing something worthwhile.

"Come on, Grace, let's go," said one of the women.

"Yeah," said Scar, "this is too sad to be fun." She spat on me again before marching away with the others falling into step with her.

I lay still for a long time, unmoving, trying not to breathe. Eventually, when the footsteps had completely faded, I uncurled a little and immediately wished I hadn't. My back, my ribs and my face howled at the movement. Salt stung my tongue.

Footsteps approached. I whimpered and screwed myself back up into a ball. Even the fallen weren't as vicious as those humans. I tried to shut the fear out, concentrating on how my hair felt under my hands – soft, and damp with fluid that might have been human spit or my blood.

"Melita?" said a voice. It was Mrs Noyer. "Oh, spirits, she's hurt really badly. Thadeus, go fetch Teya. We've got to get her to the doctor." Light footsteps ran off. I felt a warm hand take mine and squeeze. "I'm sorry you had to go through that alone, Melita."

"Better me than any of you," I said, smiling up at her. She didn't smile back.

The next few minutes were a bit of a blur. Mrs Noyer helped me to my feet and half-carried me up the track and into the doctor's office. The office walls were lined by enormous wooden shelves packed full to bursting with medical texts, which blocked all the windows, leaving the place murky, soaking in gloom. Selia, the doctor, had brought a wheelbarrow of books with her when she fled her home, whilst Teya and I had retrieved more from an abandoned surgery down in Tenebro. One bookshelf, opposite the only clear window, was filled with medicinal plants – green, purple, and red herbs growing in small black pots. An enormous desk occupied much of the room, with two doors behind it. One led to Selia's apartment, the other to the surgery.

Mr Vidal and his kid huddled in one corner, but relaxed a little when they saw we weren't human. Selia poked her head up from behind the desk, took one look at me through askew spectacles and gasped, which was a little worrying. She sprang to her feet, clicking her tongue, and waved me through to the surgery.

Mrs Noyer helped me through the door and propped me up against a raised metal table. My vision blurred, my gaze focussing on trivialities. A hand basin. A chem-powered heat exchanger. A rack of glinting, pointy devices affixed to one wall.

Selia scrubbed her hands, then pulled on a white apron and tied back her short, greying hair. "Onto the table, please, onto the table. Clothes off as well, please. Off with them."

"What, all of them?" I asked, wincing at every movement.

"Well, I suppose you can keep your underwear on if you insist, but I must say it's very irregular."

I winced as I struggled out of my clothing.

"Onto the table, come on, onto the table," said Selia.

"Ow, ow, ow, arrrgh," I said, hauling myself up before lying flat on my back.

"Mm, very nasty," Selia said, peering at me over her glasses. "Very nasty indeed. I'll give you something for the pain, one moment."

I opened my mouth to speak, to tell her that the pain really wasn't that bad. But the movement opened up the cut in my cheek and it was all I could do to stop myself screaming. Selia jabbed a needle into my arm. I barely noticed the sting, and I started to feel fuzzy almost immediately. Selia started applying some ointment to my bruises, which smelled of thyme and was so cold it made me shiver.

"Excuse me," called a voice from outside. I thought it was probably Teya, although I couldn't be completely certain about anything with my head feeling quite so strange.

"Teya, is that you? Come in, come in," said Selia.

The door to the surgery slid open and my friend walked in. Sweat beaded on her forehead, her cheeks were flushed, and a couple of coils of hair had slipped free from her headwrap. Her gaze swept the room for only a moment before she focused on me and strode forward. "Melita, are you okay?"

"No," said Selia, "she isn't. Now, take this will you, Teya? I need to work on a few technical things and I could use an assistant."

Teya nodded and moved around the table. Selia held out a glass jar of black ointment.

"What's that?" Teya asked.

"A witch made it for me. Apply it to the bruises, then remove it with that little rubber spatula on the table next to Melita, there. Don't, don't touch the ointment once you have applied it, you understand?"

"What does it do?"

"It absorbs pain. Once used, we keep it somewhere else in case we want to apply pain for any reason later. Very safe, very simple, but if you touch any, *any* ointment that's absorbed pain, the pain will transfer to you. Got it?"

Teya nodded and started smearing the cold black ointment onto my skin. I felt the distant pain fade even further. "Is it working, Melita?" Teya asked.

"Mhm," I said, smiling.

"Can we have a small jar of this, Selia? It would be useful in our work."

"Of course, of course. I have some spare on a shelf outside, next to my emergency gin. Grab some on your way out. Call it my way of thanking our patient, here."

"Thanks, Doctor." Teya smiled down at me. "So, Meli. What happened?"

"Nothing really," I said.

"That's not what I heard," Teya said, dabbing ointment gently on my cheek. "I heard you stopped a rampaging pack of humans from going after a defenceless man and child."

"I'm not sure you can call it a rampaging pack if there were only three of them. It was nothing really."

"Well, nothing though it was, I think it's the sort of nothing that people aren't going... aren't going to forget in a hurry." Tears were running down her cheeks. She was ignoring them, concentrating on delicately covering my bruises with ointment.

"Are you all right, Teya?" I asked. "I'm sorry I haven't been around much..."

"Oh, don't worry about that, I'm fine, Meli, I'm fine. It's you I'm worried about. Those humans could have killed you. It looks like they nearly did."

I waved this away with my left hand and was pleasantly surprised when the movement didn't hurt.

"I'm serious, Melita. I'm so, so proud of you for what you did, but I wonder if it's selfish of me to ask you to take a little better care of yourself?"

I thought with a pang about the trip I'd taken into the Hungry Dark without her. "I'll try," I said.

"Thank you." Teya rested her hand gently on my head then got to work scraping a patch of ointment from my flank. "So, what did the humans want?"

"Oh, they just came here looking for trouble."

She frowned, chewing her lip. "There's a lot of trouble around at the moment. I was chatting to the Tolis family, and they said they caught grief from some humans when they were trying to trade for supplies. Had to give up half of what they had just to get the humans to leave them alone."

I groaned.

"Yup. And... well, Talvik's commitment to pacifism is great, just... just... at some point, if things get pushed too far, pacifism ends up as people getting away with whatever they want whilst you stand by and let them."

My mouth felt loose and my lips kept sticking together. "Meeting... meeting violence with violence only leads to escalation, Teya. If I'd fought... if I'd... if I'd fought back, they'd have come back. Greater numbers. Crushed us utterly. They left. They left... unfulfilled. And here we are, still strong. Still *us*. Still one with Talvik and our principles."

Teya smiled, softly. "How are you feeling, Melita?"

"Sleepy."

"She can go home in a few minutes," Selia said, fiddling around with something that felt sharp but not painful in my cheek. "I'm finishing up here."

"Will she be okay?"

"Oh, fine. I wouldn't recommend doing this again any time soon, but all things considered it could have been a lot worse." Selia stepped back. "Okay, there you go. You can put your clothes on now. You're going to need to sleep for the rest of the day."

My eyes had been drifting shut, lulled by Teya's hand in mine. Now they snapped open. "What? No, I was working at Mrs Noyer's restaurant. I was doing so well! I have to go back."

Teya squeezed my hand. "Meli, you were attacked by a pack of humans. People will understand. Would you be okay to look after yourself a little?"

I grimaced. She was right, I was being selfish. "Yes. Sorry, Teya."

"Thank you, little grebe, I'll see you home." She slipped a hand under my arm to help me up. I stood and stretched, checking for pain and finding none.

We set off back to Mrs Noyer's restaurant. It wasn't far, but even in that short distance, three people nodded to me. I was used to being benevolently ignored by almost everyone in Ekzilo, and being acknowledged felt confusing but not unpleasant.

At the restaurant Teya gently steered me towards the stairs. Mrs Noyer rushed over and thanked me so much that I found myself wondering whether I ought to get myself beaten up by a clutch of humans as a regular occurrence.

Once I was safely on my bed, my landlady discovered I hadn't eaten since breakfast and left to get me a bowl of rice, fish, and greens. This started to gnaw away at my mood.

Subtly, and without even noticing, I'd slipped. I'd been the one who looked after people for one glorious moment. Now, I was back to being the one people needed to look after. My mood started to creak downwards. The food Mrs Noyer provided felt like a rebuke and her further kindness as she and Teya ensured I had everything I needed served only to twist the knife in my mood and make me feel horribly ungrateful at the same time.

By the time I pulled the bedclothes over my head, I was fighting back tears.

Something, some sound, woke me up. In my dream-state, I was sure it had been a cry of alarm. I strained to listen, but the sound didn't come again. It was probably just a bird.

There wasn't much light coming in through my windows; it was either close to sundown or just past. I still felt dreadfully tired. If magic is used to take something from you – pain, fear, love or any one of a hundred other things. It often takes something else as well, something that you hadn't planned to lose. This time it appeared to have taken my energy. I lay on my bed, trying to decide whether I should get up and investigate.

Then I heard something else: a scream. A full throated, terrified scream. Electricity flashed through my heart, up my spine and into my brain and I was suddenly wide awake. Something was badly, terribly wrong.

I leapt to my feet, my legs screaming at me, and pulled on my clothes followed by my red leather coat. I pulled my spare stash of bones from a shelf in the corner, as well as my cave-diving pack. Shouts echoed outside, as well as the sound of boots thumping against wood, getting closer. It hadn't been a bird cry that had woken me up, I realised. It had been the cry of one of my friends. The door to my room shot open and I spun to face it.

Teya stood in the doorway, panting. "Melita, we've got to run."

"What's happening?"

"The humans. They're back."

Chapter Four

An explosion roared outside. Waves of screaming followed, washing over me. Threatening to drown me. "Three humans are doing that?"

"They brought friends this time."

I tightened the straps of my pack, then followed Teya down to the restaurant's entranceway, where I pulled on my boots.

"How's it going down there, Melita?" Teya asked. Her voice was low and even.

"Good to go!" I said, tugging my laces tight. "Got a plan?"

"Yeah, we hide in the woods till this blows over. I've got my crossbow, you've got your spear. We see off anyone who follows."

I shook my head. "Our friends will all be taking cover in the woods. Too many of us hiding in one place risks us all being discovered. We should hide in the dark. We're the only ones likely to do that, and the humans won't follow us in."

Teya shifted from foot to foot. "Fine, yes, fine, but we've got to go, come on!"

I leapt to my feet, my legs having loosened up a little. I nodded. "I'm ready."

"Good. Let's go." Teya smiled at me, and I knew everything was going to be okay.

I slid the door to the street open. Teya unslung her crossbow. She nodded. We stepped out together. It took me a long moment to adjust to the alien sight in front of me. The west side of Ekzilo was on fire. The bar and the noodle restaurant I had hid between yesterday were completely consumed. Smoke was billowing to the east. It smelt like autumn clearing fires rather than the ruination of everything I loved.

Teya and I ran eastwards along the main road, away from the flames, before turning north. We passed dark house after dark house. Hopefully, the occupants had fled. We rounded a corner and saw our little school, along with the pack of humans stalking towards it.

I dodged behind a tree, then slipped from shadow to shadow, heading north, praying the humans wouldn't spot us. Teya followed, her crossbow tracking the predators. She needn't have bothered, the humans were enjoying smashing the school's windows.

We drew level with the school just as the humans withdrew, having grown bored with their sport. I motioned for Teya to stop, but she shook her head and pointed. A woman staggered out of a house just south of the school. Mrs Vidal, carrying a massive bag. Her husband appeared next, their child in his arms.

The humans were tossing burning torches through the school's windows. Distracted, but not for long. I waved for the Vidals' to come join us but I was too late – they were already running towards the north gate. Their flight caught the attention of the humans attacking the school – predators smelling fear in the air.

"Oh, no…" said Teya. Together, we burst into a sprint. Two of the attackers grabbed hold of Mr Vidal and tried to snatch his kid out of his arms. The little boy sobbed whilst his mum tried to fight back. The humans cackled, jackals backlit by the flames consuming the school.

"Hey!" I screamed.

Only one of them looked up. I'd make them regret not listening to me. I slipped a tooth from the bracelet at my wrist, flicked it into my mouth and swallowed. Power bloomed within me. "Let them go!"

The human who had noticed me flapped a hand at her friend, who was punching Mrs Vidal. The creature turned away from her victim and saw me. She leered and said something, but her words were lost as the walls of the school burst into flames, the remaining glass windows shattering. The human took a step towards me, the rest of its cabal following. Behind them, Mrs Vidal picked herself up and scrambled to help her family, who lay unheeded behind the humans.

"Look at what we have here! Is that the one who attacked you, Grace?" growled a human, her shoulders rolled forward, her hands clenched – claws glowing amber in the firelight.

Grace had a scar on her cheek. I took a step back. The last time I'd seen her she'd been kicking me in the chest. I swallowed, the memory of the pain still fresh. Behind the humans, the Vidals slipped through the north gate and disappeared into the night. A tingling panic that had been keeping me from thinking clearly began to fade.

"Get them!" Scar roared.

"Melita?" Teya asked, raising her crossbow.

"Close your eyes, Teya." I'd used my power as a tool of defence once before, but I'd hurt them. I had to be more controlled this time. I raised my hand and concentrated. If I could pour my power into a beam, rather than a flash, I could dazzle the humans and not risk blinding them. I gritted my teeth as the power gathered in my palm. I could feel tingling, then burning. The power was squirming, aching to be set free. I concentrated on the image of a beam of light. The power burst from my hand into a tight needle of light, then a beam, then a shaft. I gritted my teeth, trying to reel the edges in, but something snapped in my head. My power shattered, flaring out. I groaned as pain stitched into my hand, but the humans *screamed* and threw up their arms to cover their eyes.

I grabbed Teya by the hand, "We gotta run."

Teya opened her eyes and grinned at me. Together, we sprinted towards the north gate. Behind us, our village burned, but it was only houses and possessions. Nothing important. We could rebuild. My heart was hammering in my chest from the exhilaration at having saved the Vidals.

Within minutes we reached the cave entrance. I paused to catch my breath, then reached up to grab the handle of the great iron door.

"Hold on," Teya said, "we might not need to go into the dark."

"What? Why not?" My voice sounded outraged, and terribly loud.

"Shh!" Teya grabbed my wrist and pulled me closer to the cave wall. I tried to stay quiet whilst my heart pounded.

"I thought I saw people moving down there!" yelled someone – possibly Scar.

The steps down to the caves were suddenly flooded with light. "Where? Near the trees?"

"Yeah. But I thought I saw some down there as well. Come on, let's check it out. We've got to drive the monsters away properly or they'll be back."

Teya winced. I pointed at the iron door to the caves. Teya nodded, reluctantly. Together, we rolled the door aside. Once we had a gap large enough to slip through, Teya fished a glow globe from her pocket, cracked the seal and held it high as we stepped into the snatching tendrils of darkness. The clean, clinical white light of the globe seared the darkness away on all sides. I took one last look behind us before rolling the door shut, trapping the humans outside.

The entranceway had grown a little since I'd last been here, less than a day ago. Rock dust and shattered pieces of limestone lined the floor. I reached down and picked up a few pieces of crushed rock and felt the fresh, dusty edges between my fingers. I dropped the rocks I had picked up one by one as we walked into the cave; they fell to the ground with a dull *clack, clack, clack*. Teya's light illuminated fresh, exposed patches of rock on the cave wall. Something had been here recently – something huge.... and that reminded me that Vakua had promised me a present.

"Hold on a second," I said to Teya, who didn't appear to have noticed the changes.

Teya swung around, sweat beading on her forehead. "Melita, they're right behind us..."

Teya's light glinted off a brass object lying on the ground in our path. It definitely hadn't been there when I'd last visited. I scooped it up. It was a gun, covered in springs and cogs connecting the trigger mechanism to a fifteen-centimetre barrel. We'd recovered several like it on previous expeditions. I'd always been tempted to keep one in case we encountered something really nasty down in the dark, but they were invaluable on the surface for hunting, so we'd always needed to trade away the ones we'd found.

Teya hesitated, but then peered down at my new find. "Remarkable... Pressure chamber looks intact. Charging handle looks good. Hang onto that, Meli. If we're going to hide down here we'll both need proper self-defence tools."

I nodded. I located the magazine release and pressed it, although it took two goes because my hands were shaking with adrenaline. A long cylinder rotated out of the barrel with a jarring click, which caused me to drop the gun. Teya caught it before it hit the ground and handed it back to me. She looked from my hands up into my eyes. "Are you okay, Meli?"

"Yes, yes." I nodded decisively and shoved the gun into my belt.

Teya smiled, but then frowned. She tugged her earlobe. Footsteps beyond the door.

"Let's go further in." I said.

We crept further into the cavern. Teya hesitated when we reached the fork. She looked from the right passageway, which led to the other ground level caves, to the left passageway which led down to Tenebro. I slipped past her down the left passageway.

Teya followed. The footsteps outside had faded, although I couldn't be sure if the humans had moved on or if we were merely outpacing them.

"Why are we heading left, Meli?" Teya hissed.

"Down to Tenebro, they'll turn back when they see the trap."

"We still don't know where that thing takes us."

"The trap's got to be better than facing the humans."

"Right, but..."

The familiar rumbling, grinding sounds of iron wheels moving against their track made my teeth grind together. The humans were opening the door. Teya and I shared a panicked look, before bursting into a sprint.

We flew down the tunnel, trusting our footsteps would echo so badly they'd be difficult to track. We reached the top of the stairs down to Tenebro without any packs of rabid humans catching up to us. I kept an eye on our rear whilst Teya caught her breath.

"You ready for this?" I asked.

Shouts echoed from behind us. Muffled, but much closer than I'd like.

Teya shivered, "Let's go. I don't want to take any chances. At least I know what's coming with the trap. Sort of."

"Atta girl, we've got this!" I flashed a smile, which Teya mirrored. I led the way down the steps, taking them two at a time. Half way down, I paused and checked behind us. We were in a bubble of light, surrounded by darkness on all sides – but the darkness wasn't perfect. A few patches near the top of the stairs looked less opaque, and the patches were growing.

I nudged Teya. "They don't give up, do they?" I tried to keep my voice calm and confident so she wouldn't worry.

Teya frowned, the skin around her eyes wrinkling. She tested the tension on the string of her crossbow. "No. They don't. I know you don't want to hear this, Meli, but they're fixated on us. They followed us into the dark, for the spirits sake! It feels like we could flee to Sirmo and they'd chase us all the way down."

It was my turn to frown. "Now that's a scary thought..."

Thudding bootsteps echoed out of the dark. Thoughts of Sirmo would have to wait. We had to get to the trap.

The bottom of the stairs to Tenebro were lined with bones – the bones of the people who got stuck in the trap. When Teya and I had first seen them, she'd suggested I take them with me to feed my magic, but I'd had to explain they were useless. The bones of the dead held no power for me, nor most other witches I knew. The bones were still useful in some ways, however. The humans would see them and turn back. They'd have to turn back.

In the past, Teya and I had stood on the last safe step, held hands, and stepped into the trap together. These days we knew the anticipation only made things worse. Driven on by the thudding footsteps of our pursuers, Teya and I stepped down.

Chapter Five

Darkness. A crisp, cold breeze played against my cheeks, bringing with it smells of wood smoke, autumn leaves, and olive flowers. A wood fire cracked and crackled nearby, whilst bell crickets chirp-chirp-chirped – their clear call ringing over the sounds of waves lapping on a beach.

I opened my eyes. I stood on the beach of a lake - only just visible in the twilight. Twin moons hung above me, their light struggling to break through the clouds. I felt puzzled for a few seconds. There'd been something I was supposed to remember. Nothing came to mind. Oh, well. If it was important, it would come back to me.

I turned and... had that campsite always been there? A ring of stones bordered a crackling fire, over which perched a metal table and a bubbling pot. Two chairs, one of which was occupied, sat facing the fire. Gravel crunched under my boots as I approached. A small, mean little headache needled at me.

The seated figure turned as I drew closer. It was Mrs Noyer, her shoulders wrapped in a shawl to fend off the cold. Her fingerless gloves gripped a metal mug and the salty tang of fish soup wafted towards me on the breeze. "Hello, Melita. Come, sit with me."

I stared at the empty chair next to her. Something was wrong with it, but I couldn't work out what. My landlady had a steaming bowl of soup sitting in her lap. She must... she must have made that for her husband? I couldn't see him anywhere.

Mrs Noyer looked from me to the bowl and back again. "Are you hungry?"

My stomach growled, which made Mrs Noyer smile. She held the bowl out towards me, but at quite a low height so I couldn't quite reach it from where I stood.

My legs were burning, and my heart hammered in my chest. I didn't want to sit down, I wanted to run from whatever was wrong in this situation. But there was nothing wrong. How could there be?

"Sit down, Melita."

"Mrs Noyer..."

"Sit down." Mrs Noyer's face was as calm as it usually was when she wasn't thinking about her children, but...

The night was cold. She'd been holding that bowl of broth very still and... the tip of her thumb was dipping ever so slightly into the soup – the soup that was still steaming from the heat of the fire. If that were my thumb, I'd have wrenched it away from the steaming liquid with a wince. Her face was completely still. She wasn't even breathing...

"You've worked it out, haven't you?" she said, her voice flat.

"I've worked *something* out..."

She rolled her eyes and dropped the bowl back onto the table. "Ah, well. I'll get you next time. How have you been, anyway? I haven't seen you for a week or so."

"I come here often?"

"Well not *here* but, well, basically yes. Don't worry about not being able to remember – I block myself from your memory. Oh, that reminds me, we talked about this last time you were here. Hang on..."

Mrs Noyer's face shifted slightly – she suddenly looked a lot less like my landlady. She pointed past me. I turned and looked. Above the lake, the

clouds were clearing. The fat, full moons shone down above us, surrounded by a chorus of stars. Off in the distance stood a mountain; its snowy peak
was reflected perfectly in the lake.

Mount Senmorta. I'd only ever seen photographs and heard stories of
its beauty. I shivered at the sight, feeling both tiny in the presence of the
mountain and part of this perfect, placid moment at the same time. "It's
beautiful..."

Mrs Noyer peeked into my peripheral vision. "I'm glad you like it."

"Did you make this happen?"

"I did."

"For me?"

"Yes."

"Why?"

"Because no matter how many times I try to get you to sit down – to fall
into sloth and never rise again, to be consumed by the Hungry Dark when
your light inevitably fails – you're always nice to me. You've seen through
my trap... oh, it must be thirty times now. You always see through it, and
you're never angry at me. I've never had such kindness from my victims."

My heart was still pounding, and I could still feel adrenaline racing
through me, but that horrible sense of wrongness had fled. I still didn't
understand where I was, but that was okay. No one had ever created something this beautiful just for me.

Not-Mrs-Noyer wanted to kill me, she had said so herself. That being
said, wanting to kill me wasn't really a problem. I wanted to kill myself
frequently. If anything, Not-Mrs Noyer wanting to kill me just meant we
had something in common.

Mt. Senmorta's snowy peak towered up and up and up above me. A
breeze played on my face. The campfire crackled in my ears. No-one who
could create this perfect moment could be all that bad. I flung my arms

around Not-Mrs-Noyer and drew her into a hug. "Thank you... just... thank you."

"I'll definitely kill you next time," Mrs Noyer said, and I could hear a smile in her voice. She drew me tighter into the hug. "Or maybe the time after that. Come back soon, okay?"

I blinked... and I was standing amongst the bones of those who had fallen into Not-Mrs-Noyer's trap. The floor under the bones was lined with stone, intersecting blocks bound by dark mortar. The blocks were irregularly shaped, forming a pattern that swirled away from me into the darkness. Instead of passageways and chambers, I stood in one enormous cavern. Light from Teya's glow globe illuminated the walls on either side of the staircase we'd descended. These walls hadn't been eroded over thousands of years by water, they'd been cut using enormous earth moving machinery on a scale that was difficult to fully grasp. The ceiling of the cavern was so high that Teya's light couldn't reach it. In the middle distance, hulking shapes of decayed bio-fuel tanks huddled. We were no longer in a cave system. We'd entered the dead city of Tenebro.

No-one in Ekzilo knew who exactly had built Tenebro, but it was generally agreed that they'd been geniuses who'd built technology and magical artefacts on a scale not seen since, outside of Talvik's great cities. Tenebro's list of techno-arcane miracle inventions included the Hungry Dark, along with the traps and creatures they'd created before the Great War to prevent warlords on the surface from invading their city and stealing their tech. 200 years ago, either through sabotage or terrible accident, the dark had escaped and swept through Tenebro, consuming everything in its path. Well, nearly everything. Legends persisted of a settlement named Sirmo, where survivors of the dark had fled. Teya and I had never found it, but the legend was still alluring.

I missed the breeze from the lake shore. Already, I could feel my memories of the trap fading. All I was left with was a feeling of peace and comfort at having spent time with someone who loved me... until I recognised the pounding noise approaching from my back.

"Mm..." Teya blinked and rubbed her eyes. "What..."

I grabbed her hand. "No time. Humans nearly on us. Come on."

"Hey!" shouted Scar, her voice not nearly distant enough. "Come back, we just want to talk to you."

"You'll turn back if you know what's good for you!" I yelled, before bursting into a sprint.

Teya shook her glow globe, its clinical white light seemed much dimmer than it had only moments ago. She pointed to the towering silhouette of a bio-fuel tank. Confused, but not wanting to argue I followed her, slipping into the metre-wide gap in between the bio-fuel tank and the cavern wall.

Teya slung her crossbow over her back and leaned against the wall, getting her breath back. Dust plumed, gravel skittered to the ground and over the back of her coat. She winced and hung her head forward, trying to keep the detritus out of her hair. "Right," she said. "We're down in the dark."

I peered back the way we'd come. There was a shimmering patch of darkness where the base of the stairs should be, but I couldn't make out any detail. "Looks like the humans didn't listen to me."

"What a surprise. All right. Some of them might make it through the trap, but they're locked in it for now. Should we try and go back up?"

I clicked my tongue. "Not a chance. The trap would snare us on the way back, and *they'd* wake up first. Besides, then we'd be back at ground level, where the *other* humans are. We should go deeper in." An image danced through my brain – a glowing riot of tumbling colour, hidden depths and the light which could reveal them. Then, another idea followed on the heels of that first one. I snapped my fingers. "Sirmo!"

Teya started. "What?"

I beamed at her. "Sirmo! When I was getting stitched up, you said that past a certain point, pacifism just meant letting people do whatever they wanted whilst you stood by and let them. You're wrong, Teya, but given what just happened to Ekzilo, you're not quite as wrong as I'd like. We need to clear the humans out of Ekzilo and make sure they never come back, preferably without shedding any more blood. Everything we've tried has failed. So…"

Teya frowned. "So you think if we find Sirmo…"

"If anyone could help, it'd be the descendants of the people who made this place!" I grinned, flicking my hands out into a 'ta-da' pose.

Teya peered out at the trap. "We're not ready, Meli."

"Sure we are! We can't go back up yet anyway. If Tenebro is going to be our hiding spot, we should make the most of it. Besides –" I bit my tongue, stopping the thought I'd just had in its tracks.

Teya peered at me. "What? Besides what? Tell me."

My freshly bitten tongue felt thick in my mouth. "I thought… if we were searching for Sirmo anyway… we might find some sign of what happened to Kyrene. Her notebooks talked about it a lot."

Teya's expression froze. I shouldn't have said it. I knew I shouldn't have said it. She held up a hand and shook her head. "I appreciate the thought, Meli. I'm not… lost causes aren't… never mind. Sirmo is a good idea."

She checked back at the trap again.

In the silence, I thought I heard stirring. "Let's go," I hissed.

Teya nodded. I led the way to the next tank, but Teya's glow globe had faded to the point where I was barely able to make out the floor beyond the tanks. I swallowed a tooth and held up a hand. Teal light, far more vibrant than the pale glow it replaced, shone out of my fingertips.

"Meli…" Teya was staring back the way we'd come, her crossbow held ready. "Melita… can you shed any light on this?"

I pointed in the direction her crossbow was aiming, illuminating a trail of russet stains on the ground. "Blood?"

Teya nodded. "Can you see any more?"

"Nope."

"Well, that's a problem. Whatever left that trail was letting itself bleed freely. A cave raider would have bandaged their wounds. Plus, there's no bones. Put those two together and it seems like there's a fallen wandering around."

I grimaced. "Ah. Now, I may have dropped into the dark last night. A fallen found me, so I broke its arm. That's probably the source of the blood."

"Spirits, Meli…"

"Oh, it's fine. I got away, didn't I?"

"You did, yes. Can you reel your light in a little? I'd like to dodge the fallen's attention."

I visualised drawing my power back around me and Teya. On a bad day, imposing this sort of subtle restriction on my power felt like trying to stop myself sneezing – almost impossible without making embarrassing 'bzzt' noises. Thankfully, I was able to maintain my concentration as I hauled my power in and wrapped it around me like an affectionate python.

Teya nodded, lowering her crossbow. I grinned and led the way away from the humans, along the wall of the cavern. The pale limestone glowed a muted blue with faint hints of red at the periphery of my vision. This made me check on my hand, where a fraction of my power was coming from. A red halo glowed around my fingers. I smiled, but froze when a guttural rasp echoed through the cavern. It sounded dreadfully familiar.

I crouched instinctively, feeling my teeth grind together. I reached for the gun Vakua had left me, but it slipped from my hand as I drew it, clattering to the ground. Another rasp, followed by gulping snarls, stumbling foot-steps, drawing closer. I felt about on the ground for my gun – my fingers brushed against it, sending it skittering. Teya rested a hand on my shoulder. She held a finger to her lips, then splayed her fingers, lowering them slowly, deliberately.

I nodded. I reeled my light back in. The dark drew in on all sides, tendrils probing what light remained, seeking weaknesses. We didn't have to stay hidden forever. We just had to stay hidden for longer than...

Back near the stairs, one of the humans shouted something, a guttural noise, completely unintelligible. They might have been shouting at us, or maybe they'd turned on each other. The fallen didn't care. It howled, then charged away from our hiding spot, bearing down on the humans. In the distance, a cry of alarm morphed into a cacophony.

"If anything's going to get the humans to flee to the surface, it's going to be a rampaging fallen," Teya whispered. "They bought light with them or they wouldn't have made it this far. Hopefully, they didn't bring firearms. Okay, the western steps are that way, the worker's lodgings are up ahead. What's the plan?"

I finally managed to scoop up my gun. "Right." I shuddered, "Plan. So... So, I met another creature last night as well as the fallen. A creature that could talk. She called herself Vakua. She's the one who left the firearm for me."

Teya stared at me. "Meli... are you okay?"

"What? Yes, I'm fine."

"You're sure?"

"Of course! Look, maybe this creature Vakua knows something? She said she lives in a castle down on level two. Kyrene's notebooks said we could get down there using the canal network."

Teya frowned. "Didn't those same notes say a creature lived in the canals?"

The humans' cries were steadily turning from bellows to screams. The fallen seemed only to be growing angrier. "Right, but we can probably dodge it. The canal network is huge. Come on, we don't know how long the humans are going to distract the fallen."

Teya took in a deep breath and then let it out again. "You're right. Sirmo... any tech which can keep Ekzilo safe would be... You're right. We can do this. All right. We heading to the next cavern?"

I nodded; shoving my gun back into my belt. Shouts and screams filled the air around us. I held up three fingers, then two, then one. As my hand dropped, we sprinted for the doorway to the next cavern.

All that existed, in that moment of glorious flight, was me, Teya, my light and the dark doorway we were hurtling towards. The sounds of my sprint were a song. The rhythm of my run, a dance. My future was illuminated, one step at a time. My light reached the stone doorway – an intricately sculpted archway decorated with carvings of plants, animals, and the caves in which they lived. Fragments of shadow clung on in the recesses of the carvings until my light brought their true glory to life.

We hurtled through the doorway and into the next cavern, which was a little smaller than the one we had just left, being merely enormous instead of gargantuan. My light still didn't reach the ceiling or any of the far walls. It did illuminate row upon row of traditional Talvik houses. Wooden beams and sloped tiled rooves all winked back at me as my light reached them. It couldn't possibly rain down here, so I had no idea why the houses had been built with rooves. Maybe they'd reminded the occupants of life where they'd originally come from.

These houses were where Teya and I had spent most of our time when exploring down in Tenebro. When the Hungry Dark had consumed every-one who had lived in this city, precious artefacts had been left behind. Most of these artefacts were far more advanced than anything craftswomen on the surface were able to make, at least in our area. Such artefacts were precious in Ekzilo and the surrounding areas, and it was by trading these relics that Teya and I were able to survive beyond what charity Ekzilo was able to provide.

I led the way down a row of houses that curved southward. Each houses' door was marked by a small chalk cross – our mark to show that we'd already checked it for artefacts. In a matter of moments, the houses had blocked my light from the sight of any would-be pursuers. After a few quick turns down long dead side streets, we slowed to a walk. Other than the persistent faint sound of the air swirling around us, propelled by the silent gnashing of the Hungry Dark, we moved in near silence.

"Hang on," Teya said from behind me. After checking to make sure that my light was shielded by buildings I turned to see what was up. She'd pulled a compass from a pouch on her pack and was studying it intensely. "You said 'east' right? We're a little off course." She pointed, down a different street to the one I'd been heading towards.

"Good spot," I grinned. Teya grinned back. The first house in the street Teya had pointed out was marked with a chalk cross. We'd been midway through exploring the next house when we'd been ambushed by a fallen. We'd still managed to retrieve a crystal that reflected sound and a torque amplifier. The house after that was unmarked. I cracked the knuckles on my left hand, one by one. We'd finally entered a part of Tenebro which was new to us. Soon, I spotted the tell-tale shadow of a passageway. The eerie silence that had taken the place of the fallen's screams spurred me onwards.

CHAPTER SIX

Chapter Six

Teya and I approached the doorway to the next cavern cautiously. Darkness loomed, but as I drove it back, lights winked at me out of the void.

I pointed, "You see that, Teya?"

She hefted her crossbow, repositioning her grip. "I see it. Natural light?"

"Let's find out!"

The Hungry Dark resisted my light as best it could, but it was clearly struggling. The space beyond the doorway was a murky grey rather than remorselessly dark. Twisted, hulking grotesques towered over us. Straggly tendrils swayed in the breeze – the fresh breeze. The crisp, clear breeze. I looked up. Delighted tears prickled at the corners of my eyes.

Lights winked overhead, faint pinpricks together with twin silver disc s... the cavern must be open to the sky. I let my light flare, and it burned through the dark around us. I shivered, and couldn't have stopped myself grinning if I'd wanted.

A perfect circle, maybe the size of Ekzilo's rice fields had been cut in the ceiling of the chamber. Fresh, clear air bathed us, moonlight cradled us and the stars shimmered, celebrating our achievement in making it so far into Tenebro.

In the sudden, safe twilight, hulking shapes that had loomed at us were revealed as merely rusting cranes, barges, and shrivelled ropes. It looked as if we were standing on a loading dock.

Stone steps flowed down to a row of jetties a little way into the cavern. Dark water lapped at the jetties – the moonlight reflecting from dancing ripples reminded me of feeling unquestionably safe but I couldn't remember exactly why.

We descended the steps, burning the fragments of Hungry Dark that stood between my light and the water as we moved. The darkness was forced back and back until the cavern was nearly entirely mundane. Off in the east wall, the canal flowed through a large, lintelled doorway. Bio-luminescent lichen lined the walls, glowing a thin white light.

Teya approached the nearest barge and gave it a cursory glance. "Looks like it might be still operational. That's... odd"

I left Teya to her mechanisms and explored the rest of the cavern. The wooden boards of the jetty creaked cheerily as I walked. As I stepped from jetty to dock, a board snapped under my boot, pitching me sideways and very nearly into the canals. I wobbled, but steadied myself on a decaying crane.

"You okay over there, Meli?"

"Oh yeah, I got it," I said, trying to look as if I had everything under control. I peered down at the dark water I'd barely avoided. A layer of mulch lined the bottom, presumably silt and leaves that had blown into the cavern. I frowned.

Kyrene's notes had definitely mentioned some sort of creature or creatures in the canals. I'd had the notebooks for a year, but I'd never been able to study them as closely as Teya had in the wake of her wife's disappearance. I'd been able to read a few pages just fine, usually the maps, but then the fog in my head would start swirling and I'd find myself reading page after page without actually taking anything in. Sentences slipped past me like shadows in fog.

I was more careful where I walked as I crossed the remaining docks, towards a few lurking shapes still shrouded in darkness. The Hungry Dark put up a token resistance before fleeing.

Cages. Cages had been bolted to the walls along the northern edge of the cave. Cages large enough to hold big game animals – or maybe humans.

"Teya?"

"Mm?"

"This creature. Can you remember what Kyrene's notes said about it?"

"Not sure. Dangerous and intelligent, maybe? Why? have you found something?"

"I think I've found something, yes."

The cages looked as if they'd once been impressive, thick barred affairs. Now, they were less secure. Bars had been torn away from each cage and lay discarded across the dock. One or two stuck out of the cavern wall. I crept closer, letting my light sweep away the last of the dark. Swirling shadows cleared, revealing the bodies inside the cages.

I wanted to throw up. My heart was racing. I had to do something to help. I ran forward, and that was when I saw that none of the bodies had heads. I fell to my knees. Distant pain. The sight couldn't be real. It couldn't. My glorious adventure in the dark turned into a nightmare. Swirling shadows. Oozing blood.

My vision swam. My palms smacked the floor, stinging shock fizzed into my head, focussing me. I looked up, retched, and had to close my eyes. I breathed. I steeled myself. I opened my eyes again.

There were about twenty bodies. Some were lying in the cages, some just outside. They lay on the ground, limbs splayed unnaturally. Men and women. I couldn't tell how old any of them were. Blood glittered in my light. Behind me, I heard Teya vomit. Tears poured from my eyes. A strange keening noise filled the air around us, and it was only when I ran out of breath that I realised I'd been the one making it.

I reached out and grasped at the thick cloth sleeve of the nearest splayed arm. The cloth was rough. Scratchy on my skin but tough. The sort of thing a cave raider would wear.

Footsteps next to me made me look up. Teya was looking down at the bodies, her cheeks grey. "What did this?"

"A fallen?" I asked. My voice sounded as if it was coming from an awfully long way away.

"N-no." Teya knelt down next to me and put her arm around my shoulders. "No bruises. Clothing intact. This was something new. Just wanted their heads." She released my shoulders, leaving me feeling exposed. She reached out and folded the arms of the nearest body over its chest. Shuddering, she stood. She moved to the next body, leant down and folded its arms too. I watched, stunned as she walked from corpse to corpse. It was only when she was done that I realised she wasn't just paying respect to the lost.

"Is Kyrene among them?" I asked.

Teya shook her head. "I didn't think she would be, but it's good to be sure."

The shock was starting to fade. "When we find her, where do you think she'll be?"

"*If* we find her... I don't know. She'll probably be surrounded by devastation. Dozens of fallen, shredded buildings. A glorious last stand. She wasn't the sort to go out quietly."

She shook her head, then turned to look at the cages. I moved to stand next to her, not sure if I should reach out and hug her.

"Are you okay, T?"

She shook her head. Her expression as she poked at the cages flitted between stoic interest and devastation. Despite the death that surrounded us, the fizzing, jumping joy of my magic still made me feel *alive*. Still, it might not be worth this. "Do you want to go back to the surface?"

Cyan sparks glittered in Teya's tears as she shook her head. "You were right, Meli. If we can find a way to keep Ekzilo safe, we should do that. No-one else can. And seeing this..." she cast her hand around at the devastation. "Grim as it is, they're bodies. Identifiable. I'd always assumed that if I found Ky's skeleton down in the dark, I'd never know if it was her. Maybe that's not true. Maybe there is hope, after all. Let's press on, as long as you're okay."

Smiling, I rested a hand on her shoulder. "Let's go. It doesn't feel safe here. The bodies are still... fresh. The Hungry Dark is weak here but there are tendrils of it everywhere. More than enough to strip these bodies down in a few hours. Whatever did this isn't long gone."

Teya reached out and poked at one of the bars of the cage that had been bent away from the main structure as if it was made of paper. "I agree."

"Do you think you can get one of those boats moving?"

"I'll give it a go. Although..."

"You think the creature that lives in the canals might have done this?"

"Maybe? But no, I don't think that's right. I think Kyrene probably would have included in her notes if this creature were the sort to go decapitating people all over the place. I'll get to work on one of the boats."

"I'll keep watch." I drew my firearm and checked the mechanism before stepping around the bodies and back to the centre of the cavern. Teya stepped carefully down onto one of the jetties, then into the sturdiest-looking boat. I wasn't sure if I should be keeping an eye out for threats from the water, or back from the way we'd come.

Ripples glinted in the canals, but they seemed to be moving out and away from Teya's boat. Meanwhile, back the way we'd come from... "Crap."

"What's up, Meli?"

"There's a light approaching from the west."

"The humans?"

I adjusted the grip on my gun. "I can't think who else it'd be, but they couldn't have made it this far, could they?" My voice sounded too high, even to me. I raised my gun, but then drew in a breath between my teeth. I'd made a mistake. If I could see the light, whatever held that light could likely see me, a shining cyan star in the dark.

Reeling my light back in, I ducked behind the rusted hulk of a crane and tried to calm my breathing.

Footsteps echoed out of the darkness. Footsteps, and voices. Approaching quickly.

"You sure you saw light in here, Jaeson?" said a gruff woman's voice – it sounded like the woman I'd met yesterday with the bald head. My heart picked up its pace, but my breathing slowed.

The other voice sounded young and scared. "I don't know, okay! I don't know. Can we go back? Please?"

"No, I told you, we've got to punish them for what they did to me. You need to do this, Jaeson! You need to step up!"

Teya looked up from her work on the boat. "Melita, does that sound like a kid to you?"

I nodded, my mouth hanging open. What sort of monster would bring a child down here?

"Nearly ready," Teya whispered.

I crept down to the jetty and stepped onto the boat. Teya was working away at the engine, so I levelled my gun at the entrance to the cavern.

"Er…" said the young voice.

"What is it, boy?"

"I think something changed up ahead."

"Come on then, boy! Quickly!"

My light only dimly lit the area around the western doorway, so it was obvious when a new light source started mingling with mine. The lights frothed like two waves crashing into each other. Then, when the light had settled, two shapes came into focus. Baldy was holding a knife, its blade glistening with blood. The other human appeared male. He couldn't have been older than sixteen, although he was so curled in on himself he might have been even younger.

Two humans. I could deal with two humans. I just had to not show fear. I pointed my firearm at the humans as they stepped into the cavern, trying to look like a swashbuckling pirate hero. "Stop right there!"

The humans flinched at the sight of my gun, and raised their hands. Behind me, on the barge, Teya smacked something mechanical. A rattling purr started, but then coughed back into silence.

"Look..." said Baldy, "I know we've had our differences..."

"You attacked our village!" I cried, channelling the crash and thrash of the sea into my voice. "You came into my home and burned everything you saw. You pursued us down into the darkness. If that's 'having differences' with someone, I'd hate to see how you treat someone you're truly vexed with."

"Nearly there," Teya muttered from behind me. "Keep it up."

"Look, there's something down here with us. It killed two of my friends and it just won't die. We can't stop it. You've got to help us!"

"Why didn't you run back to the surface like good little humans?"

"And go through that... nightmare again? As soon as we stepped down into that field of bones, we found ourselves somewhere else – two of us didn't get back up again and then that *thing* attacked us!"

"Oh, you mean you didn't want to go through the trap again because there was a fallen out there..." I said, scratching my temple with the rear sight of my gun. "Yeah, that's actually fair enough, but if you want to see the sun again you don't have much of a choice."

"It's still coming! It'll come for you too. It's right behind us, please..."

"Got it!" Teya cried. An engine thrummed into life and our barge lurched away from the humans. I flung out my free hand and grabbed the barge's aft rail. The humans shouted in alarm and ran towards us. I thought our sudden movement had caused this reaction at first, but then I saw a creature emerging into their bubble of light – a creature I recognised.

My companion from my last visit to the dark, hadn't fared well since I'd last seen it. Its right arm hung limply by its side, and part of its jaw was missing. It was limping, presumably because of the large knife that was still embedded in its thigh. Still, its temperament was undiminished and it bore down on Baldy with stuttering, juddering fury.

The principle of pacifism was a little more flexible down in the dark than it was on the surface. Had Baldy been by herself, I'd have been tempted to let the two monsters destroy each other. Severely tempted, given what Baldy and her friends had done to Ekzilo. Leaving a child to fend for himself in the company of two monsters... that was something else entirely. "Come on, come on!" I shouted, moving to cover the fallen with my pistol.

The kid sprinted towards us. Baldy hesitated, before following. The fallen limped after her, hatred retching out of its throat. Our barge was picking up speed, but the humans were closing the gap.

"Melita?" Teya asked, from behind me. "Did you just invite the humans onto our boat?"

"One of them is a kid, Teya."

"Ah."

"Move!" I shouted to the humans. They were blocking my view of the fallen. The boy dodged out of the way. I levelled my gun at the non-human monster and pulled the trigger. My gun let out a *CRACK* and blood plumed from the fallen's leg. I scowled. I'd been aiming for its chest.

The human child reached us, but we'd picked up a decent amount of speed and he looked as if he'd lose his footing if he just jumped aboard. I stuffed my gun into my belt, held onto the railings with one hand and held out my other hand to the kid. He snatched at it, grabbed on and I hauled him aboard.

The kid rocked as he stumbled onto the boat but turned to watch Baldy as she staggered towards us. "Come on, Ada!"

Baldy must have been injured by the fallen. She was struggling to catch up to us. The fallen's wounds were far worse, but it was keeping up, rasping in time with its juddering canter. The kid reached out his hand and Baldy managed to grab it. With a heave from the little human, Baldy struggled aboard. She collapsed in a heap on the deck next to the kid.

I drew my pistol and pointed it at her. "Don't move."

Baldy raised her hands. She opened her mouth but closed it again without saying anything.

"How's it looking back there?" Teya called over her shoulder.

I poked the kid without looking at him. "Where's the fallen? Is it still keeping up?"

"Y- yeah. Might even be gaining on us," he said.

"Hear that, Teya?"

"Yup. Hang on, I think I've found the flow controls..."

With a rumble, the barge picked up speed. We surged into the tunnel leading out of the docks, the Hungry Dark closing in around us. I flared my light up to compensate. Soon, the barge was surrounded by a fierce oasis of light, the rich yellow of golden oak.

My light reflected back at us from the arched roof of the tunnel, the gentle chugging of the engine the only disturbance in the oasis. A scream thundered out of the darkness, although it wasn't directly behind us anymore. It felt unbalanced. There was a tow path running along the east wall of the tunnel, only just visible above the waterline. The fallen must be following the path. No matter, we'd be free of it soon.

I kept my pistol trained on Baldy, who clutched at her side and kept her eyes on the deck. Next to her, the kid fidgeted. The sounds of the barge's engine filled the space between us.

Eventually, the kid took a small step forward. "Look, thanks for... but you can let us go now. We just want to go home."

"Go ahead," I said.

The kid shifted on his feet. I didn't pay him much attention; I was focussed on Baldy. I wasn't sure what I'd do if she tried anything. I couldn't shoot her, but I didn't know whether she knew I was bluffing.

"I'm not leaving without Ada," said the kid.

I shrugged, not moving the gun away from Ada's bald head. "Please take her. I don't enjoy her company."

"You're holding her at gunpoint."

"That's right. I don't trust her. If she wants to leave, she can leave. If she wants to try something else, we'll have a problem." I didn't mention it was mostly me that would have the problem.

The kid took another step forward. He stuck his chest out. "But you attacked her!"

"I attacked *her*?"

"Yes! She came to your village, only wanting some breakfast, and you started a fight. She only just got away."

"Is that what you told her, Ada?" My grip on the gun tightened. "How... interesting. See, Teya back there saw the results of your little visit. Maybe we could have her weigh in on this?"

"No, no, I don't think that's necessary," Ada said. She clambered to her feet, using the railings to support herself. She looked as if she was barely holding herself together. She grabbed the kid's arm. "Let's go. Leave these freaks to die in the dark."

The kid leapt off the barge and onto the tow path. Ada had a little more trouble – when she leapt her trailing right leg didn't quite reach the path and she nearly fell into the water. The kid ran forward and helped her up onto dry land. Ada fiddled with a glow globe, and a thin white light bloomed just as my bubble left them behind.

"They gone?" Teya called over her shoulder.

"They're gone."

"Good riddance."

"Yup. Did you hear what the kid said?"

"That you attacked the humans? Yup. Probably the humans who attacked you didn't think returning after nearly kicking a pacifist witch to death was a sufficiently heroic story so they might have elaborated on certain parts of it."

"Why would they do that?"

"Oh, Melita, I don't know. I don't understand those people."

I shook my head at the darkness behind us and turned to see what was ahead. The passageway was curving around slightly, but otherwise was much the same as it had been when I'd last seen it. Except I could see more of the tunnel roof than I'd expected. I frowned, then realised the tunnel ahead of us was heading down at a slight incline.

"Looks like the tunnel's going to take us down to the second level," Teya said. "Hold on, this might get a little choppy."

Our barge rocked as the stream around us picked up speed. Teya cut the power to our craft and let the current pull us along, making adjustments with the barge's tiller to avoid us crashing into any walls.

"They must have used this tunnel to transport goods down from the surface," Teya said. "It must be fed by a natural spring or something. Or..."

"Or what?"

"I thought I heard some pumps working just then, somewhere nearby, but it couldn't have been. Any tech like that would have seized up over a century ago. Hold on." Teya shoved the tiller across to the left as a fork in the tunnel loomed out of the darkness. I staggered and caught myself on a railing, which drove the breath from my chest.

The air I drew in afterwards was tangy and had notes of plum blossom and oak. "Errr. I think there's magic ahead."

"What does that mean, Melita?"

"I don't know! Maybe we should –"

Chapter Seven

My world swayed. Huffing and chuffing filled my ears. Scuffed floorboards and battered metal walls... I blinked, confused at how I could have forgot where I was. I was on a train. That shouldn't be the sort of thing a person could just forget.

We were in some sort of cargo carriage. It was lit evenly by glow globes in the ceiling but stars shone through the windows and both moons were low in the sky. I was standing at one end of the carriage, near an imposing metal door. In between me and the door, Teya was crouched. She was fiddling with the door lock.

"Melita, how long's left on the clock?" Teya asked, without looking up.

I found myself looking down at a pocket watch. A red line had been drawn on the glass and the hands of the watch were perilously close to the line.

"Two minutes."

"We're going to have to blow the door. Everything we came here for is on the other side."

I nodded. We were here to plunder this train for all the riches it carried. Wait... that wasn't right. "The solution to our human problem is on the other side of the door?" I asked, confused.

"Melita, there isn't time. Do you have the explosives?"

"Yes," I said, slipping my pack from my shoulders and dropping it to the floor. I opened the clasp and flicked the leather rain cover free. Inside were sticks of compressed gunpowder as well as more advanced biological agents that could destroy just about anything. I removed a small tin from my bag and brushed past Teya. I gave the lock a quick once over and, yes, it was definitely a lock. I popped the lid off my tin and found a lump of red putty inside, which I shoved onto the lock. My fingers worked all by themselves, shaping the putty and slipping two silver detonation rods into the explosive.

Teya and I took cover behind a piece of machinery and stuck our fingers in our ears. We waited five seconds for the metal in the detonation rods to begin a chain reaction in the putty, which would cause an enormous...

BOOM

I peeked out from my hiding place and nodded in satisfaction. The door had been blown wide open, and was swinging forlornly from its hinges.

"Okay," said Teya, "okay, let's do this. The treasure is on the other side of the door."

"Treasure?"

"Yes, what we came here for."

"Are you feeling okay?"

Teya turned to me. Her eyes shone with delight and barely contained energy. "Yes, why?"

She walked towards the door, but I stopped her. "Seriously. What treasure are you talking about? We're here... why are we... Sirmo. It's something to do with Sirmo..." I was having trouble concentrating. Mist rose from the floor, making my thoughts move slowly and shoot off in unusual directions.

"Okay, what exactly is it that you want?" Teya asked. "I know I haven't had one of you down here in a while, but I didn't think I'd been gone that long. What do you want? Treasure? Or a weapon? Look through the door,

Melita! Everything we could ever want is through there. All we need to do is step through and take it!"

I peered in the direction Teya was pointing. Piles of precious stones, works of art and deadly looking firearms were on display, ready for the taking. I frowned. The word Sirmo was important, but there was also another word. Another person. Was it Kyrene? Or was it something else....

"I can't remember, Teya."

Teya glared at me. "Okay, I'm going to have to let you have a bit more of your memory back. I'm done talking at cross purposes with you."

Teya was going to let me do what? She'd just said something, and it had sounded very wrong to me, but I couldn't remember exactly what it was. The mist withdrew ever so slightly, and my memories shone into sharper focus. I snapped my fingers. "Sirmo! We need to find Sirmo so we can save Ekzilo!"

Teya moved quicker than I could have imagined. She grabbed me by the lapels of my jacket and hauled me so that we were nose to nose. "You're going to go into the treasure room, and you're going to steal something."

"What?"

Furious-Teya snarled. "I'm hungry. You're going to go in there and do whatever it is that you people do with these treasures. Come on. They're just there. Aren't they tempting?"

The pile of relics looked... well, they *were* tempting, but they also appeared formless. A hulking mass of machinery, fuel tanks, barrels, spurs, spars, cogs, and gears. I couldn't see any one piece of tech that I recognised. "No," I said, looking back at the snapping eyelids of the person wearing Teya's face.

"I'm hungry!" growled Evil-Teya. "Let me eat!"

"I've got some mochi in my pack..."

Evil-Teya snarled in frustration and pushed me away from her. I staggered, trying to stay upright. "I can't eat food, you fool. I need your soul."

I felt for my pistol. My belt was empty. My stomach dropped. What stood in front of me wasn't a person. It was a monster that had escaped the dark. The rules of pacifism didn't apply here. I raised my fists. "You want my soul? Come and take it."

"That's not how it works!" Not-Teya growled. "Just go through the door. Go on! please!" The treasure room had doubled in size. Woven baskets overflowed with gold and silver coins just past the entrance. As traps went it was pretty obvious. It made me wonder whether there was a second, more subtle trap hidden somewhere, given I was being distracted by the obvious one.

I lowered my fists and shrugged. "I'm not going through that door. Sorry, not sorry."

"Well, I'm not letting you go, then! You'll go through eventually." As soon as Desperate-Teya spoke, she clutched at her head and screamed. "No! You can't make me! I'm starving!"

I hesitated. I wanted to rush to her side and see whether there was anything I could do, but from the sounds of it the only thing I could do to relieve her distress was to step into the treasure room, which I badly didn't want to do. "Are you okay?"

She didn't even look at me. "No, no, no! I won't do it. I won't let her go. I won't. I don't care about the rules. She might be the last. I've already let the other one slip free. I'm going to hang... onto..."

She looked up at me, and I realised that the distance between us had grown. I was sure I hadn't moved, but Not-Teya suddenly seemed as if she was standing on the far side of an enormously long room. She sprinted towards me, but even as her legs pumped and her arms thrashed, the distance between us stretched. The treasure room was now the faintest glimmer in the distance.

"Come back!" cried the monster, her voice barely reaching me over the distance. She was tiny now, and the space had warped around her. I was only just able to see the door to the treasure room slam shut in between us.

I was back on the barge, huddled in a crouch at the prow. The incline of the tunnel seemed to have levelled a little. We were still descending, but at a less frenetic pace than we had been.

Pain thrummed in my legs. My muscles felt like tight strips of molten steel. I couldn't move, and they *burned*. My chest ached and my head was pounding. How had things got this bad? I needed to push through.

"Are you back with us, Melita?" Teya asked. I looked up and saw her working the tiller.

"Teya..."

"I got through the trap a few minutes ago. We'd just been drifting along for... I don't know how long but I stopped us from ramming any walls."

A railing was just above my head. I reached up, grabbed it and tried to haul myself to my feet. It was too much, too fast. I had to push through. I had to push through.

"Hey, it's okay, Meli, you can take it easy. I don't think we're in any immediate danger."

I shook my head and staggered to my feet. "What sort of trap was that? I can remember that one. I never remember what happens in the trap on the first level."

Teya shrugged, keeping her gaze on the tunnel up ahead. "I was in a castle – one of the twelve great castles. There was a room I was breaking into and in that room was everything I ever wanted, but I opened the door, and it was just stuff, nothing that would help rescue our friends, or find out what happened to Kyrene come to that. The trap wasn't happy at all when I didn't take any of it."

"Same here, but the trap tried to keep me there."

"What? Traps aren't sentient are they?"

I shrugged, helplessly. "Any sign of the mystery canal creature?"

Teya shook her head. I turned and looked back up the tunnel. A faint trail of light spun into the dark, where it faded until being finally smothered. What was that? I slipped a tooth into my mouth and swallowed, shivering in delight at the seed of power blooming inside me. A rich, green core blossomed at the centre of my sphere of light, slowly pulsing outwards until the barge was swallowed by the colour of young bamboo. The trail of light behind us grew brighter.

The tunnel walls must have been coated in something, probably some bio-chemical agent that reacted to light, or possibly magic. Much of it had decayed over the two hundred years since Tenebro fell, but some of it evidently still worked. My light was bringing patches of this chemical to life, augmenting my glow with contrasting colours, and leaving a slowly fading trail of light behind us.

My power reached my legs, causing the pain to fade and *finally* I was able to stand. I drew in a deep breath of air – cool and humid, but tainted a little by the scent of burning bio-fuel from the barge's engine. I closed my eyes, leaned over the railing to breathe in an uncontaminated lungful and sighed contentedly, then I opened my eyes. I released the railing and stepped sharply away from the edge. "Teya," I hissed, trying to have my voice carry over the chuntering of the engine, but not carry any further into the darkness.

"Yes? What's up, Meli?"

"I think there's something in the water."

Teya hesitated for only a moment before throttling down the engine and whispering, "Hold us steady." She peered down into the water, then frowned and leaned to the left and to the right. She was probably having trouble because the reflections from my light and the photo-reactive chemicals on the passage wall were only illuminating the water so much. I took the tiller and tried to watch the tunnel ahead whilst I thrust my left hand out over the edge of the barge. I eased power into my left hand. A vibrant green glow wrapped around my fingers before dissipating into the air.

Teya returned to my side. "I think whatever it is, it's alive," she said. "It's moving with the water but not being pulled along."

"We've found Kyrene's mystery creature?"

"Maybe. Tendrils and spirals of flesh. Let's take the next turning away from the main passageway. We don't want to draw this thing's attention."

I nodded. My heart pounded as I speculated about what might be beneath us, lurking in the river. Was it some monstrous aquatic plant that was lying in wait, ready to snap closed around us when we reached the right spot, like a fly trap? I shivered. At any moment, Teya and I might be under attack. We'd fight for our lives. My light would save us. In that moment, I'd be truly, truly alive.

I teased a tooth free from my bracelet and slipped it into my mouth. I didn't swallow just yet, I still had plenty of power from my last little top-up, but I wanted to be ready for the combat that was to follow. I needed to be sharp. Getting injured down in the dark was a serious problem because it slowed us down and would mean future adventures would be more frustrating than invigorating.

"How are you doing, Meli?" Teya asked.

"Never better. You?"

"Not great. Can't see any turnings ahead of us. Can you keep an eye on the beast below?"

I handed back the tiller and returned to the railing. The last I'd seen of the tendrils in the water, they'd been thin coils of solid matter. Now, the coils were gone. Instead, the riverbed seemed to be lined with layered, shiny... something. Scales? They reflected my light back at me and seemed unending, other than a few strange patches here and there which oozed a thick, white liquid which absorbed all colour from my light.

"Is there some long dead massive fish lining the bottom of this canal?" I hissed to Teya.

Teya winced. "A fork in the tunnel would be great any moment now... let me know if it moves, Meli."

Slowly, as we drifted, the scales morphed, losing their shine and colour. Scales gave way to white, smooth flesh. Not just flesh - a very human-looking waist. A woman's torso bathed in my emerald light. Arms lay by her side, drifting in the water. Finally, our barge sailed past her head.

Her hair was far longer than that of most women I knew. Still, she had the strong jaw and powerful cheekbones of someone who knew how to get things done. Her eyes were open but no bubbles rose from her nose.

"Teya," I hissed, "it's changed. It's a woman now. It looks like she's dead."

"What? Are you sure the woman is part of the creature?"

"That's what I'm seeing..." I said, turning back to where the woman... wasn't. We must have sailed past her. I checked behind the barge.

"Teya," I said, "can you start the engine again please?"

Teya followed my gaze. She nodded and, ever so slowly, she eased the throttle open. The barge rumbled and accelerated subtly.

Behind us, the face watching us from the surface of the water kept pace with us. Her eyes shone in my light, green and glittering. Hair plastered her face and spilled into the water. Her mouth bobbed just above the surface of the water.

I rested one hand on my gun but didn't draw it. The face was watching us, and I didn't want to make it angry just yet.

"What's it doing?" Teya asked.

"Keeping pace with us, but not approaching."

"Well, that's interesting. Still, this river has taken us a long way underground. We've gone through another trap. We must be on level two of

Tenebro by now. We'll probably reach another dock or some gates soon. When we do, that creature might well catch us up."

The wake behind our barge was growing in size as we accelerated. A wave washed over the face in the water. I must have blinked without realising, because one moment the face was there and the next it was gone. Instinctively, I drew my gun.

"Teya!" I called over my shoulder. "She's gone." I peered over the railing of the barge and saw movement in the water. "I think she's underneath us."

"Ah. Okay."

A roar from the barge's engine echoed throughout the tunnel as Teya dropped the throttle. We surged forward. Below us, the water was a churning green maelstrom. I could smell the citrus tang of burning bio-fuel melding with the crisp scent of fresh water.

"Talk to me, Melita!" Teya called, over the noise of the engine. "Have we lost her?"

The barge rocked. I staggered and looked around to see whether we were under attack, but the barge seemed normal... except at the prow, where a hand was gripping the lowest railing. A creature of the dark, something I'd never seen before. Air hissed between my teeth. I didn't know if I should rush to meet it or grab Teya and jump over the side of the barge. Another hand reached up and scrabbled at the deck. It couldn't get a purchase, so it flailed up at the railing, where the other hand was latched on.

I raised my gun and aimed at the arm. I hesitated, but this was a monster. If I didn't shoot it now, it would attack us. I aimed carefully, exhaled, and squeezed the trigger.

A thunderous crack split the air and caused the leaf-green light around me to pulse in time with the echoes as they rolled around the tunnel. The arm of the creature didn't move. I thought for a moment that I'd missed, but as I aimed to take a second shot, A three-centimetre metal bolt lodged in the creature's pale forearm, like a thorn in a fox's paw.

The crown of a head rose into view, slick hair plastering a pale face. I waited for just a moment until I saw her eyes, then I pulled the trigger a second time.

I didn't wince at the crack of expelling air from my gun this time, but my aim was also a little off. My projectile struck the creature in the cheek and lodged there. She blinked. She reached up, faltering, wrapping her arms around the barge's railing.

"Please," she said, "please don't shoot. I'm..." Her eyes rolled back into her head and one of her arms slipped from the railing.

A marvel of the dark, like Vakua, and one who needed help. Without thinking, I dashed forward and grabbed her other arm. I held on as her fingers weakened and slipped off the railing. It was like trying to maintain a grip on seaweed.

"Did that thing just talk?" Teya called over the noise of the engine.

"Yeah!" I yelled, trying to keep a hold of the cold, slippery arm.

"Melita, what are you doing? It's a creature! It'll try and kill us!"

"She's too weak to hold onto the railings, let alone kill us! She might be able to tell us something about Sirmo!"

I risked letting go with one hand so I could reach through the bars and grab her other arm. I hauled her wrist up so that her hand was resting on the lowest railing of the barge. She grasped at the railing, faintly, and I clamped my hand on top of hers, keeping it in place.

I could feel my light fading around me, so I swallowed the tooth I'd placed in my mouth and grinned as the tunnel around the barge bloomed back into life. Under my hands, cold and aching from the effort of gripping this slippery woman's arms, I felt a hunger – an empty space that felt familiar. It had felt like this when I'd brushed my skin against Vakua's face. My magic had made her skin glow. Would it do the same for this creature?

My power rushed towards the emptiness in the way water rushes to fill a hole in its path. Panic leapt up my throat. My magic felt out of control. I gritted my teeth, fighting for a grip on my power. My vision went fuzzy at the edges as I had to suddenly get to grips with making my power move in a way I'd never needed to before. A thread of power slipped away and into the woman clinging to life at the prow of the barge.

Her eyes flickered, and then opened. She gasped, and I felt the muscles in her arms tighten. Suddenly, I wasn't fighting to keep her out of the water, although her weight still dragged at my grip.

The woman managed to open her eyes and stare up at me, through her sodden curtains of hair. "More... Please. More. I can help..."

"Do you know where we can find Sirmo?"

The woman's head lolled for a moment, and her eyelids drooped. I took in two deep breaths. I didn't know whether I could use my power to keep her alive, but I was definitely going to try. I loosened my grip on my power, sending another thread her way, and I felt it immediately snatched from under my fingers. The woman's eyes opened again. "Sirmo? Yes, I know where that... I can... I can..."

"You can what?"

"Anything..." The woman's eyes were drooping again. "Please. Whatever you want..."

"Teya!" I called, "Activate a glow globe please! Things are gonna get dark!"

The barge wavered on its course, as if Teya had just taken her hands off the tiller. The engine throttled down and I heard the tell-tale crack of a glow globe seal breaking. I waited until the clean, clinical white light from Teya's globe washed the glorious green of mine away before I gritted my teeth and poured power into the woman.

It felt as if I was pouring water out of a bucket. The meagre amount of power I had in my body was nowhere near enough. Her body drank and drank of my power until my vision swam and I felt faint. A horrible gaping emptiness spread inwards from my fingers, where they gripped the woman's hands, to my limbs, to my heart. I felt as if everything important about me was being drained. I grinned at the feeling. My ego, my pride, all this was nothing in the face of what I was doing.

Her eyes rose like the sun. A smile glowed on her face and a shiver ran from her head, down into the water.

"Thank you," she said, her voice soft and sonorous, "thank you. You have no idea how much this means. There's a dock up ahead. Meet me there. I'll open the gates for you."

She released her hold on the bars and slipped into the water with barely a splash. Then, at the edge of the glow globe's light, she broke the water's surface, heading downriver at speed. Her human head, arms and torso leapt from the water, followed by the rest of her. Her body was smooth and fish like, ending in tendrils, tentacles and an enormous tail which splashed down on the river's surface as she plunged deeper. As she disappeared, I realised that her body had been smooth all the way down – the holes I'd seen earlier, the ones oozing white fluid had all closed.

"Wow," said Teya.

"Right?" I was finding it hard to stand. I felt drained of energy as well as magic. I remembered, in a dark, distant kind of way, that I'd been fleeing for my life for... was it only hours? It felt like days.

"You okay, Melita?"

Keeping my eyes open was a struggle. I thought about the look in the creature's eyes as she drank my magic. "Never better."

"Don't fall asleep, Meli! We're not out of danger."

My eyelids shot open. "What? I wasn't falling asleep."

Teya smiled, warming the cool air between us. I pulled myself to my feet. Pain shot up my legs but settled down to a background ache once I was moving properly. I had to keep moving.

The river was still rippling in the creature's wake. Before long, a pair of water gates loomed out of the darkness, open and inviting. Our new friend was waiting on the far side, her human body bobbing in the water. Beyond her was a dock, similar to the one we'd left behind on the first level.

Teya threw the engine's throttle into reverse, and our barge slowed. We drifted next to the only pier which wasn't clogged with rubble or another craft. Our friend was still keeping a careful distance from us. Teya leapt ashore as soon as the boat stopped moving, and I followed.

"Pleased to meet you!" I said, because politeness costs nothing. "I'm Melita and this is Teya. What's your name?"

"I am Yilin. Thank you for... thank you. I'd not expected such kindness from cave raiders. Now, if you will excuse me, I must close the gates, lest our voices carry up the tunnels and attract unnecessary attention."

Yilin dipped into the water and emerged again next to the water gates. She rose from the water – first her humanoid body, then her scaled, fishlike form. Water cascaded from her flesh as she rose to be eye level with me, even though I was standing above her on the docks, and then further up still until she was balancing on her tail, towering over me. She gripped the water gates, but paused. She reeled back from the gates with a cry of alarm.

This state of shock only lasted a moment before she shook herself. "Someone's approaching, carrying something large and heavy. A friend of yours?"

"Absolutely not," said Teya.

Yilin returned to the door. "Oh hey, the thing the human was carrying is another human. There's a fallen as well. I'll shut the door and keep them out." She gripped the gates and heaved.

I shook my head. The humans hadn't fled to the surface. I cursed their stupidity. Their recklessness. Their inconvenience. They'd come down here hunting me and Teya... but they were going to die down here unless we did something. We had the power to save them. If we didn't use it, that would be like killing them ourselves. "No!" I shouted to Yilin. "No one else needs to die! Please let the two humans in."

Next to me, Teya was silent. Yilin looked at me sceptically. I took a step forward, so that I was at the edge of the dock, staring up into Yilin's eyes.

She shrugged, and swung the water gate open a little, so the approaching humans could climb from the towpath past the gate and onto the docks. That, at least, was the plan. When the humans emerged into the bubble of light, I saw that it wasn't going to work.

The bald woman was limp, and the kid was doing his best to carry her. One of his hands was dedicated to dragging his elder, the other held a glow globe. There was no way he'd be able to climb past the gate and hold onto his friend at the same time. Moreover, when he emerged into our light and saw Yilin waiting at the gates, he reeled back, nearly falling. A snarl of triumph ripped through the air behind him, and the fallen caught up to him, and leapt.

Chapter Eight

The fallen drove the kid to the ground, his head thumping against the gravel of the tow path. Baldy slipped off his back and splashed into the river. She'd drown unless we did something.

"Yilin! Please save that woman!" I yelled, before jumping into the water myself. I submerged up to my stomach, shivering at the sudden icy cold, and thrashed my way towards the gates.

Yilin reached into the water and dragged the woman out with one arm. She tossed her towards me, making it look as if she was throwing a piece of paper rather than a ninety-kilo human. The body landed in the water in front of me. I scrabbled at the limp human and hauled her onto my shoulder. My hands felt numb as I fumbled to maintain a grip on her sodden clothing.

I carried baldy back to the docks, where Teya was waiting. I lifted, Teya strained, and together we managed to get Baldy up onto the dock. I climbed up after her, and collapsed, shivering, next to Baldy. One human safe. What about the other?

The kid had thrown up his arms to cover his head and protect against the fallen, who snarled and snapped at its prey. Yilin reached forward and picked up the fallen by the neck. Her fingers reached maybe halfway around the creature's throat, but she held it out at arm's length as if it was nothing. I found myself extremely glad that I hadn't given her cause to be angry with me.

"You're too loud," Yilin said. Her fingers clenched ever so slightly. The tiny movement cracked the fallen's neck to the side. The sound of crunching bone and snapping cartilage filled the air.

A yell grew in my throat and died against my gritted teeth. I didn't want to see anyone die, but that fallen wasn't anyone anymore. They were a danger to all of us, and not in a fun way. Yilin tossed the fallen further up the tow path before reaching for the kid.

I had a heart stopping moment of doubt, and next to me, Teya's hand froze over her crossbow. My doubt was misplaced. Yilin lifted the human past the water gates and deposited him, shaking, on the dock next to us. She then turned to the gates, her movements sharp and precise, not like how she had flowed in and out of the water only moments ago. I'd expected her to slam the gates shut, but instead she closed them with great care. They bumped together gently, making only the tiniest thump as wood met wood.

The lower half of my clothing was still soaked with freezing water. I shivered and rubbed my flanks. The docks down here were similar to the one we'd left up above, although clearly designed to be slightly more pleasant to look at. We were on a low wooden platform lined with posts atop which sat ancient, long faded glow globes. In the near distance was a set of stairs next to a ramp that led up to a street. Beyond the street I could make out silhouettes that looked like the edges of buildings. Stillness filled the air for a moment, disturbed only by the slight fizzing of Teya's glow globe, and the whimpering of the kid.

I stood up and made my way over to him. "Are you hurt?" I asked. My voice didn't seem to know what tone it wanted to adopt. It came out hard and brittle, but the concern I felt might have shown through the cracks.

The kid didn't respond, so I tried to examine him. He was curled up in the foetal position, with his arms clutched around his head. I couldn't see any damage. Blood wasn't leaking onto the docks. He was probably fine. Physically, at least. "He looks okay," I called over to Teya.

"Shh," said Yilin. "Not so loud." She'd swum back to the docks and was resting her folded arms on the edge of the platform Teya stood on. "There's a creature in the tunnel network. It came for me and broke through my defences. I only just escaped with my life."

"Did you keep cave raiders in cages?" Teya asked.

Yilin rose out of the water, slowly, so that her human waist was visible, then her tail. She towered over us, water pouring from her flesh. "They tried to steal from me," said Yilin. "They were useful. I traded them."

"Are you going to keep us in a cage?" I asked, drawing my pistol.

"You saved my life. I owe you a debt, so I may not threaten you."

Teya tilted her head to the side. "Really?"

Yilin hissed between her teeth, like a leaking air tank.

Teya lowered her crossbow. "Forgive me if I'm being rude, but I have not previously associated... people who live in the Hungry Dark with codes of honour."

Yilin smiled, thinly. "You must not have met many of us."

"We're looking for the lost city of Sirmo," I said, taking a step forward. "Any information you can offer, along with our freedom, will settle our debt."

Yilin's jaw clenched. "You may not be pleased with the results of that trade. I have never been to Sirmo myself."

"But it's real?" Teya asked. "It exists?"

Yilin nodded. Teya's eyes flashed. My heart leapt. Teya and I glanced at each other, the joy on her face was mirrored in mine.

"Yilin," I said, "please, what can you tell us of Sirmo?"

She shifted uncomfortably. "I have told you everything I know. That is why I said you wouldn't be happy with the trade. But I know of someone who might be able to help you find it. If you find her, and tell her that I will owe her a debt, she'll likely escort you straight to Sirmo."

"Someone?" Teya asked. "What sort of someone?"

"A cave raider, like you. I've traded with her in the past. Her name is Kyrene Teresi."

My lungs clamped tight. That couldn't be possible.

Teya swayed on her feet. "Kyrene Teresi is dead. She went into the dark two years ago and never returned."

Yilin frowned. "I'd wondered why I hadn't seen her for some time. You're sure? She did not seem like the type to fall to the dark."

Teya's voice was tight with tension. "Have you seen her since then?"

"I don't track years, I track progress. Another security feature added; another deal brokered. I have not seen Kyrene for some considerable time."

I shook my head. "We need recent information. Do you know anyone else who can help us find Sirmo."

Yilin shook her head, slowly. "No-one that wouldn't obliterate you on sight."

I thought of brushing this off, but 'obliterate' stuck in my head. I took a step back.

Teya glanced at me, then turned back to Yilin. "Tell me about Kyrene Teresi. Where did you meet her?"

"She snuck her way through my traps and made me an offer of trade."

"Where was this?" Teya asked, her eyes narrowing.

"In my harbour."

"The place with the cages? Were they full at the time?"

Yilin paused, pursing her lips. "Yes. Kyrene and I traded whilst the other cave raiders called for aid from my cages."

Teya narrowed her eyes. "Did any of them call to her by name?"

"I don't believe so."

Teya shrugged. The chill in her expression swept through me. Teya was a pragmatic person, and that had kept us both alive for years now. Sometimes her pragmatism made me think she was unfeeling or cruel. In those moments, I tried to remember how often her attitude had saved my life.

I also remembered those moments when I'd been in my room, unable to stop crying, and Teya had brought me food, told me everything was going to be okay and embraced me. I remembered when she'd taken me into the caves, even though she had more important things to do, because she knew I needed a break from the misery.

I remembered watching fireworks with her at the winter solstice festival. I don't know whether she'd meant to, but she'd held my hand as the bellflower and amber lights shimmered in the night sky. In that moment, I'd realised that she'd lost her wife and very possibly needed me as much as I needed her, for all that I was a burden.

"The last time I spoke to Kyrene," said Yilin, drawing me back to the present, "she was heading to a castle on the second level. She'd heard rumours of some powerful artefact that held the key to defeating the Hungry Dark once and for all. I traded some tech with her, in exchange for secrets and favours, and she left my lair unharmed."

"You have a *lair*?" I said.

"Yes, the docks on level one. That's where you came from, is it not? You borrowed one of my barges."

"Yes, but you call it a lair. That's *amazing*."

Teya's face moved from amusement to impatience and back to amusement in the space of a couple of seconds. "Can you tell us anything else?" she asked Yilin.

Yilin shook her head. "The good news is that the castle is close by. It's just to the north of here." She then rattled off a string of directions that I found impossible to follow.

Teya nodded and rolled her shoulders. "Thank you for your time, Yilin. If we meet again in the future, I hope we can continue this cordial relationship."

A smile crept across Yilin's face, much like it might on the face of a grizzly bear. "Of course," she said. "But I have one piece of advice. You came across me in an hour of great need and were kind to me. I will not forget that, but know that I would not have been so polite were circumstances different. With that in mind, if you ever find yourself on level four of Tenebro, stay away from the great reservoir. My mother lives in there and she can be... cranky."

"How cranky?" I asked. I usually enjoyed meeting people's cranky mums.

"She'd obliterate you in a heartbeat if you dare enter her lake."

"Huh," I said, unsure if she was exaggerating. Possibly not. I couldn't seek out the lake if it would put Teya in danger, but maybe if we found Sirmo I could –

"Come on, Meli," said Teya.

I shook myself. I'd got distracted again. Teya nodded in the direction of the castle. I made to follow, but then paused. "Wait, what about the humans?"

Teya started, having apparently forgotten about our erstwhile pursuers. She looked from me to the child human, who was slowly emerging from his foetal ball of terror. "They can do what they want as long as they don't attack us, we're not their dads."

"Wait..." said the kid. "Wait, please, you can't leave me down here. There are *monsters*." He shuddered and looked up at Yilin, who nodded to him.

"You were perfectly happy to leave earlier," Teya said. "Why are you even here? Last we saw you, you were heading up to the surface."

"Yes, but then that *monster* wouldn't stop chasing us. We just tried to get away and then there was this nightmare and then Ada wouldn't wake up and then..." The kid shook his head. He looked between Yilin, Teya and me, his mouth opening and shutting. He stood, and his foot bumped into an inert glass ball. It was the glow globe he'd been carrying through the canals. The chemical reactions that sustained its light must have faded as Teya and I conversed with Yilin.

"Oh no..." he said, "no, no no. Please. You can't leave me down here. The darkness..."

"So use another globe."

The human patted his pockets, frantically. His lips opened and I saw tears bead at the corners of his eyes. Teya closed her eyes and pinched the bridge of her nose.

"How's the woman?" I asked.

Teya opened one eye. "Dead. I think. She won't wake up and her hands have been... replaced."

Gold. Baldy's hands were solid gold. I scratched my chin. "Hey, kid, did Baldy fall into the trap?"

"I don't know what happened!" the kid wailed. "One moment we were running away from that monster, and then I was... somewhere else... and then I was back in the tunnels and Ada wouldn't wake up and..." He trailed off.

Teya shrugged. "Well, she won't be seeing the sun again."

The kid sobbed. Yilin rose from the water to peer at the body. "Interesting."

"Hello?" called a voice I didn't recognise from the other side of the water gates. "Is anyone there? I need help!"

Yilin started, spun around to face the gates, and then turned back to face us again. "You need to go. Right now." She looked down at Ada's body and grabbed her arms. She plucked the body from the dock.

"What are you doing?" the kid asked.

Yilin didn't even look at him. She repositioned the body on her shoulders and swam towards the water gates. "I said get out."

"I need help!" said the voice beyond the water gates, noticeably louder than previously. "Is anyone there?"

Someone else needed help. My debts were getting lighter and lighter. I walked to the edge of the dock. "Open the gates. I want to help."

"Get. Out. Believe me, you don't want to see what's on the other side of those gates. And you don't want it seeing you."

"Look at her face, Melita," hissed Teya, in my ear.

I turned. Yilin's jaw was clenched. Her eyes were fixed on the door. Her chest was rising and falling far quicker than previously.

Teya pulled at my arm. Confused, I allowed her to drag me away from Yilin. Every instinct I had was screaming at me to stay and help the voice, but I knew that was wrong. It felt like another trap.

The Hungry Dark swallowed Yilin. Anxiety rose inside me, but I clicked my fingers to interrupt the cacophony of guilt. Yilin lived in the dark. She wouldn't die if left alone with it. The human, however, was at the edge of our light. He realised this just in time and sprinted to join us. We fled up the ramp, towards the doorway to the next chamber.

"Is anyone there?" The voice reached to me out of the dark, then wood splintered under a single massive impact. I glanced behind me, and saw pinpricks of light burning through the Hungry Dark. I saw them... and I got the feeling that they saw me.

"Come on, Melita!" Teya said.

I nodded and sprinted to catch up to her. The three of us ran down a rough stone passageway. After only a couple of minutes, we burst into an enormous cavern. Our light didn't reach the walls, so I couldn't know how large it was, but the air moved around in a gentle, teasing breeze. For the air to move like that, the cavern had to be either truly enormous or open to the elements.

Spread out ahead of us were familiar two-storey houses. I only caught snatches of detail as we ran. There, a lantern with a family sigil hung next to an entranceway. There, a row of plant pots resting next to a walkway – the Hungry Dark had left nothing but soil.

We ran down an alley between the nearest two houses. I paused at the far end and looked out into the street. "Looks clear."

Teya nodded, and then rounded on the human. "Who are you and why were you following us?"

The human's gaze darted from point to point but avoided looking at Teya. He drew himself up. "My name is Silas."

"What? Like the warrior who dressed as a woman in order to fight in the imperial army?" I asked. "That's amazing. Your parents must have had big plans for you."

"Yes," said Silas. "Now who are you?"

"I'm Melita, and this is Teya," I said.

"You don't need to know our names," said Teya, at the same time.

Teya and I looked at each other. She frowned at me and nodded towards the human. 'Why are you being friendly with this human?' she didn't say.

I tilted my head to the side and nodded down at the human's belt and hands, which didn't hold any weapons. 'He's unarmed, he's not a threat,' I didn't say.

Teya's eyes flashed wide, exasperated, and she flicked her hands open and away from her body. 'It's so very much not our problem,' she didn't say.

I rolled my eyes and exaggeratedly stared around at the darkness that surrounded us. 'What are you going to do? Leave him here? In the dark? He's just a kid!' I didn't say.

"What are you doing?" Silas asked.

Teya turned to him and folded her arms. "Why are you still here? Are you going to slit our throats in our sleep?"

Silas took two sharp steps back. "No! Look, it wasn't like that. Ada said I needed to come with her."

"Mm," Teya said. "Well, bye then. Go back to the surface. Go back home."

"I can't, I've got no light."

Teya rolled her eyes. She unclipped a glow globe from her belt and held it out to the human.

Silas didn't take the glow globe. "You want to send me back to the surface alone?"

"Do you want to go home or not?" Teya asked.

Silas drew himself up. "Of course!"

"Well, there you go."

"But..."

Teya turned to me, her eyebrows raised. I thought about what it would mean to abandon our quest to take the kid back to the surface. This was further into Tenebro than we'd ever been. What might we find if we pressed on?

The thing was... Silas needed our help. But then again, he'd come here with people who wanted to kill us. When creatures of the dark did that, I didn't hold it against them, but these humans had attacked my village. They weren't good people.

"We're not going to escort you back to the surface, Silas," I said, firmly. "We've got things to do. People to find. Forgotten civilisations to discover. Precious towns to rescue from packs of rampaging humans."

"Take the glow globe, go back home and never threaten Ekzilo ever again," said Teya.

Silas looked at the glow globe in Teya's hand, then cast his gaze to the floor. "I can't."

A furious roar echoed between the houses. It sounded distant, but not nearly distant enough. Teya unslung her crossbow. "Sounds like another fallen. Let's move."

"What? There's more than one of those things?" Silas said, his eyes wide.

I smiled at him. "There are hundreds. How many have we had to deal with on our little trips, Teya? Seventeen?"

"Sixteen," Teya said. "You're counting the one that just turned out to be a particularly aggressive cave raider. Lead on, Meli, I'll navigate."

I nodded and drew my gun, whilst Teya fished out her compass. I checked the pressure gauge, which had dropped since I'd fired at Yilin. I worked the pump, and then checked the magazine. Seven rounds left.

"That way," said Teya, pointing at one particular patch of the Hungry Dark.

I grinned at her, stepped out of the alley and scanned the street. No movement. No threats. I waved the other two to follow, before scurrying across to the alley on the far side of the street.

"Wait! You can't leave me alone with one of those things," Silas said, running after us.

"We're not leaving you alone," I said, "we're going about our day. It's up to you whether you go back to the surface or stick with us."

"I'd rather you went back to the surface," said Teya.

I nodded. "So would I, but if you're worried about the fallen you can stick with us for a little while."

"But..." said Silas, "but..." His footsteps trailed after us.

Another fallen scream cracked the stillness around us. It sounded a lot closer. I kept my breathing even. One fallen wasn't a problem with both me and Teya prepared for it. If anything, knowing that it was around was keeping me sharp. In the moment. I was maintaining my concentration.

My legs were loose. The weight in my chest was… well, it was still there but it was definitely manageable.

We stalked through the alley and into a wide street lined with smooth, elegantly sculpted paving stones. I caught a glimpse of moving shadow – less defined than a fallen. A swirling patch of darkness. A wraith of night.

Teya drew in a breath. "I don't like the look of that."

"A large open area with no cover which looks like it has some unknown peril lurking somewhere within and a furious, unrelenting creature tracking us, what's not to like?" I asked.

Teya smiled. Silas whimpered.

"Is this the way to the castle?" I asked.

"It's the most direct route, yes. Should we outrun the fallen or try to lose it in the houses?"

"Outrun," I said. "We don't know this level well enough to hide, and we can't control your glow globe well enough to smother our light safely."

Teya tested the tension on the string of her crossbow, before nodding. "Sounds good. Silas, try to keep up. Or don't. I don't care."

"Wait…" Silas said, but I was already moving. We crossed the street and took shelter next to a wall, painted white apart from the supporting posts which were a rich wisteria-brown. Teya held up a hand and consulted her compass. She frowned at it, before shrugging and pointing east. I nodded and followed the wall in that direction. The stone reflected the brilliant light of the glow globe back into the street. This seemed odd, but I was too busy running to spend any time puzzling over why.

I paused at a gap in the wall. Wrought iron gates hung wide open, inviting us inside. "What do you think, Teya?"

Teya glanced at her compass. "We should go in. The walls will hide our light, and we have no idea how big the detour will be if we go around. Yilin said the castle was to the north, so if we cut through here, we'll be taking the direct route."

"Sounds great!" I slipped through the gates and waited until the other two were through, then I closed one gate whilst Teya hauled the other shut. There was a bolt set into the gates, which I slid shut.

"Aren't you locking us in?" Silas asked.

"No," said Teya, "we're locking that out."

Silas looked up and reeled back. The fallen had finally found us. It sprinted across the street, slammed into the gates and scrabbled at them, trying to get to us. I took two quick steps backwards, grinning as my heart picked up its pace.

This fallen must have started its dive in winter, because it wore thick cotton trousers, a shirt, and an insulated jacket. Its eyes were white and filled with hatred. Its hair was long and matted. On its head was... "Huh." On her head was a headband made to look like a set of cat ears.

"Melita, come on, let's go!"

Teya's shout broke me out of my fascination. We ran down the path the gates had guarded. We'd only travelled a few metres before an enormous two-storey building loomed out of the darkness. Its shape was instantly familiar – large windows set into a robust wooden frame, topped by a flat roof. It was a grander version of Ekzilo's school. Teya sprinted up the three steps that led to the enormous wooden entrance doors.

The doors were shut and didn't budge when Teya tried to slide them open. She rammed her shoulder into the solid wood, but the doors stayed resolutely closed. I joined her at the doors, spurred on by the screams of the fallen behind us.

"Three, two, one," said Teya. We both charged at the doors, together. Pain spiked in my shoulder as it met the wood, which rattled, but didn't budge.

"Something must be blocking it on the other side," I said. I turned to look back at the gates. Swirls of darkness obscured much of my view, but I saw a stygian shape trying to break down the gates in much the same way we were trying to break down the doors.

"Let's climb in through a window," said Teya.

Next to her, Silas shuddered.

I clapped him on the shoulder. "Come on! It'll be an adventure!"

I led us along the east wall of the school, until we came to a bank of windows that looked into a classroom. The gates rattled behind us, the sound echoing from wall to wall to wall.

"It's climbing the gates," said Teya.

I reached up and tried to slide the nearest window open. Jammed. Teya joined me and we both put our weight into it. Without warning, the window shot open. Teya held her hands out at knee height. I placed a foot in her waiting hands, and she boosted me up and over the windowsill. Teya's light didn't reach the classroom, so I swallowed a tooth and brought my own light to life before the dark could snatch at me. The vibrant blue light made the classroom seem bright and full of life instead of empty and dead.

Silas climbed in after me and stopped as soon as he saw my glowing skin. "You're a witch?" His voice trembled, and he turned to the window. He might have been thinking about fleeing from me, but Teya climbed in at that moment, blocking his path.

"We've got to move, gang, the fallen's over the gate and is looking for us."

"I'm not going anywhere with a witch," Silas said.

Teya shrugged. "Okay. I'll leave you the glow globe. Good luck." She dropped her glow globe, unceremoniously, at Silas's feet. Ignoring the human's incredulous stare, she strode to the classroom door, slid it open and stepped into the corridor beyond. I paused in the doorway and waved goodbye to Silas.

Past the kid, in the dark, the fallen screamed. Silas scooped up the glow globe and looked from us to the window. He hesitated, but a cry of triumph split the darkness outside. Two bloodied hands gripped the windowsill and the fallen's face rose into view.

CHAPTER NINE

Silas reeled back from the fallen, bumped into a desk and tripped. He sprawled, scattering furniture and his glow globe spun off into a corner of the room. The fallen climbed onto the windowsill.

I leapt forward, grabbed Silas's arm and dragged him to his feet. The fallen screamed in triumph and leapt at us. Thankfully, she landed in amongst the mess of chairs and desks that Silas had scattered. This gave me the time I needed to haul Silas out of the classroom. Teya shut the door behind us.

A corridor stretched away, our every sound echoed from the wooden floors and permeated the paper walls. Windows in the north wall looked out over darkness. Silas wrenched himself out of my grip and backed away from me.

Teya shook her head and took my hand. "Let's go, Melita."

"We can't leave Silas here!"

"Melita, look at him! He's terrified of you. He's made his decision, respect it."

Silas backed away from us, glancing from me to the Hungry Dark behind him and then back to me, clearly unsure as to which he should fear more. Leaving him would be a death sentence, but he clearly didn't want to come with us. What was I going to do, kidnap him?

A rattling from the classroom door caused Teya to swear and leap forward. She grabbed the door with both hands and braced herself against it to keep it closed. I drew my pistol and aimed it at the area where I thought the fallen was likely to be. My aim was thrown by a hand shattering through the flimsy timber and paper of the door.

Teya grabbed hold of the arm with both hands and pulled, so the fallen's torso was dragged into the far side of the door.

I aimed past Teya and yelled "Ears!"

Teya clapped her hands to her ears. I could only cover one before firing another shot. The *crack* of my gun firing was agonisingly loud in the confined space, even with one of my ears covered.

A scream cut through the door and the creature's arm thrashed in furious agony. Teya jumped clear, so I shot again, leaving a high-pitched ringing in my ears as the roiling crack of the gun faded. The fallen's arm slumped but refused to stop moving.

Teya motioned for me to take a step back, before reversing her grip on the door. She shoved it half open - the monster's arm was still thrust through the door so she couldn't open it fully. The door slid aside, and the fallen was tugged with it, dragging it off its feet. It slumped to its knees. It probably would have collapsed entirely had its hand not been caught in the door.

Teya stepped around the monster, who made a weak swipe at her. Its breath was ragged and shallow. One of my shots must have caught it in the lung. Teya ran to the corner of the room, snatched up the glow globe that Silas had dropped and returned to my side.

"Do you see that?" I asked, pointing at the fallen's head, where the cat ears I'd spotted earlier sat.

"Huh," Teya said, before frowning, shrugging, and dodging past the fallen, out of the classroom.

The creature made another swipe at Teya but was noticeably slower. Her eyes closed. Teya slid the classroom door shut once she was back in the corridor. The fallen's arm slipped from the hole and into darkness.

The stillness of the air around me made me realise just how shaky I was. My vision was getting fuzzy, and I was drenched with sweat. I unslung my pack and fished out a canteen. I drained half of it and offered the rest to Teya, who accepted it gratefully.

"Were those cat ears on that fallen's head?" I asked, as Teya drank.

Teya nodded, still drinking.

"I don't get it. How could the headband have stayed on since the darkness took her?"

I eased the classroom door open a fraction and peered through. The fallen on the other side let out a rasping roar that failed to impress as she was evidently unable to rise from the ground.

"Don't make it angry!" Silas hissed.

I stared at the headband on the fallen's head. It was a perfectly normal headband of the sort usually worn by teenagers. It didn't seem to be tied onto the fallen's head in any way.

"Melita, is this important?" Teya asked.

"You know, I think it might be..." I reached forward and twitched the cat ears from the fallen's head. She took a swipe at me, but her movements were slow and easily dodged. I retreated back out into the corridor but didn't close the door behind me.

I turned to Teya. "She's not quite dead. If she follows us, which she probably won't, it'll be interesting to see what happens with those ears."

"Why do you care about any of this?" Silas asked, still hovering at the edge of our light.

"Last chance," said Teya. She bowled the glow globe she'd rescued to the human, who scooped it up inexpertly. "Go to the surface. Go back home. You can't stay here; you're going to get us killed."

I nodded. "Yeah, and you're not allowed to get Teya killed."

Teya took in a breath... but didn't speak. Silas stood still. Teya shrugged and set off down the corridor.

I caught up and walked with her, shoulder to shoulder. "So, this castle Yilin mentioned..."

"What about it?"

"You know I mentioned a creature I met last night? The one I thought might be able to help us find Sirmo? She said she lived in a castle on level two. I'm guessing there aren't two castles down here."

Teya frowned. "Interesting. I wonder why Yilin didn't mention that."

"Good question. Maybe she didn't know? Anyway, hopefully we'll find answers there, either about Sirmo or Kyrene."

"Ideally both, we'll have to see." Teya frowned, then shook her head.

I nudged her. "Problem?"

Teya smiled, ruefully. "No, I was just wondering if Ky had become a fallen. I must be losing my grip. She was far too stubborn to give herself over. Ha! The very idea of it... Anyway, how are you feeling, Melita?"

My hands were shaking. I placed one of them on my heart which was still pounding unnaturally fast, but it felt like it wasn't about to explode. "Yeah, I'm having a lovely time."

"How many teeth have you got left?"

I checked my wrist. "Plenty. You have enough glow globes to keep us going?"

"Seven left. We need to make sure we have enough to get us back to the surface."

"Wait!" said Silas, his voice cracking.

We turned around. The light from Silas's glow globe was only just mingling with my beautiful blue dome. Tendrils of the Hungry Dark were probing at the tiny overlapping zone of light, seeing whether they could force us apart.

"What?" I asked.

"You can't leave me here!"

Teya shook her head and turned back. We started walking eastwards again, with Teya checking her compass. "We need to head a little north," she said, pointing at the wall on our left. There were windows set into it. Shapes loomed on the other side – the Hungry Dark must be thinner out there, but it was hard to tell why.

"That looks like a central courtyard," I said.

Teya nodded. I heard running footsteps behind me and turned to see Silas catching up with us.

"What do you want?" Teya asked, not turning round.

"I'm staying with you."

"Are you sure?" I asked. "I'm a wiiiiiiiitch." I waved my hands in the air; a little trail of dancing lights followed in their wake. This came as a surprise to me. I'd never been able to leave persistent effects like that before. Still, I'd never had my light active for this long before either. Maybe I was finally gaining some measure of control over my power.

Silas swallowed. "Even... still. You can't leave me!"

Teya spun around to face Silas. She took two quick steps towards him. He took two shuffling steps back.

"Look," Teya said. "I don't want you with us, but we're not going to stop you following us. Right, Melita?"

"Right."

"I don't blame you for not wanting to go into the dark by yourself, but you can't slow us down. Okay? If we tell you to do something, you have to do it."

Silas nodded, eagerly. "Anything, anything, just please don't leave me down here."

"I'd like an apology," I said.

Silas hesitated, before nodding. "I'm sorry! I apologise!"

"What are you apologising for?" I asked, folding my arms.

"Attacking your village, even though I didn't actually attack anyone."

I narrowed my eyes. "Look, I have a question. Answer this one and I'll think about protecting you. Why does your village not care about preserving the principle of pacifism? Did you not get taught about the great war in your schools or something? Do you think it doesn't apply to you?"

Silas drew himself up. "If you don't fight you make society weak! People need conflict to make them stronger."

I raised my arms into an X in front of me. "No. No, no no. As a country we've only grown stronger since the great war because we're not killing each other every five minutes. Look around you! Tenebro fell because warlords on the surface kept attacking them. We're currently walking through what happens when people think it's okay to just attack people and take what they want. Your village, and its allies exiled almost everyone in Ekzilo. You made it too dangerous for us to make the journey to other, less horrible parts of the country. And you think that's strength? It requires real strength to be the better person and shut violence down by not rising to it than it is to get into a scrap over nothing. Do you really believe that nonsense about conflict leading to strength?"

Silas was quiet for just a moment too long before he said, "Yes! Of course! Why are you asking me about any of this anyway? I should be angry at you! You're the ones who attacked Ada! She's dead because of you!"

"Ada was the bald woman who we left with Yillin? Who was she to you?" Teya asked.

That took the wind out of Silas's sails. He was quiet for twenty seconds before saying: "She worked at the place where I grew up. She took care of some of us."

Teya raised an eyebrow. "You know, when you're deliberately vague it just makes me curious. Where did you grow up?"

Silas's gaze fell anywhere except on Teya. On the ancient wooden floorboards. On the glass pane set into the wall that looked out over darkness. Up at the ceiling, into which was set a long-dead glow globe. He muttered something.

"I'm sorry?" Teya said.

"A foster home."

"Oh, okay."

"Wait," I said. "How does a foster kid end up following someone who cares for him with an angry mob to attack a village of committed pacifists?"

"No, that's not what happened! Ada came back yesterday and said she and her friends went to get breakfast at your village. You attacked them, so they got a bunch of us together and said you all needed to be taught a lesson."

"A lesson? They were busy burning Ekzilo to the ground when we left," I said. "A bunch of you chased us into the Hungry Dark. Even if I did attack Ada and her friends, which I didn't, you don't think that might have been a bit of an overreaction?"

Silas didn't reply to this. Teya and I exchanged exasperated looks, shrugged and started walking again.

Over her shoulder, my friend said: "Silas, you're tagging along with us and we're not taking revenge for what you and your friends did to our village. Unless you have a better apology for Melita, you should really keep your mouth shut."

A strangled rasp from behind us made me start. I glanced around, past the kid, but couldn't see anything approaching through the darkness. I turned back to Teya, who nodded and increased the length of her stride.

A doorway loomed out of the gloom in the north wall. Teya paused as we reached it and nodded to me. I drew my pistol and reeled my light back in. Anything could be beyond that door, and we didn't want to attract attention if we could help it. Teya held up three fingers, then two, then one.

She slid the door aside. The scrape of wood on wood died quickly in the still air. I stepped through onto a stone path. To either side were gravel beds that might once have contained plants. Ahead of us was the slightly thinner patch of darkness I'd seen through the windows. A rushing sound soothed the space. Was that running water?

I walked forward, slowly, and softly. Teya's footsteps were barely audible behind me, given they were mostly masked by Silas, who appeared to have lead feet. Before long, we were far enough away from the school that I couldn't make out the buildings through the darkness, and the fallen's furious rasps were distant and muffled.

As we moved further down the path, my light picked out a large wooden archway and timber floorboards that rose at a soft incline. The arch was colourless in my blue light, but when Silas brought his glow globe closer, I saw that the structure was actually red – a brilliant strong vermillion. The colour took my breath away.

We passed under the arch. I reached out to brush my fingers against the painted wood, whispering a prayer for light in that moment of peace. Moments later, my light pushed back the dark from the path ahead to reveal a bridge – vermillion, like the arch, a flowing, elegant design. Constructed with skill, maintained with obvious care and dreadfully, dreadfully wrong.

"Teya," I hissed, as we walked closer.

"Mm?"

"Tenebro has been dead for hundreds of years, right?"

"Mm."

"There's no one down here?"

"Not unless they've found a way to stave off the darkness, no."

"Then who painted this archway? Who's been maintaining the bridge?"

Teya frowned. "That's a very good question. There's no way that paint's two hundred years old. There's a stream here; the moisture from that would have caused any wooden structures to decay decades ago."

We stepped onto the bridge, our footsteps thumping on the solid wood, reminding me of autumn walks through Ekzilo. The bridge crossed over a narrow, rushing stream, before the path sloped down into the thinner area of darkness. Above us, a fissure had been carved into the rock which led to the surface, through which I could see one of the moons, looking quite a bit smaller than I was used to, along with a cluster of stars. During the day, light from the fissure must drive the darkness back.

"If it looks like we're going to stay down in the dark for a while, we could come back here and camp during the day," I said. "We wouldn't need to use any artificial light."

Teya nodded. "I agree. Let's hope it doesn't come to that. The longer we're down here, the more our friends on the surface are in danger. I'd like to get out tonight if we can."

Behind us, Silas made a strangled 'I have something to say' sort of noise. I ignored him. Ahead of us, my light picked out the branches of an enormous tree. It towered above us, maybe twenty metres tall. Its branches seemed bare until I drew closer, and my light revealed thousands of gnarled buds, as if it was a bush waiting for the first heat of summer so it could flower.

"I'm amazed this can survive down here," Teya said. "It obviously gets light from the fissure, but... do you think it furls its leaves up into those pods during the night?"

"Maybe," I said, not really paying attention to Teya's words. The tree was ancient, a monument to life surviving in the harshest of conditions. Still, I didn't like the idea of what the tree had needed to do to itself in order to survive.

"Is it moving?" Silas asked from behind us.

The tree's branches were, indeed, swaying as if in a breeze. I took a step closer, bringing the tree's trunk into my light. Its bark was thick, dark, and twisted.

"It's beautiful…" Without thinking I lifted a hand towards it.

Teya rested a palm on my shoulder. "Don't touch it, Melita. Something's off about this tree."

I hesitated, considering the spoilsport's advice, then nodded and drew my hand away. Back the way we'd come, the fallen roared.

"The fallen's still following us. Can't incapacitate those things for long, can we?" I said, turning in the direction of the scream. "Shall we see if she still has the cat ears on?"

"Yes," said Teya, "and if she does, we need to kill her."

I frowned. "What? Why?"

"Why are you people talking about cat ears?" Silas asked.

Teya ignored Silas and turned to face me. "If the fallen has put her cat ears back on, that means that part of the cave raider - who she was before she gave herself to the Hungry Dark - is still in there. It means she's not just a pawn of the dark, some part of her is still alive. And if some part of her is still alive, she's currently got a punctured lung and a shattered collarbone. She's in absolute agony and the Hungry Dark won't let her pass out from the pain."

"So, we should knock her out rather than kill her!"

"I don't know if that's even possible. Can you heal her like you healed Yilin?"

I shook my head. "Yilin's own magical abilities healed her, she just used my power. I can't do anything like that here. We need to try knocking her out. She might be able to come back."

"The word 'might' is doing a lot of work in that sentence, Meli. She gave herself over to the dark. We have no idea if anyone can come back from that.

Even if we could purge the dark somehow, she's still going to have a bullet in her lung."

"Then we could..." Hundreds of suggestions leapt to my lips, but I clamped my teeth shut. I was letting myself get carried away. We couldn't perform surgery down here to remove the bullet, even if any of us knew how. If we made any attempt to remove the shard of metal, we'd probably only end up getting the wound infected. Tears beaded at the corners of my eyes. If there had been an opportunity to save her, I'd lost it when I'd shot her. I looked from Teya's eyes to her crossbow, not feeling strong enough to say the words out loud.

Teya nodded. She turned as another rasping scream sounded nearby. She raised her crossbow and waited. I took a step back, not wanting to be close to this, but also not wanting to shut my eyes to the burden my friend was taking on because I wasn't strong enough. I'd have let the fallen live on in agony because I wanted to preserve life at all costs. I frowned at that thought.

The fallen screamed, I caught a glimpse of the cat ears perched neatly on her head, Teya loosed a bolt from her crossbow. Behind me, Silas screamed, "Look out!" and tackled me, knocking me to the ground. I lashed out at Silas, who squealed in surprise. I pushed the human off me and leapt to my feet. Teya was frantically loading another bolt into her crossbow. At her feet was the fallen, who wasn't moving. Teya wasn't looking at the fallen, however. She was looking at me. *Past* me.

"Melita! Duck!"

I threw myself to the ground. A glancing blow stuck me on the way down. Teya fired her crossbow, the bolt whistled over my head and thunked into the tree. I rolled over - the tree's branches were thrashing around in some breeze I couldn't see. One raised high into the air directly over me.

"Oh no..."

I rolled to the side and leapt to my feet as the branch smashed into the ground. I dodged a second, ponderous but powerful swing and nearly bumped into Silas, who was cowering nearby.

Teya sprinted to my side and grabbed my shoulder, pulling me back away from the tree. Together, the three of us retreated out of range of the tree's branches. It thrashed in our direction but couldn't reach us.

"Did you know trees could do that?" panted Silas.

"No," I said. "Sorry I hit you. I thought you were attacking me again."

"Is it getting lighter?" Teya asked.

Angular shapes loomed in the distance, probably the walls of the school buildings. The world around us was brightening. I was finally able to get a good feel for our surroundings – we were in a courtyard, surrounded on four sides by two storey school buildings – paper walls around a wooden frame with dark windows looking out over us. We'd been following the only path that led through the courtyard, past the enormous tree and to a large pair of metal gates to the north.

Silas grabbed me by the arm and pointed at the tree. "Look!"

The tree jerked from left to right, its bark expanding and contracting. Out and in, out and in. Its movement was ponderous, but grew more frenetic with each wrenching movement. The darkness around the tree was fading. I blinked and tried to focus – it looked as if the tree was drawing the Hungry Dark into itself.

"That's impossible," Teya said.

I grinned. "I know! Isn't it amazing!"

"We need to go, right now. Whatever that thing is doing, we know it doesn't like us."

"Right! Let's circle around it. It's just a tree, we can stay out of reach of its branches."

An enormous root ripped free of the ground and slammed down onto the gravel. The root braced itself against the ground as the tree leaned towards us. The ground around it shifted alarmingly. A terrible moan echoed around the courtyard. It was low, melancholy and ear-splittingly loud.

"Never mind!" I said. "Run!"

I led the way, although with the Hungry Dark this thin, we probably would have been safe even without my light. I ran past the tree, heading to the north wall. The tree's branches swiped at us, but it couldn't reach us from so far away. It hauled more and more roots free of the ground, moaning in agony as it did so. Before long, it was able to lift itself up and pull itself completely free.

"Wow, that's huge!" I shouted over my shoulder to Teya and Silas. The tree thrashed towards us, its movements unsteady as it overbalanced and tottered first one way, then the other. At every movement, more pained groans split the night air.

I reached the north wall and ran along until I reached the gate, which was closed. "Teya! Get the gate open! I'll keep the tree busy!" I ran past the gate, then turned and waved at the tree, trying to attract its attention. Teya and Silas reached the gate and tugged at it. Silas's glow globe was fading, even without the Hungry Dark pushing it back. Strangely, the tree didn't even pause as it staggered past them. It seemed entirely fixated on me.

I sprinted south, towards the bridge over the stream. This would give me plenty of places to run. My light was shifting colours – it had been blue but pulsating spears of yellow were shining out of my skin.

The tree charged at me. I stared up at the tower of night-clad bark and whipping branches, my heart pounding and my vision sparking. I wondered whether I might have been a little overconfident by drawing the tree's attention like this.

I slipped a tooth from my bracelet into my mouth, my heart momentarily freezing as I felt how many gaps there were in the row of bones at my wrist. I was getting through my teeth far faster than I normally did, and they'sd be exceedingly difficult to replace. Still, I wouldn't need to replace them if I died down here, so best to use them as and when I needed them rather than hold back and possibly have my adventure cut short.

The tree thundered towards me before swinging its branches. I dodged to the right, but the twigs still battered at the leather of my jacket. Pain shot through my shoulder and up to my collarbone. I yelped, but I didn't have time to think. I dove out of the path of the charging tree. I rolled as I landed and leapt to my feet. I was in time to see the tree completely fail to stop, and cannonball into the south wall of the school. Wood crumbled under the impact. Glass shattered. Wooden beams creaked and groaned before, slowly, the roof of the school collapsed. The tree thrashed in the wreckage, howling in agony as it was swallowed by thousands of kilos of wood.

I winced at a stab of pain in my shoulder and felt the area gingerly. The leather of my coat hadn't been broken, but I could tell I was going to have a nasty bruise there for at least a week. I rolled my shoulder, wincing as the movement caused another stab of pain.

"Melita!" Teya called. I shook the cobwebs in my head free and ran to join her and the human.

They'd managed to open the gates; an intricate mechanical lock lay on the ground, its securing bolts sheared through. I joined them on the far side of the gates and together we dragged them shut.

We'd emerged onto a broad street. Teya checked to make sure I wasn't severely injured before using her compass to check our heading. We walked in silence, following street after tomb-like street.

"Did you know trees could drink in the Hungry Dark like that?" I asked.

Teya shook her head. "I read this book once about the origins of magical humanoids like you, Melita. This book said that maybe, if a living creature stays in an area saturated by magic long enough, the magic and the creature bond together."

I frowned. "But I was born in Plogsworth, and I was born a witch. There's nowhere less innately magical than Plogsworth. I've asked everyone."

"The book said that actually there's a lot of background magic about, it just gets sunk into certain creatures and places. In your instance, Meli, the magic might have chosen you when you were in the womb. As a theory for where witches come from it makes more sense than any other I've heard."

I nodded, wondering whether this changed anything about who I was. "Okay," I said, filing that question away to think about later, "but what about the tree?"

"Well, if we know magic bonds with living things, how's this for an idea? Hundreds of years ago, maybe even before Tenebro fell, plants started to grow on the surface near the mouth of that fissure. The Hungry Dark leaked up there, not enough to devour the plants but enough to be troublesome. The magic accelerated the plants' evolution, and they developed traits that enabled them to survive, such as bark that was resistant to the darkness, and the ability to hide their leaves inside that bark when the sun wasn't out. If they did this – and I need to stress that's a big 'if' – before long, darkness resistant seeds would have fallen into Tenebro. Trees bloomed down here that were already darkness resistant, but that just meant they absorbed more of the magic. The tree we saw might be the result – a tree that unfurled its leaves during the day and sustained itself on the magic contained in the darkness during the night."

"Okay, but it tried to kill us."

"I'm not sure it did. You heard it, it was in agony. I think the darkness inside it wanted to kill us."

A massive set of wooden doors, bordered by a low wall with a sloped tiled roof loomed out of the darkness ahead of us. I unspooled more light, revealing hints of a towering structure beyond the wall. We'd made it to the castle.

A metal sheet had been riveted to the left door, and on the metal sheet someone had painted the words: 'Welcome! Please knock for admittance.' We stared at the sign. There was no way this sign was an original feature. Talvik's castles were legendary. The twelve monuments to the great war stood as living reminders that our country must never again give in to war. Clearly the people of Tenebro had wanted to have a similar reminder down here, if they built their own castle, but no-one building a monument to pacifism would rivet a sheet metal sign to its front gate. I'd never seen anything quite so strange in my life, and I'd just seen a tree get crushed by a school.

"So, do we knock?" Teya asked.

"Sounds like a good start." I took a quick step forward and knocked. The sharp rap of my knuckles against the wood flew into the dark and were swallowed. I waited. The gates didn't move.

"Do we try and open the gates?" asked Silas.

"Who's there?" said a new voice. It was low, gentle, and unmistakably Vakua's.

"Vakua! Hi!" I said "It's Melita Eklumigi."

"Melita? You found me! Consider me impressed. And I was impressed at your handling of the fallen earlier. I am now doubly impressed. Impress me once more, and you win a small prize."

Teya frowned, but didn't say anything.

"Thanks!" I said, "I've come because I wanted to ask you about Sirmo, we've had some trouble up in Ekzilo... oh, that reminds me, I brought friends!" I turned to Teya and Silas and whispered: "So, on the other side of the gate is Vakua. She's not human. Her appearance is... unusual but she seems nice. Silas, try not to panic."

Teya raised her eyebrows. I nodded to her and Silas. Teya shrugged, then took a step forward. "I'm delighted to meet you, Ms Vakua. My name is Teya Teresi."

Vakua didn't reply. I nudged Silas. "And my name's Jaeson Eyler!" called the human.

I was surprised for a moment. "Isn't your name Silas?" I asked. The look on the poor little human's face was a picture. It only took me a couple of seconds to work out why. "That name you gave us... It wasn't your name, was it?"

Jaeson shook his head, bashfully.

I rolled my eyes. "Paranoid humans. That story you tell each other about witches being able to eat people's souls if we know someone's true name is made up, you know. We can only do that if we also know a human's date of birth and are presented with copies of two identification documents."

"Don't tease Jaeson, Melita," said Teya. "Look." She nodded at the gate, which wasn't opening. Come to think of it, Vakua hadn't said anything for a while.

"Vakua? Is everything okay?" I called.

"Yes," said Vakua, "yes. It's just... my castle is a sanctuary to those I invite, and I worry about letting too many people in. I'm not going to leave anyone out in the dark, but I don't like how... I've had too many people look at me and see..." She trailed off.

"I'm so sorry, we can probably find somewhere else if..."

"No, no," said Vakua, her voice tense. "You are all welcome to my castle, but I must ask that you do not enter the keep itself. I will confine myself in there. You may stay for as long as you like. There is a food store and bedding in the outbuildings. The light will remain for as long as you stay with me. Melita, you may visit me in the keep if you wish. I trust you."

"Thank you, Vakua!" I called.

A mechanism clanked on the other side of the wall, and I felt a soft rumble through the soles of my boots. Above me, strings of glow globes blossomed, slowly at first but soon the darkness was driven back, and I was standing, along with my friend and a human child who kept changing his name, in front of a glorious, shining castle.

I walked towards the gate but Teya caught my hand. "Melita, I don't like this. Why is she only letting you into the keep?"

"Because I met her before, maybe? Look, I know this is a little dubious, but she left me the pistol. This might be the only chance we have of getting help for Ekzilo. Plus we might find answers about Kyrene."

Teya nodded, slowly. She shouldered her crossbow. Without a word, she walked through the gates.

Chapter Ten

I climbed the path which led up towards the keep with Teya and Jaeson alongside me. Hundreds of glow globes hung from cables above our heads. In the distance, I could hear the low rumble of a pump. Someone with serious technical skill had created a network of globes that could be fed biofuel through the cables. We'd be safe in the castle as long as the pump stayed active.

At the top of the small hill was a courtyard, paved with flat stones and bordered by a parapet, which looked out over the Hungry Dark. In the centre of the courtyard stood a great keep, its stone substructure occasionally visible amongst the cedar walls. Strings of glow globes wound up and around its rafters in glittering spirals that reached all the way to the cavern roof.

I'd never seen one of Talvik's legendary castles outside of drawings, and to see such a magnificent structure here and now with Teya beside me gave me a very immediate but distant feelings, as if I'd brushed up against history without knowing if I was a passive participant or someone who could involve herself. Sparks jumped and danced in my light, tiny fireworks celebrating our arrival.

I turned to Teya and the human. "You'll be okay here if I go and talk to Vakua?"

Teya nodded. "We'll have a poke about in the outbuildings. Try to find some food. Don't worry, I'll make sure no one gets into any trouble."

I nodded to my friend, turned, and walked up the slight slope towards the castle keep. The entranceway stood open, door-less, perpetually welcoming, so I walked inside, accepting the welcome. Inside was an antechamber – stuffy and formal, polished wood and fading cloth banners. A set of battered wooden cupboards sat against one wall, looking rather out of place in the precise traditionalism of the space.

Another door-less doorway the size of a decently sized house led through to the rest of the keep – an expanse of cedar floorboards, plain walls and a staircase leading up a fair way in. As a keep, as a legendary monument to peace, it was surprisingly boring.

"Vakua?" I called, wondering if I'd managed to miss her enormous, impassive face somewhere in the empty chamber.

"Ah," said my friend. "Welcome. I'll just come downstairs."

Her flawless, porcelain face slipped into view at the head of the stairs. Then, she descended, moving smoothly, like a snake. Her face topped a slender snake-like body. A shimmering turbulence of darkness. She looked like the sea under a moonless sky. Arms, twice as long as I was tall, brushed against the bannisters, and then the wall of the keep as she descended. Her face turned, saw me, and approached.

"Hello!" I said, desperately not wanting to seem rude in case Vakua took offence. "Sorry for staring."

She approached, slithering and unstoppable, poised and delicate. "You look about half as scared as I'd have expected."

I felt out of step with the world. My vision prickled, pins and needles at my world's periphery. "Only half?"

Vakua chuckled as she stopped a stone's throw from me. "No, Melita. Thank you for coming, and before you start to worry, I'm not angry that you brought friends. Please forgive my shyness, I merely wished to spend time in the company of someone who wouldn't look at me as if I'm a monster. Can I get you anything? There's water in bottles stacked under the stairs if you're thirsty."

I was about to decline, but the mention of water made me realise how dry my mouth was. I retrieved a bottle from its storage place and drank from it, self-consciously. Once I was done, I let my gaze dart around the room, completely unsure of what to say. "Who polishes your floors?" I asked.

"My floors?"

"They're beautifully maintained. Do you take care of that?"

"Me? No. There's a cave raider who lives down here. She takes care of that sort of thing for me in exchange for trade and protection."

My chest tightened. Hope was the first step on the long, long road to misery, but I had to be sure. "A diver lives down here?"

"Has done for years."

"Is her name Kyrene Teresi?"

Vakua's face tilted, slightly. "Now that's interesting. Why would you think that her name was Kyrene Teresi? You had another Teresi with you, didn't you? Are you searching for Kyrene?"

I hesitated. I really wasn't sure whether I wanted to answer that question until I knew what Vakua wanted. I scrunched my toes up and then relaxed them once, then twice. I concentrated on the sensation of my feet in my boots. I could feel the solid wood of the castle floor through my soles. The floor felt solid – real. It reminded me of why I was here. I could try to engage in a battle of wits to get at the information I wanted, or I could just ask her. Asking her required trust, but she hadn't given me a reason to distrust her. Yet.

"We're looking for Sirmo, and we're hoping to find information on what happened to Kyrene."

"What happened to Kyrene..." Vakua said, her voice low and rumbling. "You knew her?"

"Very well."

"Do you know…"

"I know many things. I know where Sirmo is. I can show you the way, if you'd like."

The knot of tension that had been building in my stomach burst into fizzing, jumping relief. I hadn't dared believe that our quest might actually be possible. "We would be extremely grateful if you could take us to Sirmo." Images sang to me – our triumphant return to Ekzilo bearing miracle devices which would ensure our safety. The festival held in our honour.

Vakua leaned forward. "There's just one thing I need you to do for me first."

A jolt ran through me and I was suddenly back in the room – entirely present and alert. Vakua's voice had sounded eager. Hungry.

"Oh?" I said, trying to keep my voice casual. My escape route should be clear - I'd have to find Teya and Silas… no, Teya and Jaeson. His name was Jaeson. How was I supposed to keep that human's name straight if he kept changing it every five minutes? I would get those two and flee for the gates. Had the gates closed behind us? I hadn't been paying attention.

Vakua swayed, before backing away, her tail retreating into the far corner of the keep, the rest of her body coiling up, ready to spring. "No need to look so worried," she said. "It's nothing that will hurt you or anyone you know. You'd just be doing me a favour, that's all. A favour for a favour."

The inviting chill of the night air tickled the back of my neck. "What's the favour?"

"Do you see, at the edges of my face, there are four catches?"

"I don't see…"

"Look closer."

If this were a trap, I'd probably already fallen into it. Her shimmering white skin drew me closer. There was something there. Yes – two places on either side of her face where the white of her skin bit into her twilight body.

"I think I see them," I breathed. "Vakua... is your face..."

"It's not my face. It's a mask. My mask is attached to my body, which is made from magical darkness similar to, but not entirely the same as, the Hungry Dark. The catches are the parts of my mask that attach one to the other. Please undo them."

"Why?"

Vakua turned ever so slightly to face me. "It's not that I can't undo them myself, it's just there is a small ceremony of renewal that I like to perform. For the ritual to be effective I need the help of another. I wondered if you would do me the honour of helping me? Before you ask, it does not involve any great sacrifice on your part."

A minor sacrifice, then. There are many things that a person such as Vakua might consider a minor sacrifice. The question was whether I'd agree. Still, every good deed I completed meant my list of debts and favours was one step closer to equilibrium. I smiled at Vakua, and nodded.

Vakua turned her head to the side, exposing the seam where her mask met her flesh. "Then please, undo the catches."

I reached up to the top catch and, as my hands approached, the storm of darkness calmed, and drew back, exposing a simple, vertical edge that had been lodged in Vakua's skin moments before. I stood on tip toes to grasp it with both hands and tugged.

With a gentle *clack*, the catch sprang free. I reached down and released the lower catch in the same way.

"I have power, Melita," Vakua said as I moved around to the other side of her mask. "but a large amount of the power resides in my mask. Whoever controls the mask, controls the power. Power is fleeting, however, and slips away easily."

Power. I'd always thought of my power as something which lived within me – me and not me at the same time. Vakua spoke as if her power was a coat she could choose to wear or leave behind. I released the third catch. Vakua shivered.

"Does this hurt?" I asked.

"No, it doesn't. I've worn this mask for a long time and have grown used to its little ways. When you release the final catch, please grasp the edges of the mask itself and pull."

"Why does your ceremony require someone else?" I asked. "It seems a curious quirk of the magic to force you to rely on the kindness of strangers."

"Magic delights in giving with one hand and taking away with the other. You are a witch, Melita, that much is obvious. Presumably, your clan has some sort of curse?"

I nodded.

"Do you mind if I ask what your curse is?"

I stayed silent. What happened in my head with my Kaskado Disorder was my problem to deal with, no one else's. It was also deeply confusing to me. In the past, when I'd tried to explain what happened in my head to doctors or friends, I'd always ended up getting frustrated. I could never seem to coherently convey my symptoms.

"Of course," said Vakua after a moment. "Forgive me for asking. My point was merely that you have great power, and your curse is presumably significant. What magic gives, it also... takes away."

I nodded and released the final catch. Vakua sighed, contentedly. I reached up and felt for the edges of her mask, the flawless, unnatural texture felt uncanny under my fingers. Like ice cream on a hot day, or a diamond-toothed saw biting into glass. I found the edges – whisper sharp, but safe. The edges were choosing not to cut me, for the moment. I pulled.

The mask adhered to Vakua's face for only a moment. I closed my eyes... I remembered when I still had parents... we'd gone to the beach. Rolling waves, shimmering sun and enticing caves. I'd been so small I'd held onto my mum's index finger with my entire fist. She'd led me to the spot on the shore where the waves broke, and smiled down at me. I'd let go of her hand and stepped into the surf. The mask held onto Vakua for only a moment, before letting go.

I opened my eyes. I was left holding an artefact of magical porcelain three times my height. I barely had time to wonder whether I was to be crushed under its weight before the mask shrank in my hands. The world rippled, reality confounded by the speed of change. Grey and silver spots pulsed in my vision until the mask settled in my hands, small and harmless, like a festival mask. Magic thrummed deep within.

Vakua's revealed face was churning darkness. She sighed, and her voice sounded from the depths of twilight. "Please, take the metal saucer from under the stairs and douse the mask with water. The water will purify the object of power you hold in your hands."

I nodded. I tried to hold Vakua's mask reverentially in both hands, but I needed a hand free to pick up the saucer. I returned to Vakua and placed the saucer on the floor. I retrieved my bottle, and gently poured water over the mask.

Clear water beaded on the smooth surface, before running in thin streams down to the edges. As the water dripped from the mask into the saucer, Vakua sighed once more. "Thank you, Melita. Believe me, not many people would do this for me. I knew I was right to trust you with this."

Power hummed under my fingers. I gritted my teeth. I should take the mask from Vakua. Down in the dark, power was vital to survival. If not for myself, I should do this for Teya and Ekzilo. I would do anything to re-unite my village, to make it a safe home for everyone.

Anything?

"What power does the mask hold, Vakua?" I asked, my mouth dry, my lips cracked, my nerves snapping.

"Strength. Such strength. It also renders me nearly invulnerable to harm. It's a blessing unlike any other."

The last of the water dripped into the saucer. The sound of the final splash was strangely loud in the still air.

I had to give the mask back. I couldn't get power through theft. Not even if it meant potentially sacrificing everyone I loved. But.. it was one thing to think about risking my friends' lives in the abstract, but when I held the power to protect them in my hands, to keep them safe from humans for as long as I lived, it felt different. Vakua was silent as I stood, my eyes locked on the mask. She had trusted me, just as Teya trusted me. Just as Mrs Noyer and everyone in Ekzilo trusted me. Could I betray someone I had no grievance against to save everyone I loved?

"It's done," I said, my voice catching in my throat.

Vakua was silent for a while longer. Eventually, her voice, soft and faint, said: "Simply release the mask, as if to drop it. It will return to me."

I opened my hands, letting the mask fall. After a quick blur of movement, it returned to Vakua's face. It didn't grow to fit her face, instead it seemed as if it had always been that size.

Vakua was very still. Her face – no, her mask was impassive. She didn't seem happy at having completed the purification ritual. Maybe she was just tired. Still, I'd held up my end of the bargain.

I looked up into Vakua's empty eyes. "So, Sirmo..."

Vakua dipped her mask, slowly. "Of course. Kyrene Teresi visited this castle many times. She left a pack here on her last visit. It contains records of her movements, areas she frequented in Tenebro and her visits to Sirmo."

"May I see this pack?"

"You have Kyrene's wife with you. You may have the pack. She would want her wife to have it. Do you plan to remain down here long?"

"It's not safe on the surface. That's why we're searching for Sirmo. Unless you would be willing to protect Ekzilo for us in return for help with future rituals?"

Vakua seemed absent for the longest of moments. Eventually, she returned, her gargantuan arms shifting, her body retreating. "The pack is in a cupboard by the entranceway. Kyrene left it there when she last visited, and I have not been of a mind to move it."

Her voice ached with melancholy. I couldn't understand why. Maybe I'd hurt her by asking whether she'd protect Ekzilo. "I should check and see how Teya and Jaeson are doing."

"Oh, yes. Please do. Thank you for your help with the ritual, Melita. Please do come and see me if you'd like to chat again."

I bowed, returned to the entranceway, and retrieved Kyrene's pack. My chest clenched tighter and tighter with every passing moment. Uncertainty gnawed into me. Had I made some sort of colossal mistake? Vakua had seemed so grateful and then she'd shut right down. I'd felt as if Teya and I were so close, *so* close to Sirmo, but instead I only had a pack which contained notes which might possibly help, if we were excruciatingly lucky.

The courtyard outside the keep had two gates set into the walls – one directly opposite the keep's entrance, through which was a shrine. Paving slabs outside had been laid in rows with the standard grey stone alternating with a rich plum red. I thought it unlikely that Teya would shelter in a shrine – she'd never really clicked with our faiths and worried about disrespecting them. I walked through the eastern gate instead.

If Vakua's ritual had been a trap, it had been a very strange one. What had Vakua wanted? Had she let me out of the trap because I'd done what was needed? She'd only asked me to take her mask off and pour water over it. Traps generally start by pointing someone at something they want and then hitting them with a stick or something when they try to take it. I was having trouble working out what the thing that I was supposed to have wanted was, and what the stick might have been.

The only thing, the *only* thing that it could have been was that she wanted me to steal her mask. Maybe she had a curse on her, and she could only eat people who stole from her. If so, that was a dreadfully convoluted way of going about things. It was far more likely that I'd missed something. Maybe she'd drugged the water she'd offered me.

Through the eastern gate was a courtyard. Winding paths led through a gravel garden dotted with colourful glass spheres and artfully placed pebble sigils. A guard tower was set into the far wall - a tiny version of the keep. A likely place for Teya and Jaeson to shelter in.

Approaching the tower, I heard crying from inside. Was Vakua keeping prisoners? I crept closer and peered through the open door.

A simple room, wide and open, marked by windows through which the Hungry Dark stared. Blankets, pillows and futons spilled from a cupboard, and weaved straw mats had been laid out across the floor. Jaeson was sitting on one of the mats, weeping quietly to himself. Teya was stretched out on a futon near the far wall, eating a rice cake and looking embarrassed.

I waved at my friend, who looked up and padded over to me, grabbing a tray from a cupboard as she passed. The tray was piled with paper parcels. I unwrapped one, revealing a rice cake. I hadn't realised how hungry I was. I demolished the cake in three bites – the soft rice drew out the umami flavour of the seaweed which nestled at the centre.

I only noticed Jaeson was watching me after I'd devoured three more cakes. Tears streamed down his face. I held out a paper parcel to him, but he shook his head, dropped his face back into his arms and resumed sobbing. I ate the rice cake myself.

"What's going on?" I whispered once I was done.

"I think he had a panic attack when I gave him some privacy," Teya whispered back.

"Mm. Poor him. So, I have news: Vakua gave me one of Kyrene's packs. Apparently, there are notes about her movements inside. Sirmo-related notes."

Teya's eyes lit up. "Good work, Meli! And well done for getting through whatever that ritual was with the giant masked snake."

"You spied on my conversation with Vakua?"

"Yes. Yes I did."

I didn't know whether to be impressed or annoyed. Teya would never have done such a thing in Ekzilo, but the rules of polite society were fragile down here. To me, that meant we were even more bound to uphold them. To Teya, they were the first thing to be abandoned if our survival might be on the line. Teya's attitude had saved our lives multiple times. My attitude had kept our spirits up and our minds focused on who we were and what we wanted, which had less of a dramatic impact on our survival, but it still helped. Hopefully.

I frowned at my friend, who was delicately munching on a rice cake. "You seem very calm. I nearly had a trouser accident when I saw Vakua for the first time."

"I'm not going to lie, Melita, I'm not doing brilliantly. When I saw who you were talking to, I had to stuff my hand into my mouth to stop myself screaming. I think I would have had a fit if I hadn't met Yilin earlier today. Tonight. Whatever the time is."

I nodded, but then my memory poked me. "You spied on us? Vakua specifically asked you not to do that."

"She told me not to go into the keep, I didn't. I watched through one of the windows. I wasn't going to let you go in there and just hope everything was fine, Melita. I was sure it was a trap."

"Was?"

Teya nodded. "I'm not sure now. Still thinking. Anyway, what's in the pack?"

I unslung the pack and opened it up. Inside were a cluster of angular shapes wrapped in oil skins, as well as a netting bag stuffed with glow globes and a small leather bound notebook.

The notebook's pages were cramped with Kyrene's spidery handwriting. It seemed to be half diary and half structured notetaking.

'12th day, Month of Decay. Supplies fine, restocked stashes on L3 and L4. Mermaid in reservoir continues trouble. Dodged Capper. Still working on distractions. *Seven round pipes enter into numbered lists before devastating...*' I squeezed my eyes shut and pinched the bridge of my nose. I shook my head and tried re-reading that last sentence. 'Seven glow globes rendered useless by decay, replaced *wetly before timing into squils and rantils porfingly. Streenit is blubling –* ' No, no it was no use. I couldn't focus on the book for more than a few sentences. I could read the words well enough but my head was so foggy that they just wouldn't transition from the page to my brain. My head felt heavy. I dropped the book and let my face fall into my palms.

"Hey, hey," said Teya. She wrapped an arm around my shoulders. "Why don't you have a sit down and take a rest? I can work on Ky's pack. You've had a pretty serious time of it, little grebe."

I'd let her down. I'd let everyone down. I always did this. Still, I didn't feel strong enough to argue. I grabbed four rice cakes from the tray and went to sit with my back to a wall, turned slightly away from Teya so I couldn't see her doing the work I'd failed at.

I started to feel a little better after four rice cakes and a quiet cry. Thankfully, my crying was masked by Jaeson's, which was turning out to be quite persistent. Eventually, I came back to myself enough to take pity on him.

Standing, I stretched and went to sit next to him. He didn't stop crying. "I don't think we're heading up to the surface any time soon, lad," I said. "We're trying to find a place that can help us stop future attacks by your lot. We've hopefully just got a lead on that, as well as Teya's missing wife. That's our priority for now. I'm guessing you'd like to go back to the surface so you can get back home?"

Jaeson looked up at me and nodded.

"Well, I don't know if she'd be willing, but we can ask Vakua if she'll escort you to the surface."

"Who's Vakua?" Jaeson asked.

"The person who lives in the castle."

"Is she a witch?"

"No. I don't know. You know, I'm not actually sure what she is."

"She's not human?"

"Oh no, don't worry, I wouldn't send you to the surface with one of you lot, not if I wanted you to get there in one piece."

"Do you want me to get to the surface in one piece?"

I thought about this for a few seconds. I weighed the arguments for and against. "Yes," I said, eventually.

"Do you trust this Vakua?"

"With your life? Absolutely."

"How about with your life?"

"Without hesitation."

Jaeson thought about this. "And what about Teya's life?"

"Ah. Now that's a more interesting question…"

"Why is the answer different for Teya?"

"I like Teya more than I like either of us."

Teya didn't find this as funny as I'd hoped. To my surprise, Jaeson laughed instead of my friend. "You're a strange witch, you know that?"

I huffed and folded my arms. "People have told me this before. So, are you going with Vakua?"

"Could you describe Vakua for me, please?"

"Her body is made from churning, whirling energy. Her face is formless, like the rest of her body, but it's covered by a mask, white as unbleached silk, and expressionless. It's only broken by two eye holes."

Jaeson nodded. "So, my choices are sticking with a predator and an outsider, who are on a quest that will probably lead me further into danger, or going back home in the company of someone who sounds like a creature from my nightmares."

"I didn't say sticking with us was an option."

"Is it an option?"

"If you give me my apology, yes."

Jaeson thought about this. He pursed his lips. His jaw tightened. He looked up at me. "I'm sorry that my people attacked your village and hurt your friends," he said.

The tone of his voice didn't contain any actual contrition and he was pretty clearly just saying what he thought I wanted to hear. But, and this was important, he'd managed to say something I did actually want to hear. He didn't mean it, but it was a start. "Okay," I said, "if Teya agrees, you can come with us."

Teya had set the notebook aside and was midway through stripping an oilcloth from an item which consisted entirely of exciting bulges and strange angles. She looked up at the mention of her name, and the oilcloth fell away from the shape, revealing a hefty rifle. Its barrel took up more than half its length and was surrounded by a protective mesh. Gauges and bio-fuel reserves were dotted along its length. Teya's eyes gleamed.

Tearing her gaze from the gun, my friend stared at Jaeson for a long moment, before saying: "Okay. We'll do our best to protect you. If you get caught by a monster, we'll try to rescue you. You need to know, going in, that if Melita or I decide that it's too dangerous to rescue you, we're going to leave you behind, okay? I want you to know that in advance in case you get the bright idea to try and curse us or something as a swarm of fallen are descending on you. Or worse."

Jaeson blanched. "Worse?"

"Probably. Melita and I haven't seen most of the things that live down here, but Ky had. Look."

Teya picked up Kyrene's notebook and flicked to a page near the back, which she held up, so that Jaeson and I could see. The page was dominated by a pencil drawing of a twisted shadow, its claws reaching towards us. Teya turned the page. Another drawing – a panther sitting regally, a human head staring at me. The next was a skeleton in a traditional boy's robe. It held balloons in one hand. No, not balloons. Human heads bobbing along on the ends of the strings. Underneath the picture was the word 'Capper.'

"The Hungry Dark is full of strange creatures, and our best chance of getting out alive is to avoid them as best we can."

I nodded, before thinking of something. "Is there a picture of Vakua in there?"

Teya closed the book. "No, and that's interesting, isn't it? Both Vakua and Yilin said that Kyrene came to this castle. Why wouldn't Kyrene make notes about a creature as interesting and intelligent as Vakua?"

"Are there notes about Yilin in there?"

"Yes, there are, but that's not all. Kyrene seems to have mapped out this entire level of Tenebro. There are only occasional mentions of Sirmo, but she's made notes about stashes she's been keeping on lower levels. If I understand the structure of her notes, I think those stashes will have other maps. If we find those, we might find clues to finding Ky and Sirmo."

"Great!"

"Right? Still, I'm interested as to why Ky's pack was left in the castle, when it's not marked in her notebook as one of her bases. Maybe I'll ask Vakua about it. Anyway, are you happy with the plan, Melita? Jaeson?"

"Yes!"

Jaeson nodded, slowly. "I don't have much of a choice."

"Of course you have a choice. If you don't want to come with us, go back to the surface. Don't come with us unless you're sure it's what you want."

Jaeson looked at his hands, and then back up at us. "It's what I want. The plan sounds fine to me."

Teya closed her fist, decisively. "Good! One last thing. How many hours of light will your remaining teeth give us, Melita?"

I checked my wrist. "Depends. Maybe fifteen hours?"

Teya nodded. "There are glow globes in Ky's pack. About ten hours' worth at a guess. Combined with your teeth that means it's safe to continue looking for Sirmo unless you want to get back to the surface and try to help in some other way?"

I shook my head. "I know the longer we leave Ekzilo alone the worse things are going to get, but we need a permanent solution. We need to either find Sirmo or… accept that Ekzilo won't be Ekzilo when we make it back."

Teya nodded, her expression sombre. "I agree. So, I suggest we all rest up, eat, sleep, and relieve ourselves. This might well be the last safe place we come across; we should use it as best we can. We shouldn't take more than a few hours, but we'll never find Sirmo if we're sleep deprived. Jaeson, do you want to sleep somewhere else or are you okay in here with us?"

"I'm fine here."

"Good. Melita, are you going to try and sleep?"

I nodded.

"Great. I'm going to keep going through Kyrene's pack for a little while, but I can do that with low light. There was a pump adjustment on the wall I think, one moment."

Teya rose and fiddled with a brass wheel set into one of the bio-fuel pipes, whilst I pulled down a straw mat and set up a futon on it, as well as three blankets. Feeling a call of nature, I located a bathroom, attended to matters, then took advantage of the castle's running water to have a badly needed wash. The room was dimming to a half-light haze by the time returned.

"Goodnight, Teya," I said.

"Goodnight, Melita," said my friend, winding a silk scarf around her hair.

I slipped between the futon and blankets, delighted at how soft every-thing was.

Movement.

My eyelids felt glued shut. I could hear shuffling. Where was I? My futon felt different. There was light. Why was there light?

I remembered where I was, at the same time as I heard footsteps. I wrenched my eyelids open, scrabbled for my gun, and pointed it in the direction of the movement.

"It's just me, Melita," said an indistinct shape. "I can't sleep, so I'm going for a walk."

Teya's voice. I lowered the gun and slumped back onto the futon.

"Sorry to wake you," whispered Teya. I made an indistinct 'Mmm.' noise as Teya crept from the room. I dropped my gun and turned over.

I tried to go back to sleep. I wanted to sleep. I *needed* to sleep. I was so tired. Every part of me felt like it had shut down. Even my head was quiet, which, given the sort of things that usually happened in there, was a relief. Still, I lay on my futon, unable to move but also unable to sleep.

The fog that normally clouded my mind seemed to have solidified into bristles of wool. My legs hurt. Were they painful or just aching? I couldn't tell. A cold, empty feeling had risen up through me at some point over the last few hours and I hadn't even noticed. I was used to the feeling, I felt it near constantly on the surface, but I wasn't supposed to feel it down in the dark. Down here, I was meant to be free.

Deep within me, resentment simmered until it started to boil. I was on an adventure in the dark. I was supposed to have left my Kaskado Disorder behind on the surface. What was the point of my adventure if I was just going to experience the same misery, the same fatigue, the same pain and the same jumbled thoughts that I always did?

Saving Ekzilo. That was the supposed to be the point of my adventure. Guilt rose to join the boiling resentment. I lay, stewing in my own feelings for maybe twenty minutes before I had to accept that I wasn't getting back to sleep anytime soon.

I rolled over and hauled myself to my feet. The light in the room was still dim, which annoyed me at first, before I remembered that if the room had been completely dark, then the Hungry Dark would have eaten us alive. I shook my head, trying to clear some of the fuzz, then worked up enough energy to get up and see what Teya was up to.

I pulled my boots on, starting to feel properly awake, which would have actually been useful back when I'd been trying to read Kyrene's notebook, but currently was more aggravating than helpful. The feeling of begrudging wakefulness turned into a jolt of fully alert shock when a deafeningly loud scream blazed through the room. It seemed to contain multiple pitches at once. It felt as if it was born of rage, anguish, and fear. Whatever had made that scream was in serious trouble. I froze, not sure what I should do.

"What's going on?" asked Jaeson, scrabbling out of his bedclothes.

The scream ended, leaving fading echoes in its wake. Jaeson's panicked grimace and the anguish in the echoes focussed me. I grabbed my belt - my gun was missing. I spent precious seconds panicking until I remembered I'd needed it earlier in the night. I found it lying next to my pillow. Where had the scream come from? Some distance away. What direction?

Footsteps outside – running. Frantic. I dashed to the doorway - Teya was sprinting towards us. A second scream split the air. Teya shouted, but the scream obliterated her words. Teya winced at the sound and made a repeating circular gesture with her right hand – the gesture she used when we had to move in a hurry.

I slung on my jacket, then my pack. I tossed Teya's pack to her. The scream ended, then another began almost immediately after.

"What's happening?" I yelled.

"Danger. Imminent. Will explain later," Teya shouted.

"Explain now!" Jaeson shouteed. His eyes were screwed shut and he was clutching at his ears.

"No time, Jaeson!" Teya shouted. "Come with us or don't. Your call!"

I slipped a tooth into my mouth, readied my pistol and nodded to Teya, who smiled, grimly. The third scream ended, granting us a second of peace before another began. Under the scream, I could hear thrashing and crashing.

I held up three fingers to Teya and counted them down. When my last finger dropped, we fled our room, and ran up the ramp to the upper courtyard, where gusts of dust and debris were billowing out of the castle keep. I wanted to call out to Vakua but Teya anticipated me, grabbed my hand, and ran towards gates back to Tenebro.

I swallowed my tooth as we reached the gates, and a sickly green light, the colour of willow dye, worked out of my pores. A nearby rumbling made all three of us look round at the keep, which was rapidly disintegrating.

"Er... run?" suggested Teya.

Chapter Eleven

We sprinted out the castle gates, and then through Tenebro, past houses, shrines and shops. Distance was near impossible to gauge – we ran, my bubble of light the only real thing in this dead city. Buildings flashed by, the ground fled under our feet.

Once Vakua's anguished screams had faded to merely loud, rather than deafening, Teya diverted us into an alley sandwiched between two houses. Jaeson leaned against a wall and heaved in deep gulps of air.

"Okay," said Teya, once she had her breath back. "I owe both of you an apology."

"Really?" I asked. Usually, it was me that did the apologising.

"Really. I made a mistake."

A crashing rumble echoed out of the darkness. It sounded as if something enormous had just collapsed.

"What sort of mistake?"

"Well, I couldn't sleep last night, I kept going over our plans, and wondering about what sort of power Vakua's mask had, and whether I'd need it to find Kyrene."

"Okay."

"Yeah. So, I was passing by the castle, and I thought I'd drop in to see if Vakua had changed her mind about chatting to me."

"Why would you do that?" Jaeson asked.

"Vakua was asleep. She didn't move when I approached. So…"

I nodded, remembering the temptation I'd felt when holding the mask. "So, you thought you'd try her mask on, just for a moment. You were going to give it right back, and when she woke up, you were going to ask her if you could have it, but you needed to know if it actually contained any power, because otherwise it would be wrong to bother our host with trivialities."

"Right."

Jaeson opened his mouth, then closed it again. Little flecks of wisteria-coloured light shone from my fingers and tumbled around, zigging, and zagging with little care for their jagged reflections in the nearby windows. "What happened next?"

"I unclipped one of the clasps on Vakua's mask. She woke up. She did not react well when she saw me."

Jaeson opened his mouth again, but I held up a forestalling hand. "Teya's not done."

"So, I'm sorry, Melita, Jaeson. I let… I just… I didn't feel in control, even though I was. I wanted that power so badly. It felt like the difference between life and death. I was wrong."

The wisteria pinpricks illuminated a furrow in Teya's forehead.

I listened for sounds of Vakua's distress, but the air was finally still. "Okay," I said.

"That's it?" Jaeson asked, his voice shrill.

"If you've never done something, knowing at the time that it was a bad idea but still doing it because it felt like a scab you had to pick at, then please, by all means, cast judgement, Jaeson," I said.

"It'd be okay if you were angry at me, Meli," Teya said. "I messed up. I messed up badly. I cost us an ally. I know that's bad. So do you."

I felt my mouth twist. I was tired and I wanted to go back to sleep. I wanted to be on an adventure where nothing mattered except me, Teya and the dark. I wanted to get back to how things had been. I shook my hands loose and smiled at Teya. "Don't worry about it. So, where do we go now?"

Next to me, Jaeson was mercifully silent. Teya nodded and unslung her backpack. She fished out Kyrene's notebook and flicked through the pages.

"Hello?" cried a voice. "Is anyone there?"

The three of us froze. A reply formed in my throat and died just as quickly. Something about the voice had sounded familiar.

"I need help. Can anyone hear me?" cried Yilin.

Teya dropped Ky's notebook and clapped her hand over my mouth. My eyes were wide. I saw the recognition I was feeling reflected back from Teya's eyes. "It's not Yilin, Meli. It's a trick. Don't reply," she hissed.

"Isn't that the mermaid's voice?" Jaeson whispered.

"The only water we've seen nearby was the stream that ran through the school. She'd never fit in a stream that small. This is a trap. I'm going to let you go, Meli please, please don't reply."

I nodded, and Teya removed her hand.

"Hello? I need help. Is anyone there?"

"It doesn't sound like Yilin..." I whispered, as Teya picked up Kyrene's notebook. "It's her voice, but that's not what she sounded like. Even when she was at death's door, she was..."

"I can hear you," said the voice. "Please? Can you help me?"

A shudder skittered through me. A spike of fear rammed up through the soles of my feet, pinning me in place. Teya flicked through the pages of Kyrene's notebook with renewed urgency. Not too far away, I heard strange, clicking footsteps. They were getting closer.

"We need to go," said Jaeson.

I nodded. I wanted to speak up, to agree with him, but the creature had reacted when I'd spoken. Had it heard me and not the others? Was I putting everyone else in danger?

The *click, click, clicking* footsteps stopped. Teya let out a shuddering breath and turned the notebook to catch my light a little better. She stabbed a finger at a page and turned the book, keeping her finger in place. On the page was a map, and her finger was pointing at a specific location.

"Hello?" said the voice. It sounded as if it was only a street or two away.

I squinted at the map. We'd fled from Vakua's castle, turning *there* and *there*... so we were probably just north of the magistrate's court. I drew my pistol and tiptoed down our alley, away from the voice, dearly wishing I could whisper a prayer to the spirits. As we left the alley, I heard one more: "I need help. Is anyone out there?"

Frozen pins and needles crept down my back. There was something out there calling for help. It didn't sound desperate, as if its life were in danger, it sounded sad. It sounded as if it was lost down in the dark, just as we were.

If I'd heard the voice on the night when I'd come down into the dark without Teya, I wouldn't have hesitated. I'd have run to help the person in need. Even now, I wasn't sure, not completely sure, that I shouldn't be doing just that. Still, the strange likeness of Yilin's voice filled me with an alien and unfamiliar fear. I never wanted to see what could steal someone's voice like that.

We turned five more corners, passing houses and small, dead gardens. Massive claws loomed out of the dark, only to be revealed as twisted husks of wood which might once have been trees. We crossed eight streets, each curving in a slightly different direction, but each lined with houses that looked dispiritingly similar. Wooden beams, dark windows, wooden beams, dark windows, wooden beams, and dark windows. These houses, like the ones up in Ekzilo, were beautiful when looked at individually. They were mini works of art and took skilled craftswomen hundreds of hours of work to build. As we ran, these works of art blurred together and lost any touches of individuality.

Finally, after Teya had finessed our direction twice, my light fell on something new. An archway, painted vermillion red, and beyond that a stairwell. I paused for a moment to give Teya time to catch up, and then several moments more to give Jaeson time to catch up.

We trotted down the stairs quickly enough to put distance between ourselves and the creatures on level two of Tenebro, but not so fast as to risk tripping and tumbling into the darkness. The walls down here were smooth, straight, and reflected my light back at us companionably. The colour of young bamboo filled the tunnel and for a moment I imagined I could smell rain and fresh green shoots. We emerged into a passageway lined with wooden lanterns, which led to a cavern. In the distance, my light picked out the shape of a large building. I couldn't see many details of the structure, but its silhouette was all sweeping curved lines and elegant protrusions. I held up a hand and my companions slowed to a walk.

Teya cleared her throat. "The first of Kyrene's bases is through the passageway up ahead, then maybe three hundred metres into the cavern beyond. With any luck we'll find some clues there as to Sirmo's location."

The path we followed circled near to the beautiful silhouette without approaching directly. Three sets of footsteps crunched against gravel in a steady rhythm. My light added definition to the silhouette as we passed, slowly revealing it as a temple with a single, enormous ground floor and a swooping teal-tiled roof supported by wooden pillars. There wasn't much decoration to speak of. The air around it was still. Peaceful.

"Come on, we haven't got long," said Teya. We walked from the gravel path to stone paving, our footsteps sounding soft and lonely, then up three stone steps. "How are you feeling?"

"A bit shaken," I said.

"That's understandable. Don't worry, everything'll be fine. We just need to do what we've done a hundred times before. Do you need anything?"

"No, I'm good." I glanced around at the darkness behind me. "Are we missing someone?"

"Don't think so." Teya slid the door open for me. I stepped through and found my path illuminated by lanterns, hanging silent and still in the cool air.

"That jacket's all wrong," she said, once she'd joined me.

"Is it?" I asked, looking down at my trusty red leather coat.

"Yes, we're home for the first time in, what, nearly a year? It's a celebration. We need something better. Hang on." She slid open a door and slipped through. At the sight of Teya vanishing, I drew in a sharp breath through my teeth. My stomach clenched tight, as did my fists. Why was I suddenly so nervous?

My friend returned moments later, carrying a white coat with silver and gold threads criss-crossing it. "Here you go," she said. I slipped the coat on. It was lighter than my red leather affair, which was thick with padded plates. I bounced on the soles of my feet, the wispy garment flowing around me. I wasn't completely sure what was happening, but Teya rarely led me astray, and even when she did, we always wound up in interesting places.

"Great," said Teya, "here's your wand and here's a femur to get you started. Before you ask, it was lost in an accident. I'll give you the name later."

She handed me a polished steel rod which tapered to a spike. I twirled it experimentally before slipping it into my belt. I then took the leg bone. It sat heavy in my hands, power humming within it.

"Go on, swallow it," said Teya, "it's nearly time." She turned and walked up a wooden staircase, leaving me alone with my meal. I opened my mouth. I hadn't eaten a bone like this in some time and it took a little effort to unhinge my jaw. It felt like cracking seized knuckles. I raised my head and, like a snake eating a rodent that was just a little too large, I slipped the femur down my throat.

I smacked my lips and licked my fingertips. I closed my eyes and smiled as the bone's power rose within me, then spread out and out and out to every cell in my body. I let out a long, shivering breath before following Teya up the stairs, wondering what other delights awaited me there.

After climbing three flights, I found my friend perched on a stool, holding a violin loosely in her hands.

"Are you ready?" she asked. She fished her bow out of her robe and held it loosely in between her thumb and forefingers.

"Yeah, I'm ready."

"Great. Can you hear them?"

I listened. I could hear the babble of a crowd. It seemed to be both extremely large and waiting in anticipation of something. A voice emerged from a focus crystal affixed to the wall. Tiny echoes made their way in from outside, making it sound as if the voice was speaking out there in the same way at the same time.

"Men, women and those who have evolved beyond the binary," the voice said. "Children of all ages, are you ready?"

Voices roared.

"Are we ready?" I asked Teya.

"Oh yes, we're ready."

"Great, I love being ready."

The noise of the crowd died away, as the voice spoke again: "I am proud to present tonight's star. You know her, you love her. She's just returned from a tour of Selen, Okan, Akoma, and the great flotilla which sails the Jade Sea. Here she is..."

"Let's go," said Teya. She stood and walked through a door I hadn't seen before. I followed.

"Melita Eklumigi, with tonight's musician Teya Teresi!" cried the voice.

I gasped. I'd emerged onto a raised platform... no, not a platform. An expansive stage, bordered on three sides by vast, mirrored walls. To my left, the stage was set, and beyond the stage was a group of people. It was quite a large group. At a conservative guess I would estimate there being around seven hundred. They were cheering.

I wondered who they could be cheering for. I was alone on the stage except for Teya, who was kneeling at a corner, watching me and applauding gently. I bowed, experimentally. The cheering intensified.

I smiled at Teya. She smiled back. I turned to the crowd but couldn't see any faces. There wasn't enough light.

"Ready!" cried Teya, her voice carrying across the stage and the crowd, even without magical projection. She drew her bow across a string on her violin, letting the note sing out through the empty air for a precious second, before moving her bow in a quick flurry, sending notes soaring over the crowd. Behind me, and behind the massive wall of mirrors, someone started beating the ever-living hell out of a drum.

I let out just a fraction of my power. My light curled up and around the metal wand until it pooled at the very tip. I'd seen my power behave like this hundreds of times during my shows, but it still thrilled me, because a part of me still remembered that sad time in my life when I could only shine uncontrolled, unfocussed light from my skin.

The music built around me. It grew and grew until I was ready. I took a deep breath in... and expelled it, along with a magnificent explosion of power. Green light thundered out from my exposed flesh. I gave my wand the tiniest flick, and light spun out in elegant strands.

My light curled over the crowd, bathing them in cyan. In the corner, Teya plucked out higher notes that soared across the don-don-dokko-don of the drums. I flicked my wand up, bringing light to the sky.

This was merely a warmup – I had so much more to come. With the light from my wand playing across the sky, I turned my back on the crowd. I swept my wand down and around so that the light played across the mirrors. Suddenly, instead of one stream of light there were dozens, reflecting back and forth between the mirrors before flying out into the crowd.

I twirled my wand, letting the light fly out in spirals and stutters. I was danced to the violin, making the wand arc and swoop as the music soared. I turned away from the mirrors and saw the crowd – they were on their feet, reaching for the shapes of light, screaming in delight.

I formed my power up into my left hand and let it take shape. What would this crowd like? What would be perfect for us all on this night? They'd come to see me on my return from the Jade Sea so... let it be something that reminds us all of home. I opened my palm and concentrated. A mote of pink light sprung into being, before curling up and out into the small, humble shape of a petal of plum blossom. I blew the petal towards the crowd. It multiplied as it flew. From one petal came two, then four, then eight. Soon, a huge tumbling, twirling arc of blossom was dancing over the crowd, swooping down to pass just over their heads before climbing back up and forming into an enormous cloud. The crowd swayed and laughed, reaching for the petals.

I raised my hand and then lowered it. Slowly and gently, the blossom tumbled down towards the crowd. It settled on shoulders and rested in outstretched palms. I grinned at their delight. In the corner, Teya played a ripple of descending notes. It was time for something truly special, something this crowd would never forget. I clapped my hands together.

Nothing happened. I blinked. The crowd were gone. The drums had fallen silent. Teya's violin was gone. She was now sitting on the edge of the stage. I looked around the stage, wondering what could have happened. The air was still. Shrouded in silence. I turned back to Teya, who motioned for me to join her. Cold air prickled against my bare arms.

"What's going on?" I asked.

"Come sit with me, Melita."

I sat, feeling lonely in the enormous space.

"So, what do you think just happened?" Teya asked.

My hands were shaking. "I... I don't... there was a crowd, and I was performing for them. It was wonderful."

Teya smiled. "It was more than a performance, Melita. It was a triumph. It was everything you could be. What I just showed you was you at your absolute best. If all the stars had aligned and everything went perfectly, what you just saw was what your life could have been."

"Really?"

"Really. What you just saw was your perfect life. Performing for a crowd. Making them happy. Do you recognise that dream, Melita?"

"...yes."

"But it's more than that, Meli. You want to make people happy using your magic. You have this talent within you, and you want to do something with it. You want to know, not *hope* but really, absolutely *know* that you're doing something useful with your talent. That's important, because it means your talent is real, you're not just some poor sap who can make pretty lights come out of her nose. And to you, doing something useful means making people happy. I like your dream. Making people happy – that's a better dream than most have. Usually, if someone makes it this far into Tenebro they dream of power or money, which is basically the same thing. You don't want power; you want to use your gifts to bring people joy.

"I don't understand why it had to end," I said, tears silently streaming down my cheeks.

"It had to end, Melita, because your dream is impossible. It'll never happen. To control your magic in the way you just did, you'd not only need extremely rare bones, you'd have also needed to train for years to gain the fine control required. Remind me... when was the last time you trained to improve your skill with magic?"

"I..."

"I know it's not your fault, Melita. Your Kaskado Disorder means you can only train infrequently – fatigue and chronic pain will make sure of that even before you account for mental symptoms. That's a hard truth. Here's another one: no one cared about your gift in Ekzilo and it's likely no one will care if you ever make it to Sirmo. In the dark, in Tenebro, it's useful, but only as useful as a glow globe. Congratulations, Melita, you are precisely as useful as a device that can be purchased from Tolis' General Store for five Bilono, barter available to good customers." She clapped, softly.

"You've got problems, Melita. Problems that are never going to go away. Kaskado Disorder. The social stigma of being a witch. But that's just the obvious stuff, you know about all that. You also know you don't *actually* leave all that behind when you dive into the dark. No, I'm curious about one very precise question I have: when you suggested to Teya that you should search for Sirmo in order to help Ekzilo, was that the only reason you wanted to stay in the dark?

I shook my head. "No, I... I hoped I might be able to find out what happened to Kyrene. Closure. For you."

Teya stared at me for a long moment. "Oh yes," she said. "Closure. I was forgetting. Well, leaving *that* to one side for a moment, we'll come back to it, I promise - was there another reason you wanted to drag Teya into the dark with no plan and no preparation? Were you, perhaps, risking the life of someone you love so you could chase an impossible fantasy of being a shining star in the dark?"

I couldn't force words past the knot in my throat.

Cold-Teya stood and stretched. "You don't have to answer, Melita, it's just a thing to think about. Now, returning to that point you made earlier, did you really think giving Teya false hope that she might learn Kyrene's fate was a good idea?"

"I—"

"Melita, please, I'm trying to make a point. Let's say for a moment, that you manage to find Kyrene down in the dark and, miracle of miracles, she's alive. What do you think would happen next? Because I think it's pretty likely that, when reunited, Teya and Kyrene would flee Talvik as fast as they possibly could. Unless you're holding out some hope that Teya would stick around in Ekzilo because you needed her – that she'd choose you over her wife." My friend stared down at me. She waited for me to reply. She sighed. "Do you know what I am, Meli?"

I shook my head.

"I'm a trap. You're in the Hungry Dark, in Tenebro. I'm going to let your memories fade back in a little. Do you understand what it means when I say I'm a trap?"

I felt the context of my situation fade into focus in my head. I frowned. "It means you're trying to kill me."

Trap-Teya smiled, sadly. "No, Melita. That's what my sisters do. I don't want to kill you. Let me tell you what's going to happen. We're going to have a bit more of a chat, and then you're going to kill yourself. It'll be quick and painless, there won't even be any mess because the Hungry Dark will clean everything up for us. If only everyone could die as cleanly as you."

I could barely see through the tears. I didn't respond. I didn't want to die. I didn't. Except that I really, really did. Dying would leave my pain behind.

"Think back to how it felt to stand on that stage, Melita. To feel the joy you were calling into being soar around you. Can you feel it?"

I nodded.

"Good. Now, really concentrate on what your life was, back in Ekzilo. Can you remember ever feeling that wonderful, soaring joy whilst you lived there?"

I shook my head.

"Does it hurt, living the way you do? Does it hurt to be miserable all the time? To feel exhausted *constantly*? To have your muscles ache so hard and for so long that the pain just fades into the background unless things are particularly bad? To hate your life and feel unable to change it?"

I nodded.

"There is one quick, straightforward way to make the pain stop. You don't have to live your life as others tell you. You could say that enough is enough. Enough pain, enough misery. You're allowed to just leave it all behind. To finally just... rest. Please stand up."

I stood, shaking. Through my blurred vision, I saw Sad-Teya reach out a hand to me. "Melita, in real life, outside of my trap, we are currently standing on the roof of the Temple of Peace in Tenebro. The edge of the stage here is the edge of the roof. If you want, you could take one tiny step forwards. I won't ask you to do it alone. I'll step off with you. We'll fall together. No-one should have to be alone in their last moments." She moved her hand a little closer to me.

Unable to think, unable to experience anything apart from absolute, all-encompassing, crushing misery, I took her hand.

"I love you, Melita," she said.

"I love you too," I said.

I lifted my foot. I moved it out, past the edge of the stage. She mirrored my movement. She gave my hand a little squeeze. I stepped forward and she stepped with me.

Air rushed past me. My vision blurred, and my world changed. My light had dimmed to a tearful violet haze. I was back in the Hungry Dark, just as the trap had promised. I closed my eyes. I smiled. It was nearly over. I didn't have to feel this way anymore. After years, decades of endless misery and pain, it was nearly over.

I landed on something soft. The impact knocked the breath out of me, but I didn't die. The shock left me disorientated, but one thought bubbled its way to the front of my mind and then lurched out of my mouth. "Oh, *come on*!" I yelled.

I opened my eyes. I was surrounded by darkness. I dried my eyes with my sleeve and looked around. I was lying on something twisting, turning and the colour of a moonless night. I stood, and as I did, I realised I could see faint cracks, below which my light illuminated stone. The shape I was standing on was familiar. I looked up, then further up. Vakua's mask stared down at me. I realised what I was standing on - a pair of cupped hands.

"Vakua..."

"I'm sorry for what you just went through, Melita," Vakua said, her voice cracking, "but you don't have time to come to terms with it just yet. Teya and the human are up on the roof. They're about to jump. I might not be able to reach them both in time. Will you help me?"

My death had been stolen from me. I wanted to just lie down and let the darkness take me. But Teya was in danger... I nodded to Vakua, who rose, lifting her hands until I was level with the roof I'd only recently stepped from.

Teya stood at the far end of the long, flat ridge. Jaeson was crouched on a wooden spur halfway along the roof's length. A glow globe lay discarded on the roof, its bubble only just keeping them safe from the dark.

"You get Teya," Vakua said, "I'll get the human."

Teya rocked on the balls of her feet. Her weight shifted. She was thinking about stepping off the roof. I didn't have time to think. I sprinted forwards, a terrifying expanse separating me from the life of my only friend. Jaeson stood as I approached, staring away from me, into the dark. He lifted a foot. I didn't have time to help him.

I hurtled past the kid. Agony stabbed into my side as Teya spread her arms and lifted her face to where the stars should have been. She slid one foot out over the abyss. I skidded to a halt, nearly barrelling into her. She shifted her weight, pitching forward. I grabbed desperately at her pack, snagged a trailing strap and hauled Teya back until I was able to grab onto her collar with my other hand. For one dreadful moment, we stood in equilibrium, Teya's weight dragging us towards the darkness, my weight hauling us back to safety.

I had the advantage. Teya was still in a haze of absolute misery, while I had purpose. I didn't need to win this tug of war. I sat down, dragging our collective centre of gravity lower. She wavered, then collapsed backwards, landing on top of me. I wrapped my arms around her and hugged her as if I was never going to let go.

Chapter Twelve

I held Teya for a long time while she came back to herself. I worried I was crowding her at one point, and tried to let go. Her grip tightened so much it started cutting off blood flow to key areas of my body. I hugged her back, and she relaxed a little.

I was given time to think as my friend cried in my arms. The trap had wanted me to kill myself, so I couldn't trust everything it had said. It'd clearly been biased in how it presented its information. For example, just because I'd never felt as happy as I could have on a stage whilst living in Ekzilo, that didn't mean I'd *never* been happy. The problem was... most of the things the trap had said were true. I was miserable most of the time on the surface, and I'd never achieved the fine control over my magic that I'd wanted. I'd neglected my training for years.

I was so tired. All the time. So very tired. Not just in my legs, although that's where I felt the fatigue most strongly. Most days it felt as if I only had a couple of hours' worth of energy, and there was so much that needed doing.

My problems weren't going away, and every time I dove headfirst into the Hungry Dark, I acted as if I was leaving my problems behind. My stepping off the roof was proof that my problems had followed me into the dark.

Cloth rustled behind me – Vakua resting Jaeson on the roof nearby. The kid looked in much the same state as Teya. Crushed.

The roof ridge that was, for the moment, home was hard and uncomfortable to lie on, but I ignored my left leg, which was rapidly going numb, and concentrated on making sure Teya felt safe.

My friend was not having a good time. Guilt welled up inside me as she cried. I couldn't immediately work out why, until I remembered what I'd done the night before the humans had attacked.

If I'd gone into the dark without Teya and I hadn't come back, how would she have coped? She'd already lost her wife to the dark. I hadn't told her where I was going. She'd never have known what had happened to me. Would she have lost a year of her life to searching for me in the same way she had with Kyrene? Would she have been in mourning for another year after that?

I held Teya tighter and started seriously to think. I needed to swallow another tooth after an hour, but soon after that, Teya seemed to emerge from whatever personal hell she'd been living in. She released her grip on me and I eased back to look at her.

Her cheeks glistened, and the skin around her eyes was puffy, but she was smiling shyly at me. "Thank you, Meli," she said.

"Any time," I said. Slowly, gently, I let go.

Jaeson was still huddled in a ball, crying quietly. I walked over to him and reached down, but he shrank away from me and his weeping intensified. I backed away and gave him some space, keeping him at the edge of my light.

Teya and I drank some water and ate a rice ball each from my pack in silence. The rice was soft and salty. The flakes of salmon were rich and given kick by the chili flakes I'd added during the cooking. Next to me, Teya ate with no obvious sign of enjoyment. The air was thick with words left unsaid.

Eventually, Teya cracked. "We made it to Sirmo," she said. "I was there, and Kyrene was there. It was wonderful... but she looked at me, and she asked me why I gave up. Why I stopped looking. I said I'd tried so hard for so long. She said I only tried for a year. Was that all our love had meant to me? A year?"

I growled at the Peace Trap's version of Kyrene. "You learned how to dive into the dark for her during that year. Besides, you didn't stop because you thought a year was a nice round number, you realised that you were taking too many risks and it was time to let go."

"I know."

I handed Teya another rice ball and bit into one of my own. This time the gentle flavour of the rice contrasted with the salty, sour flavour of pickled plum.

Teya stretched. "I know, it's just... giving up the search for Ky was a relief, you know? It was one thing to search the first level of Tenebro for arcano-tech to sell, quite another to make it way down here. That's what I thought. Maybe I should have kept looking. It's not actually *that* dangerous down here."

"I mean, we did all just try to kill ourselves because of a trap."

Teya paused, then nodded. "Fair point. Until that trap, our time down here wasn't that much more dangerous than what we'd been dealing with in the hungry caves. Maybe if I'd just pushed a little harder, we'd have found the castle with Ky's pack a year ago. What if she'd managed to survive for that long? What if she's still down here, somewhere? Those questions, Meli... they're eating me alive."

"Isn't it better to know?"

"Maybe. What did the trap show you, Melita?"

I told her about the stage and the crowd and the performance. I told her what the trap had told me.

"I'm sorry, Meli..."

"That's not all."

"It's not?"

"No. The night before the humans attacked. You know I came down into the Hungry Dark by myself? I'd wanted to see something beautiful. I'd wanted to leave life on the surface behind. I left *you* behind, and I wasn't planning to come back. I'm really, really sorry."

"Meli... I love you. You know that. I want you to be safe and happy. You never need to apologise for feeling... what you feel." Teya shuffled a little closer to me. Her arm brushed against mine. "I don't know if it'll make any difference, Meli, but I'd consider it a favour if you stayed in the world. I think it's a much better place with you in it."

I rested my head on Teya's shoulder. "Right back at you."

We were quiet together for a minute. Her shoulder was the most comfortable pillow I'd ever used. I reached out and took Teya's hand. Our fingers interlaced. She squeezed, gently. I closed my eyes.

"I think it'd be great if neither of us did anything like that again," said Teya.

"I think you might be right."

We were silent for a few minutes. The still night air was only broken by the persistent sounds of Jaeson's crying.

"Do you think he's okay?" Teya asked.

I chuckled, "I don't think any of us are okay."

"Yes, but... should we wait for him to come back to himself? I don't know how long we can stay here."

At this, Jaeson shot to his feet. He stood bolt upright, although he kept his gaze firmly on the roof. His arms stayed locked to his sides. His hair fell forward in front of his face.

Teya straightened a little, "Jaeson? Are you okay?"

Jaeson nodded. Teya and I shared a look. Jaeson was lying. It was obvious he was lying. I knew it. Teya knew it. The reason for the lie was a bigger mystery.

"Okay," Teya said. "Well, there's a few steps just over there. Let's see if they lead to a way down off the roof."

The steps led to a door set into the roof, and the door led to more stairs down. As we descended, I told Teya about how Vakua had saved me. The booming echoes of our footsteps against ancient wood accompanied the story, making the tale of the giant serpent catching me sound more sinister than it had felt in the moment. Teya paused on the step below me and looked as if she wanted to turn and flee back up to the roof. Behind me, Jaeson paused as well, although he didn't stop crying.

"I think she's not angry anymore, Teya," I said. "She saved me. You don't do that sort of thing if you're only going to kill someone later."

Teya nodded and started descending again. Her footfalls were noticeably more contemplative than before. As we stepped out of the temple, I took her hand. In the distance, by the wall of the cavern, lay Vakua. I was surprised at being able to see that far. My light should have struggled to penetrate the Hungry Dark to that extent. Vakua's form was hazy, but her mask was unmistakable.

"Hello," she said, maintaining her distance from us. "We should talk."

Teya and I bowed to Vakua.

"I'm deeply sorry for my actions when we last met," said Teya. "I hope to make it up to you one day."

"You can make it up to me by explaining why you tried to release the catches on my mask," said Vakua.

In the still, dark air, all we could hear was Jaeson's grief.

"I'm trying to find out what happened to my wife Kyrene," Teya said. "I thought I would have a better chance at finding her if I took your mask. I desired power. It was selfish and wrong."

Vakua chuckled. "Do you know how long I've held this power?"

"Er, no," Teya replied.

"Neither do I, exactly. It has been a long time. And truth be told, I am tired. Very tired. Once I calmed down after the shock of your attempted theft, I began to think. I began to wonder if it was time for me to retire, to stop acting as a guardian for this darkness and see what else is out there in the world. So, I have come to you with an offer. If you truly desire my mask, you may take it."

"Just like that?" Teya asked.

"Just like that." Vakua uncoiled slightly and approached. Jaeson took a step backwards, his footsteps crunching on the gravel path.

"You're not going to ask for anything in return?" I asked. I could just reach up and take the mask from where I was standing.

"If I may join you on your journey back up to the surface or down to Sirmo, that might be advantageous... but I suspect I will need some time to myself once I give the mask up. Let me ask for a few glow globes and other supplies. Whoever takes on the mask will not need such things. The power of the mask absorbs the worst of the Hungry Dark's bite."

I turned and looked at Teya. She nodded.

"Very well," I said. I tapped the first two fingers of my right hand against my right palm in a quick, excited beat. "We accept your offer."

Teya quickly stepped past me and reached up to Vakua's mask.

Vakua jerked back, "Hey, what are you doing?" she asked, her voice suddenly less serene and a lot more alarmed.

Teya froze, she looked at me. Her face asked whether she'd just made some catastrophic mistake. "I was going to take your mask," she said, cautiously. "You know, like we agreed?"

Vakua backed away from Teya, "Yes, yes, that's right, but not *you*. Either of the other two, yes, but not you."

"Why not me?" Teya asked.

I shifted, the tension in the air flowing through me. "Er... I'm happy to do it."

"Good, then Melita's going to take my mask," Vakua said.

"No," Teya said.

"What?" I asked. "What's the problem?"

Teya folded her arms, still staring at Vakua. "You can't do it, Melita. You need a mouth to swallow your bones. That mask doesn't have a mouth hole. In an emergency we won't be able to wait for you to remove the mask and swallow a fresh tooth. Sorry, you can't do it."

"Well, how about you?" Vakua asked, turning to Jaeson.

Jaeson stared up at Vakua, his eyes wide. His jaw was tight. His hands shook.

"Er..." he said.

"You'd have power," Vakua said. "More power than a human could ever dream of."

Jaeson couldn't even speak.

"I'm going to go ahead and say Jaeson declines the offer," I said.

"Oh no," Teya said. "Well, if Melita and Jaeson can't do it, then it has to be me, doesn't it?"

Vakua loomed over Teya. "It. Can't. Be. You."

"Why not?" Teya asked sweetly.

Vakua's mask was completely immobile, but her massive fingers twitched. "Okay," she said. "Okay, you can have the mask."

She lowered herself so that her mask was just in front of Teya, who reached up. Teya had only just touched the first of the mask's catches when Vakua jerked backward.

"I can't," she said. "I can't."

"Why not, damn it?" Teya asked.

"Oh, I'm going to regret telling you this, I just know it," Vakua said. She rolled her head back and pawed at her mask with her night-clad hands for a few seconds while muttering to herself. After a full minute of groaning and grumbling she faced us once more. "Okay, fine. I've been trying to get this mask off for years now. It doesn't just give me power, it's what gave me this shape. I didn't used to be like this, I used to be humanoid, like you. This mask isn't a blessing. It's a curse. It's obviously a curse, look at me."

"But you're so powerful!" I said.

"Oh yes, the power's great but everyone I meet thinks I'm a monster."

We looked up at the enormous creature with the blank featureless mask.

"This is one of the longest conversations I've had in years," Vakua said.

"But why?" I asked. "Why not just take the mask off?"

"Because I can't! The mask won't come off if I try to remove it. Watch." She scrabbled at the clasps on the side of the mask with her hands. They seemed to be locked tight. "Before I met Melita, I'd never been able to talk to anyone for long enough to persuade them to undo the catches, let alone take the mask. That's why I was so thrilled when you took the mask off, Melita. I was so *sure* you were going to take it!"

I thought back to standing in Vakua's temple, surrounded by the scent of cedar wood. The air was different down here – mustier. Closer. It felt as if the world had closed in on me.

"So, and I don't want to give you ideas here," Teya said, "why don't you threaten to kill us if one of us doesn't take the mask?"

"Oh yes, I've tried that. It doesn't work. The catches of the mask remain locked. The only thing I can think of that might work – which I haven't been able to try – is to have someone else take on the mask willingly, of their own free will."

"Ah."

"Yes, 'ah' is right. And that's why you can't ever trust anything I say if I ask you to take off my mask, because I guarantee you that I'll be trying to trick you."

"Why are you telling us all this?" I asked.

"Because Teya had worked it out pretty much anyway. But listen, listen, this is fine. Look, you know now. You're not going to take my mask. Okay? I can take you to Sirmo. You want that, don't you? To get to Sirmo?"

I opened my mouth to answer, but Teya rested a hand on my arm.

"We want to go to Sirmo," she said. "Why do you want to take us? What's in it for you?"

Vakua froze. A long silence filled the air.

Teya nodded. She took a step forward. "We'll go with you to Sirmo if you can answer two questions. The first, you already know: why do you want to take us? And the second: why wouldn't you let me take the mask?"

Vakua was already turning her back by the time Teya was halfway through her second question. She slithered off into the darkness, heading towards the stairs that would lead to her castle.

Teya sighed. "Okay, hopefully that's the last we'll see of her."

I nodded, frowning. There'd been such pain in Vakua's voice. There'd also been something in the conversation I'd missed, but I couldn't quite work out what. "I wonder if we just turned away the only chance we had of finding Sirmo..."

"With Vakua showing us the way it was guaranteed to be another trap," Teya said. "Can you walk, Jaeson?"

He didn't look up, but still made an "mm" of ascent.

Teya met my gaze, then jerked her head at Jaeson. I shrugged. He'd clearly been hit hard by what had happened in the Peace Trap. We couldn't stay here indefinitely, and he seemed happy to keep moving. Still, in the wake of that trap, we could probably all use a little kindness. "We can stay here for a while if you need time, Jaeson."

Jaeson shook his head. Without looking at either of us, he turned and started to trudge down the that we'd been walking along before we'd been snagged by the trap. We followed him, keeping enough of a distance to give him some space, but not so much as to run the risk of him being swallowed by the darkness.

"Should we ask him about what the trap showed him?" I whispered.

"I don't know, Meli. I just don't know. He's fully aware we don't really want him along on this trip. He's clearly going through some stuff. If he wants to tell us, he'll tell us. At least he's not slowing us down anymore."

Our path led us through a short passageway, impassive stone statues lining one wall. They didn't object to our passage, and their stares didn't falter as our light left them behind in darkness once again.

We emerged into a cavern where my light couldn't pick out the ceiling or walls. So far it was similar to the caverns on the upper levels, but the contents of this cavern differed significantly. Instead of broad streets and large buildings, my light fell on small, narrow, winding streets which dove between knots of small, single storey buildings. At the edge of my light, I saw a three-storey building rising out of the throng of squat structures. The height and the ornate shape of the building's roof made it obvious that it was a temple. I had to hope we weren't going to head in that direction. I'd had enough of temples for a while.

Jaeson paused at the top of a set of steps that led down to the closest cluster of buildings. We caught up and felt an unasked question hang in the air. Teya pulled out Kyrene's notebook and flicked to the map page.

"It looks like the first of Kyrene's stashes is to the north of here," Teya said, after a moment of intense concentration. "How tired are you feeling, Meli?"

I rolled my shoulders, feeling their weight. I could push through. "I've got this."

I walked down the steps and led the way into the warren of streets. Teya whispered directions behind me whilst I scanned for threats. To my relief, Kyrene's stash seemed to be in the opposite direction from the distant temple. I topped my light up with a fresh tooth and, as we walked, I realised what the buildings we were passing had once been and my light took on a bluer hue.

The street was no larger than an alley, but every structure had windows and hatches that looked out. There were stools and chairs dotted about, and inviting, yawning doorways. Signs hung above head height, boasting names and prices. We passed the remains of bars, restaurants, shops, and the occasional workshop.

"You must be relieved," I said, after allowing some thoughts to slot into place.

"Are you talking to me?" Teya asked.

"Yeah. Relieved. You. Must be."

"How's that?"

"Well, Vakua was trying to trap us into taking her mask. You didn't ruin things for us and cost us a potential ally."

"Yeah?"

"Yeah."

"I'm not sure it's that simple, Meli."

"Sure, it is. If you hadn't acted in the way you did, on both occasions Vakua tried to trick us, Jaeson or I might have put on the mask." I thought about this. Our footsteps, soft as they were, thudded in the still air around us. "Well, I might have put on the mask anyway."

"Maybe, maybe, but come on, Meli, in the moment I wasn't acting with restraint, I wasn't being cautious. I was letting my worst instincts get the better of me. I tried to steal from an ally. I knew at the time it was the wrong thing to do."

"Or maybe you knew something was up with Vakua's mask. Maybe you felt something deep down was suspicious, and you wanted to pick at it."

"I didn't."

"Teya, how long have we known each other?"

"Must be nearly five years now."

"And how many times have you acted recklessly or without thought?"

"Hey, I can be impulsive."

"Mhm."

"I can! We get up to all sorts of stuff when we've been drinking."

"Singing lewd songs barely counts."

"No, no, not just the songs. There was... er... Hold on..."

"You're trying to distract me. Look, I'm saying you might have known something was up, even if you didn't know you knew it."

The path ahead of us divided in two as we approached a stall, on which sat small intricately carved wooden knick-knacks. Teya paused before starting down the northerly street.

We walked in silence for maybe twenty minutes. The dark air around us was quiet and still. The only disturbance I sensed came from behind us, after we neared the end of a strangely long, unbending street. Something shifted in the darkness. Something huge. I'd a feeling about what it might have been, so I didn't alert Teya to her presence.

"Do you smell something?" Teya asked, after another two minutes of silent strolling.

I drew in a deep breath. Musty air, cedar wood... there was something else as well. "Maybe?"

Teya snapped her fingers, triumphantly, and pointed down a path that jutted between two shops. I led the way, covering suspicious looking approaches with my pistol. At the end was an ornate wooden wall decorated with long dead lanterns. Set into the centre was a doorway that must have been covered by a door or a cloth, long ago, but now stood open. Through the gap wafted the heady smell of sulphur and the sound of running water.

The smell of eggs long past their prime reminded me of happier days, before I was exiled from my parents' home. We'd had a hot spring a little way into the mountains, which we'd bathed in whenever we'd needed to relax. Without waiting for the others, I stepped through the doorway.

On the other side, paving slabs gave way to pure cave floor, worn smooth through long use. The walls closed in on all sides, making a natural chamber, merely large rather than cavernous. Benches lined the walls, clean and beautifully maintained, which made me frown, but only for a moment.

Stepping in, my light revealed a second, much larger, chamber beyond where rocks had been artfully placed in a sweeping curve in beds of black and grey gravel. In the middle of the chamber was a pool of steaming, milky water.

A hot spring. A little oasis of home in the Hungry Dark. I crouched at the pool and dipped my fingertips into the water. It warmed me down to the bone. I held my hand still for a long, long moment, feeling the warmth run through me. Even if I'd wanted to, I wouldn't have been able to keep the smile from my face.

"How's the water, Meli?" Teya asked, still back in the changing space, peering through.

"Delightful."

Teya shifted on her feet. Her expression softened from stern to something more open.

I stood and shook the water from my fingers. "Shame we don't have time to make use of the place."

"Meli, none of us got much sleep last night. I'm not feeling great. You look like you're about to fall over."

"Hey..."

"We've got six globes and you have more than ten hours of light. We can spare twenty minutes. We're going to burn out if we keep going."

If I stopped, I wasn't sure if I was able to start again. Even standing still for this long was making my legs feel as if they were seizing up. I shook my head, mute.

Teya looked back at Jaeson, who was standing in the doorway to the changing area, his eyes still locked on the floor. My light glinted off twin trails leading from his eyes down to his jaw. My friend pursed her lips. "How about this. We find Kyrene's pack, and if that doesn't take too long, we can take turns. One of us has a soak, one keeps watch and the other works through the pack, then we rotate. Sound okay?"

The smell of the beautiful, toasty warm water made my muscles yearn for a good soak. I nodded and looked around the changing area. There weren't many places where a stash of Kyrene's belongings could be. In fact, there was something dark hidden in the shadows under one of the benches. "See that?"

Teya nodded and stepped forward. I joined her, and the shift in my light revealed a large travelling pack.

I reached for it but Teya rested a hand on my shoulder. "Melita, look." She pointed. On the rocky ground in between us and the pack was a discoloured area of rock.

I frowned. "What's that?"

"I think it might be all that remains of a blood stain. Kyrene wasn't the sort of person to just leave her kit unattended where anyone could nab it. She might have left a trap."

I squatted down and held out a shining hand, bathing the pack in turmeric-coloured light.

Teya joined me and peered closer. "Move a little that way please, Meli?" she said. "I might have a view of something but the light's making it hard to see."

I shifted slightly, causing the shadows to ripple and move. Teya shuffled closer to the bag. "No," she said. "I think it's nothing. I'll try grabbing the bag. Maybe Kyrene was relying on this place being out of the way. No self-respecting cave raider would go searching for artefacts in a hot spring, after all."

Teya reached forward and grabbed the handles of the pack. Gently, she drew it out from under the bench.

Click

Teya and I froze at the mechanical sound, but nothing happened immediately. Teya let out a breath at the same time as I heard a gasp from Jaeson. The human had straightened. He was looking straight at me. He still stood in the doorway to the chamber, at the edge of my light. A hand had reached out of the darkness and was resting on his shoulder.

Chapter Thirteen

The hand resting on Jaeson's shoulder seethed in my light. It seemed to be made from living shadow, more of a claw than a hand. I reached for my gun. The hand yanked Jaeson out of our light and into the Hungry Dark.

"Teya!" I yelled, leaping after Jaeson and flaring my light. My power was still fresh, but it was a hollow sort of power. My most recent tooth must have had a flaw, a fracture, something that reduced its ability to hold magic. I sprinted forward, knowing that if Teya couldn't keep up, she had glow globes and Jaeson did not. I reached down to my wrist and popped another tooth into my mouth. The light that flowered in its wake was pure orange; vibrant and warm.

Jaeson screamed, his cries high and desperate. I surged forwards, but it took precious seconds for the edge of my light to reach him. Blood streamed from deep bite marks on his face and arms. A night-clad figure had its arms wrapped around him. Undefined and blurry – a dark hood shrouded where its head should have been. The only parts of it that seemed to have real substance were its arms, which were wrapped tightly around Jaeson's waist, and its claw-like hands, which were gripping Jaeson's flesh so tightly they were drawing blood.

The wraith's night-flesh hissed as my light reached it, but it wasn't immediately forced back as the Hungry Dark usually was. I felt the weight of the pistol in my hand as I ran. I couldn't shoot at the wraith – Jaeson was flailing about too much. On top of that, I'd have to stop running to line up a shot, and the wraith was unlikely to stop dragging Jaeson into the darkness in order to make my life more convenient.

I finally caught up to within an arms reach of him as the wraith dragged him out of the alley and back into the shop-lined street. The wraith hesitated, seemingly unsure as to which way it should drag Jaeson. I stuffed my pistol into my belt and leapt forward.

I knew I had to do something, but I had no idea what. The wraith wasn't fleeing my light – it didn't even seem to be harmed by it. If I couldn't use my gun for fear of hitting Jaeson and I couldn't use my light I was utterly useless. I'd just have to try and wrestle Jaeson free from the wraith's grip.

Jaeson's eyes widened still further at the sight of me hurtling towards him. I grabbed the wraith's arm - stone cold under my grip. I was unable to stop my shoulder from slamming into Jaeson's chest, but this seemed to only confuse the wraith more.

I yanked at the wraith's claws, but they were biting into Jaeson's flesh and I couldn't pull them loose. Jaeson keened in pain as the claws bit deeper. The wraith dragged him back, hissing at me. I could keep up with it but the further we moved, the higher the chance that we'd lose Teya. I had to do something desperate.

In theory, my magic could be focussed down to a single point, turning a broad light into a powerful beam, like using a magnifying glass to focus the sun. I'd never managed to do this for more than a second. The peace trap had taunted me about how I'd neglected self-improvement. If I didn't step up now, my lack of training was going to get Jaeson killed.

I poured power into the palms of my hands, focussing my light into a smaller and smaller area. A vibrant orange light like the setting sun burst from my palms, burning into the wraith's arm. The shadow released Jaeson and reeled back. My concentration slipped, and the glare from my palms lost its intensity, returning to a soft red glow. Still, Jaeson was free.

The wraith rounded on me, its cloak flapping furiously, despite there being no wind down here. Its faceless cowl glowered at me. Its cloak was translucent in my light, revealing a network of silver struts deep within the creature which might have been all it had for a skeleton.

It circled around me, arms darting forward and then dropping back as it drew closer. The arm I'd grabbed seemed fainter than when it'd held Jaeson. Good. It was a creature of living darkness. I could burn it away. I rolled my shoulders and stepped around Jaeson, towards the wraith. Behind me, Teya finally arrived.

"Come on, Jaeson," she said, "don't worry. You're safe now."

"Not yet, not yet," I said.

The wraith surged forward, and I struck out with three quick punches. I concentrated light into my fists, and my power left gaping holes in the creature. Still, it was quicker than me. It wrapped a cold, cold claw around my outstretched arm and dragged me towards the darkness. My coat sleeve protected its hand from my light, so I couldn't burn its grip on my forearm away. Still, by grabbing my arm it had pulled my hand closer to its body.

I let myself be dragged, concentrating instead on pouring light out of my captive hand and into the wraith's body. I remembered how I'd felt at the moment I'd saved Jaeson – the feeling of warmth inside reflected by the glow of my light. I concentrated on the burning sensation of my light in my hands. I focussed that light tighter and tighter and tighter. My light glowed a rich red, orange glowing at its core. Warmth washed over the street and the wraith burned. I felt alive. I wasn't going to stop until this monster was obliterated.

"Melita?"

The wraith blazed under my light. Sensations swirled around me. I ignored them, concentrating my power to a single point. It was working. I was winning. The peace trap was wrong. I could do this.

My vision swirled, distorted by the flashing, dancing golden figures that twirled at the core of my light. The wraith crumpled, and I took another step forward, forcing what remained of the dark creature to the ground. One of my outstretched arms fell uselessly by my side but my right arm stayed pointing at my target. My light was making the rest of the world seem dark by comparison.

The wraith let out a soundless scream. I slipped to one knee but didn't let my light fade until the last particle of shadow was obliterated. I smiled in triumph. My breathing echoed, obliterating all other sound. I wanted to laugh.

My shoulder hit something hard. My head fuzzed briefly with an impact. I opened my eyes. I was lying on the floor. Teya sprinted to me, shouting something. I couldn't make out what she was saying. I closed my eyes again and rested my head on the ground. The chill cobblestones felt restful.

The last of my power ebbed out into the darkness, but the light didn't fade. Someone else had probably taken over duty as bringer of light. Maybe one of my sister witches had arrived to save the day. Or maybe Teya had activated one of her glow globes. There was no way of knowing without opening my eyes and in that moment such an action didn't feel possible.

Someone gripped my arm firmly but with obvious care. They lifted me, and I felt the warmth of another body. I rocked back and forth, slumped over something rock hard.

After being rocked gently for about a week, I managed to open my eyes. Teya was carrying me on her back. Jaeson wore Teya's pack, and held a glow globe high, bathing us in cold light. He looked as if he'd emerged from his personal hell a little. That was nice.

Movement out of the corner of my eye. I shifted my head. My vision focused and, at the very edge of the light from Jaeson's glow globe, I caught a hint of something enormous and white. It looked like Vakua's mask. She was following us. I wanted to wave to her, but I couldn't move my arms.

She might have seen me looking, because her mask faded into the darkness, and I was left staring at row after row of shops, bars, and workshops. I had no idea where we were going.

I closed my eyes again and opened them when I felt warmth on my face. Sunlight made me squint. I was bathing in sunlight. A rattling gasp escaped my mouth.

"Are you okay up there, Melita?" Teya asked, over her shoulder.

"How..." I mumbled. The smell of fresh earth and crisp vegetation filled me.

"There's another fissure in the cave roof, it leads up to the surface. Looks like we've passed our first night down in the dark. Don't worry, Meli. Hush now. The sun should keep us safe."

'Should' stuck in my head like a needle between my teeth. I forced my eyes to stay open, although they dearly wanted to close. I saw bamboo, tall and dark but with vibrant green leaves. I saw a winding path. I saw a hooved foot, the size of a house, land gently on the ground around ten metres away from us. This seemed strange to me, but Teya kept walking, undeterred. I looked up and saw a creature the size of Vakua's castle bending down and pulling up a bamboo plant by the root. It was a deer – a spotted deer. They were common in Talvik and some people thought they belonged to the spirits. Even the humans from Jaeson's village would think twice before harming one. This deer seemed to be thriving down in the dark... or in the light, rather.

Another deer, even larger than the first, strolled up to its friend. Both had dark, shimmering skin, spotted with occasional lighter patches. They were clad in night, like the tree in the school courtyard had been. But... the new deer, who I internally named Maisie, gently nuzzled at the flank of the original deer, who I named Zadie. Maisie picked a patch of Zadie's skin loose that must have been the size of a carriage. Beneath the skin was brown fur with lighter spots.

Maisie bent down and picked up a dark bamboo stem in her jaws. She chewed it thoughtfully before licking Zadie's flank at the point where the brown fur was showing. Her tongue was dark with the bamboo flesh, and the darkness transferred over to Maisie's flank, patching the hole.

"They're clothing each other in night to protect from the hunger..." I said.

"Did you say something, Meli?" Teya asked.

I wanted to repeat myself but found I could only smile at the sight of Maisie and Zadie caring for each other, both utterly ignorant of our presence. My eyelids drooped. I couldn't recall ever feeling so tired but also so content in my life.

I woke to the sound of voices. The world was bright around me, even through my closed eyelids. It wasn't the cold light of a glow globe and my magic wasn't flowing. I was bathed in honest to goodness sunlight. My legs were stone. Immovable. My chest had calcified in my sleep.

"You're awake?"

That sounded like Jaeson.

"Yeah. Feeling much better," said Teya.

There was something strange about that exchange, but I was still too groggy to puzzle it out. I was lying on something soft – maybe a futon. I was on my back. My fingers had rolled into loose fists as I slept. The tops of my fingers brushed thick, scratchy cotton.

"Listen," said Jaeson. "Er... this is... When we were in the peace trap. Did you tell the truth about what happened to you? About your wife and..."

"Listening to that, were you?"

"I'm sorry..."

"It's fine. I just let you watch my back while I slept. At some point I have to let certain facts of our shared past go. Yes, what I told Meli about the peace trap was basically all there was to it."

"Basically?"

"I left out a few bits and pieces. The trap told me Meli manipulated me into agreeing to this expedition by saying she wanted to help Ekzilo but all she really wanted was to go on an adventure down in the dark."

A jolt ran through me. She knew. I needed... I needed... I needed to leap to my feet. Distract. Distract Teya. Move the quest on. Focus. I needed to, to, to *move* but I was a statue, carved from the ground beneath me. I knew I could explain to Teya if I could move. If I could open my mouth. My eyes.

"Do you think it was telling the truth?" asked Jaeson.

"Yeah. Yeah, I do."

"What?"

The bottom dropped out of my world, sparkling shards of shame flashed behind my eyes and still I couldn't move.

"Oh don't look like that, Jaeson. I meant... What the trap said might have been technically true without being what I'd call Capital T True, you know? I think the trap took great pride in never actually lying. I'm sure Meli wants to go on an adventure, but you don't have to spend much time with her to get to know what she's about. When Ky and I first came to Ekzilo, for example. We'd been there for a few days and been sorted out with a place to sleep. Ky wanted to try exploring in the Hungry Dark, so I was left on my own. Next thing I know, Meli is knocking on my door asking if she wanted me to show her the village."

"No-one else had done that for you?"

"Everyone in Ekzilo is pretty busy, Jaeson, either with work or their own problems."

"Sorry."

"Right. So anyway, Meli is showing me round, and she keeps getting distracted and looking off into the distance, and she's pretty clearly unwell, right? So I suggest getting some food and her face just lit up and we spent the next two hours chatting about our pasts and our hopes and dreams. I thought she was hitting on me at one point but it turned out she was just really interested. My point is, there's a lot of stuff bubbling below the surface with Meli, but just pay attention to what she says and does for a while. You'll see."

"Right," said Jaeson.

"Right?" said Teya.

"Yeah."

Silence reigned, and I knew that was my moment. Teya had moved on from my betrayal to possibly my kindest moment in our shared past. My brightest moment. That was when I should have leapt up, dazzling my companions with a smile. There were secret logbooks to interrogate. Mysterious stashes to raid. Lost cities to find. I could move. I could probably move. If I summoned every scrap of energy I had, I could probably roll over onto my front wriggle my arms under me, rise onto my hands and knees and, if there was a table or something nearby, I could grab that and haul myself up.

They shouldn't see me do that. Better for them to think me asleep than to see me reduced to such a state. I burned at my body's betrayal of my spirit. I needed to push through, but I'd been pushing so hard and for so long.

My head swam. My thoughts grew fuzzy. I started drifting off again, before Teya spoke. "You want to say something, Jaeson?"

"Uh..."

"You wanted to talk about my time in the Peace Trap. I told you. Why don't you tell me what happened to you, and we'll see if it's as bad as you seem to think it is."

No. I couldn't hear this. This was private. I needed to grunt or something. Let them know I was awake. A scream echoed around in my head as I learned I was unable to act with even that tiny amount of decency.

"Er. Well... I was back in my village. I was there with my foster mum and I had a lovely brother who was, I don't know, five or six. I don't have any... well, never mind, the point is, in the peace trap, our village had become the centre of a movement that had swept across Talvik. We had exiled every immigrant, deviant, waster, and witch from the country. Not just the nearby villages, we'd overthrown the governors of the cities who had allowed the rot to spread, as well as the villages like Ekzilo who harboured undesirables. Kareco and Paco, those dens of deviance, had been restored to their former glory. They were places of purity and peace."

I held my breath, wondering what Teya would do with that information. Only silence followed. Hating my weakness, my statis, I gave up. I let Jaeson's words wash over me like a rising tide over a corpse.

"It was the ten-year anniversary of the great purge. My lovely little brother took me by the hand and led me into the street. It looked exactly the same as it always had. He took me to our little clinic and showed me that our doctors were still overworked and underpaid. He showed me the children who still lived in poverty. He showed me the long hours my foster mum still had to work for meagre pay. He showed me the houses full of old people who had no one to care for them. He showed me that returning Talvik to purity hadn't actually solved any of our problems. Then, my brother, the person I loved, looked up at me and told me that what I was seeing in that moment was the absolute best-case scenario."

"Ah."

"Please. I'm not done. My brother then showed me another scenario, one he said was far more likely. We purged Talvik of the outsiders. Then we got rid of the deviants. Then we got rid of the wasters. That hadn't solved our problems, so we didn't stop there. We got rid of the socialists because they were ruining the economy. We got rid of the people who followed the old religions because they were heretics. Men were forbidden from working to make sure they concentrated on their natural roles as homemakers. People from the islands to the north and south of Talvik were blamed for our problems. Our neighbours were exiled. The people who had cared for me and my brother when mum had been working late. Then it wasn't just the islanders who were exiled. They came for the people whose parents or grandparents had been born on the islands. They came for me and did it in the name of something I'd thought was true.

"Teya... you saw your dream come true, and the trap tried to twist it against you. I saw my dream come true, and the trap showed me why I should never have dreamt for something so horrifying. My dream brought death and destruction and misery for hundreds of thousands of people, and it didn't even solve my village's problems."

"Huh," said Teya. "Yeah. That's pretty bad."

"Yeah. I'm really sorry."

"I have a question."

"Okay."

"Would it have been okay if the peace trap had shown you your dream and it *had* fixed your village's problems?"

Jaeson didn't seem to know what to say to this. Silence stretched on in the wake of Teya's question. Outside, I heard the deep *thud, thud, thud* of the enormous dear walking through the bamboo grove.

"Something for you to give a little thought to, possibly," Teya said. "In your own time, no rush." She sounded as if she was moving. Another moment I should have moved. To my surprise, I found I was able to shift slightly. Reposition my back on whatever beautifully soft thing I was lying on. Giving in, listening to Jaeson's lament without screaming at myself to just *move* might have allowed some of my energy to return.

"There's one more thing," Jaeson said, his voice barely above a whisper.

"Oh joy."

"Have you seen Melita's wrist?"

What about my wrist?

"Yes."

"There's not many teeth left, are there?"

"Nope. Don't worry, I snagged Kyrene's pack from the hot spring. There are plenty of spare glow globes in there. We've gone from having about fifteen hours of light to nearer thirty, even taking Melita's nap into account. I'm just glad she's finally resting. I shudder to think how much sleep she's had in the last 48 hours. I'd say we can afford to go a little slower than we have been, but we still can't afford to delay once the sun sets."

"Why not?"

"Three reasons. First, for every hour we spend down here, that's another hour our friends on the surface are being hunted by... well, you know. Second, we don't know how many delays we're going to face down here. Lastly, Meli's mood is going to take a serious hit when she runs out of teeth. Ideally we'd use glow globes to stave that moment off."

"She's been out for a long time."

"She'll be fine."

"Is... is she always like... that?"

"No."

"It's nice that she's happy down here."

"She's not happy down here."

It wasn't like Teya to be quite that wrong. I could have moved my hand, made it swing up, interrupt Teya's misstatement... but my strength was still so fleeting. I had to choose my moment.

"She looks happy," said Jaeson.

"She does. She's not. It's happiness's sinister sister. It's ecstasy, but it makes Meli risk her life. It stops her from living on the surface because she feels useful down here. She doesn't need to find a place for herself on the surface, because why would she? Everything she wants is down here. She's going to die down here, unless I can find something she cares about enough on the surface to stay in the light. But even that might not be enough."

That stung. Heat rushed to my cheeks, and my chest clenched tight. Teya didn't have faith in my ability to fight off the darkness. I wanted to open my eyes and give her a piece of my mind, but her voice had sounded so sad.

"She wouldn't stay in the light if you asked her to?" asked Jaeson.

"No. And staying in the light wouldn't be enough to keep her from self-destructing. She needs to slow down. She's fully burned out and she just keeps *pushing* herself."

Silence reigned. I tried to make sense of Teya's words.

"Have you found anything out about Sirmo or your wife?" Jaeson asked, after the longest moment.

"More maps, more information, some promising details but... Honestly, Jaeson, when I asked if it would be okay to throw exiles like me out of this beautiful country on the condition that you got what you wanted, you didn't say 'no', so I'm not sure why you're trying to be friendly. I'll keep you safe but asking me to like you when you're on the fence about whether I deserve to live here is a bit of a stretch."

"Sorry."

"Oh, don't look like that. It sounds like your time in the peace trap made you think about some stuff. Keep thinking about it. See what happens."

I was a little uncomfortable in the silence that followed, both physically and in sympathy with my friends. Finally, I gathered enough strength. I rolled over and groaned at the ache in my muscles.

"Are you awake, Meli?"

"Mm."

"Don't worry, little grebe, you've only been asleep for about eight hours. We've still got a while before sundown. Go back to sleep if you want."

"Eight hours?" I said, groggily. "That's eight more hours our friends have been homeless. Who knows what the humans will have been able to do in that time?"

"I know, Meli, I know, but you were unconscious. You needed to rest. Don't worry about it. You're awake now. We can get back to work when I'm sure you're better."

I nodded, still unable to open my eyes. "Okay. Thanks, Teya. Were Kyrene's maps helpful?"

"You were awake for that bit, were you? Yes, they were. She's mapped out this level and there's no sign of Sirmo. Her notes don't look that recent, but they mentioned visiting another cache on the level below this one, along with a map to its location. There are some stairs pretty close to where we are now, so we can nip down there and check it out easily."

"Wonderful."

I concentrated, and opened my eyes. We were in Mrs Noyer's Restaurant... no. Wrong. The room was a different shape and the serving counter was in the wrong place. Still, definitely a restaurant. Someone had pushed the old tables and chairs against the walls, although the cushions from the chairs had gone. I checked under myself and found a large number of cushions there. Jaeson was lying next to me on another set. Teya was stretching in a clear space in front of the counter. Expansive windows looked out over the sunlit bamboo grove.

Jaeson handed me a rice ball, which I ate in three bites. I felt much more alive after that, so I joined Teya in her stretching. Jaeson disappeared into the back rooms of the inn and emerged holding a metal box, which turned out to be full of dried fish.

"How can this possibly be here?" he asked. "Shouldn't it have rotted sometime last century?"

I took a piece gingerly and nibbled at it. It tasted mostly of salt, but my stomach approved. "Someone else must have left this here," I said, once my mouth was no longer full. "There's someone living down here."

"You sound very sure, Melita," said Teya.

I nodded. "Vakua said there was, and we've seen signs of someone for a while now. Remember the school courtyard? Someone had painted the archways there, and recently too. It would make sense for whoever it is to leave stashes like this in places where they might want to sleep. We shouldn't take too much."

Teya nodded thoughtfully. "We'll take a little but, yes, if there's someone living down here and we run across them I don't want to annoy them by stealing all their food. I've already annoyed my quota of dangerous individuals for this expedition."

We argued for a little while about how much dried fish was too much to take, before putting most of it back and gathering our kit. I didn't want to leave the restaurant but knew we couldn't stay. It was a little slice of home down here in the dark. I reached out and rested my hand on a table top. The wood was soft and smooth. I closed my eyes and could almost feel the thousands of trays, plates, cups, and mugs that had rested here before the Hungry Dark came. I frowned at the thought. I could feel a knot in my chest weighing me down, a sensation I only usually felt in Ekzilo. I shook my head, slipped my boots on, and stepped outside into the bamboo grove.

Maisie had gone, having presumably wandered off somewhere on its cervine business. Zadie was lying down in the bamboo grove a couple of hundred metres away from the restaurant, chewing enthusiastically.

I looked up at the fissure in the cavern roof that allowed sunlight to shine down into the bamboo glade. Fragments of dust danced in the light, flowing with the breeze, which brought with it scents from the surface – pine and cedar. The smells of home mingled with the creeping odour of giant deer guano.

"We should come back here after we've saved Ekzilo," I said. "Take our time. Really enjoy the place. I don't think I've ever seen anywhere this peaceful." Cicadas sang in the bamboo. Zadie's chewing sounded like a distant earthquake.

I sighed, then turned to Teya and Jaeson. "Ready to go?"

Teya took one long look up at the fissure in the ceiling before nodding. She fished out a glow globe from her pack and cracked the seal, then drew out her compass. "That way," she said.

I nodded, and took one last moment to gaze at the deer before striding into the darkness. A brisk stroll through the bamboo grove later, and we were back in Tenebro's urban labyrinth.

My chest felt heavy but my head was surprisingly clear. Sleep might have done me some good after all. Teya and Jaeson's footsteps pattered after me. I listened out for the slithering sound of Vakua, but I couldn't make it out. What I did hear, however, was the soft *click, click, click* of footsteps that didn't sound humanoid. I stopped, and turned on the spot, trying to work out where the footsteps were coming from. They echoed from building to building, sounding a little like the chattering of teeth.

"Something's coming," I said. "It might be the same thing that was impersonating Yilin."

The clicking footsteps paused as I spoke, then resumed.

"Should we run?" Jaeson asked.

Teya checked her wife's notebook. "Yes, I think so. We're aiming for that far cavern wall, Meli."

I nodded and set off at a run down an alley that led in roughly the right direction. My friends fell into step behind me.

"Are you there?" said the creature that was using Yilin's voice. "I need help. Please. I need help!"

We emerged from the alley onto a street that was more spartan than the others. The far side of the road was entirely empty, except for the familiar expanse of cavern wall.

"The stairs down to level four should be a few hundred metres away on our left," said Teya.

We ran, our flight obliterating any sounds of pursuit. We ran until rocks the size of houses loomed out of the darkness in front of us. They were covered by a treacherous scree that had spilled over the street to completely block our path. Teya moved a little closer to the cavern wall, where an enormous fissure had opened, resulting in a rockslide.

"Er.." Teya said. She drew out Kyrene's notebook again and started examining it. "Er... If we go around there's... there's a series of alleys..."

"I'm on it!" I said. I swallowed a tooth and shone a dancing orange light out of my fingertips. I turned from the cavern wall and strode along the outer limit of the rockslide.

"Hello?" cried Yilin's voice. "I need help. Can you hear me?"

"It's getting closer," said Jaeson.

"How's that rockslide looking, Melita?" hissed Teya.

"Pretty... pretty huge," I said, staring off into the distance, where the rockslide had engulfed the street beyond the initial row of buildings, and had half-submerged the shops on the next street over.

"So, what are we doing?" Jaeson asked.

I turned and saw he was hovering around Teya, anxiously. His fear crackled over to me like lightning. The pace of my breathing ratcheted up another notch and my chest started to feel tight.

"I'll see if I can find a way around the cave in!" I said. I ran down an alley and out into the street on the other side. I froze.

Not far from the edge of my light, two pinpricks of glowing red shone out of the darkness. I'd seen them before. They were fire. They pierced the darkness as if it was nothing and bore into me, pinning me to the spot.

I stood, frozen, not wanting to turn my back on the terrible lights. The clicking of footsteps drew closer. Fear gripped my heart. This wasn't the exhilarating fear of the chase, or the adrenaline rush of my powers driving back the darkness. This was the terror of knowing that there was something a handful of metres from me that was so focused and so utterly selfish I might not be able to escape it.

Click, click, click. The voice, when it called for help next, sounded as if it was just outside of my fragile dome of light. Light that was even now turning from the triumphant orange it had been only moments before into a washed out white. Still, I couldn't move. I watched, helplessly, as the creature with crimson eyes and Yilin's voice stepped into my light.

Chapter Fourteen

The creature was maybe a meter tall and wore a simple blue tunic. Its arms and legs were nothing but bone. Its head... was Yilin's. Her neck was missing, leaving her head globe-like and uncanny. Her features were twisted into a parody of distress, her mouth agape, her eyes wide and burning red. I wanted to run, but I couldn't. I *needed* to run, but I couldn't.

The creature lifted a bone hand and gripped the top of Yilin's head. It lifted, dreadfully slowly, easing Yilin's face from the skull that lay beneath. The creature then reached to a metal cable bound to its left wrist and slipped the trailing end into the empty space under Yilin's chin. Yilin's expression drifted from pained to chillingly neutral. The creature released Yilin's head, and it floated gently upwards, like a balloon, the metal cable linking it to the creature's wrist. The head joined a cluster of other heads, each secured by its own metal cable.

The monster's freshly revealed skull was clean and unblemished. Its eye sockets were a misty white. I had expected them to be filled with that dreadful red light, but instead I had to look closer to see that the lights were indeed still there, lurking at the core of whiteness like a red hole in the world, almost microscopic in size but no less terrible.

"Melita!"

I jerked out of my trance. I'd taken two treacherous steps towards the creature as I'd searched for the dreadful lights. The creature strolled towards me. Bearing down on me. Mere meters away. It unspooled a cable from its wrist. It wanted my head.

A fleshy hand grabbed my shoulder and hauled me back. I staggered, and nearly fell. Teya stepped in front of me, facing the creature. She raised the cannon she'd found in Kyrene's pack, and fired.

Whump

A wall of sound shot from the barrel of the gun. Dust and grit blasted away from us, caught in the soundwave's wake. The drift of rocks shifted and rumbled. The creature continued walking towards us, undeterred.

Teya turned and ran back down the alley. She grabbed my hand as she ran past me, hauling me after her. Feeling her hand in mine brought my brain lurching back into step with our situation. "What was that thing?" I panted.

Teya didn't slow down. "No idea, but let's not hang about to find out. We can probably outrun it."

A flare bloomed ahead of us. The yellow chrysanthemum illuminated both the street around it, and the person standing behind it. The stranger stood with her head directly behind the glowing sphere. Her tan jacket flapped in the wake of the power emitted by her light. I could just about make out her neck, which was adorned by a necklace of bones. She raised a gloved hand, and waved to us.

Jaeson ducked around behind Teya, then remembered what we were running from and thought better of it. He moved to stand next to me. I rested my hand on my gun whilst Teya's fingers twitched on her sonic weapon. She didn't raise it to threaten the stranger, but she looked as if she wanted to.

"Come with me," the stranger said. "I was sent to help you."

"Who by?" Teya asked, her tone level, her gaze unwavering.

"Are you a witch?" I asked. Magic was cascading from the chrysanthemum of fire. It felt both familiar and unfamiliar at the same time. It was like seeing a stranger across the street, before recognising them as an old friend.

"Come with me or lose your heads," the stranger said. She turned and strode away from us. The chrysanthemum moved with her. That was when I realised... the chrysanthemum hadn't been hovering in front of her head, it had been *engulfing* her head. Who was this woman?

"What..." Jaeson said.

The skeletal creature stepped into my light as we wavered. We couldn't afford to wait. I tasted the magic that still lingered in the air. It was like mine. The magic of the sun – the magic of light and fire. Whoever the stranger was, we were from the same clan of witches. Trusting her had to make more sense than standing to face the creature that had taken Yilin's head.

"Come on!" I shouted, before sprinting after the stranger.

"Are you sure?" Jaeson asked, stumbling into a jog behind me.

"She's sure, Jaeson," said Teya.

"She's my clan-sister!" I called over my shoulder.

"She's *what*?"

I caught up with the witch whose head was adorned by the sun. She was still walking, calmly, although at a pace that I somehow needed to trot to keep up with.

"You chose to live," my clan-sister said. "I'm glad. The Caretaker will not get paid without you alive and compliant."

"Are you the Caretaker?" I asked.

"I am the Caretaker."

"Is that your name?"

"No."

"What's your name?"

"Call me the Caretaker."

I shrugged. "Okay, then. Who paid you to help us?"

"Part of my payment was not revealing the Benefactor to you."

"Where are we going?" Teya said, as she ran up next to us.

"A tunnel, freshly dug by the Benefactor," said the Caretaker. "I have laid a trap for the Capper. Did it see any of you?"

"It saw all of us."

"Eyes, did it look at any of you in the eyes?"

Teya exchanged a look with Jaeson. "No."

"Yes," I said, quietly.

The chrysanthemum of fire engulfing the Caretaker's head dipped, momentarily. "Good. Come on, we go this way."

The Caretaker led us along the sheer rock wall of the cavern until we reached a shaft leading away from Tenebro. The shaft had rough walls, clearly having been carved by some machine that had been having an off day.

"Did you say that thing was called a Capper?" I asked.

"Capper. It decapitates," said the Caretaker.

"Why are you helping us?" Teya asked. I could hear the suspicion in her voice, but she was doing her best to hide it.

"You will see. Here, this is far enough."

Ahead of us, the tunnel opened up into a house-sized cave. A passageway at the far end was framed by a vermillion arch. The elegance of the arch was a curious addition to the roughly hewn cave surrounding it, and the passageway beyond it was strange as well. It was oval rather than circular and looked less rough. The Caretaker didn't seem interested in the cavern. Instead, she turned to face back down the tunnel.

Click, click, click.

The Capper's footsteps echoed around the tunnel. Red light glinted deep within its eyes. The Caretaker stood solid in the centre of the tunnel, unafraid of the approaching nightmare. Was this how she earned her name? Why not 'Defender' or 'Guardian'? They were more self-aggrandising.

Maybe she was modest. Or maybe… I thought about the places we'd been in Tenebro. I thought about the things I'd seen that didn't make sense.

"What are you the Caretaker of?" I asked, as the Capper stepped into my bubble of light.

"Tenebro," said the Caretaker, slipping a bone from her necklace into the swirl of fire that surrounded her head. Fire rose in her palms. It curled in on itself, wrapping around and around and around her wrists. The Capper stepped closer.

"Are you the one who painted the archways in the school courtyard?" I asked. "Have you been stopping the buildings from decaying down here?"

The Caretaker's head whipped around. I couldn't see her eyes beyond the churning blaze, but I knew she was staring at me. "You saw that?"

"Melita! Please stop distracting our rescuer!" shouted Teya, her voice cracking.

The Caretaker stared at me for a moment longer before turning back to the Capper. Her head dipped for a moment. Then she reached out with her hands and, with a dexterous flick, threw a stream of fire towards the Capper. The fire missed – instead striking the ceiling just above the Capper's head. I was surprised, and so, apparently, was the Capper. It stopped walking for a moment to stare up at the tunnel roof.

The Caretaker's fire hummed into a stream of pure, white-hot power. It was dazzling, bringing the summer sun to the depths of Tenebro. The Capper lost interest in the roof, returned its gaze to me, and took a step forward. A piece of white-hot rock fell from the roof, then another. A third fell onto one of the heads the Capper carried like macabre balloons. The head's expression remained placid, it collapsed in on itself with no fuss or apparent pain.

The Capper looked up at the deflating head. Its skull tilted to the side. More rock fell – fragments followed by a thick drizzle of white-hot rock. The Capper looked back at me and strode forward once more.

Molten rock gushed from the ceiling and collapsed half of the remaining heads. A white-hot rock slick poured onto the Capper's skull. It didn't appear to mind the sudden heat, staring instead at the space where its balloon heads had been. I couldn't fathom what it was doing.

Crack.

A slab of rock, still molten at the edge, cracked loose and dropped. It fell on the Capper, who stood perfectly still, even as it was buried.

I let out a yell of delight. The Caretaker staggered to her feet and turned to face me. "Let us go," she said. She strode past me.

"Wait," I said. "If you're the Caretaker, should you really have destroyed the roof of this tunnel?"

The Caretaker shrugged. "The Caretaker told you the Benefactor dug this tunnel for this purpose. It's not part of Tenebro. It's not the Caretaker's problem."

Crack

The Caretaker and I turned on the spot. The enormous boulder that had crushed the Capper shifted slightly, as if something underneath it, something extremely strong, was moving experimentally. The Caretaker gasped and slipped the second of her three bones into her mouth. She forced a jagged beam of fire from her hands and into the cherry coloured section of tunnel ceiling. A roaring, whipping noise cracked through the air as cooling rock was hit by that dreadful heat.

The Caretaker swayed, then slipped to one knee. "Not yet, not yet," she gasped. The boulder shifted again. The Caretaker would need to bring the entire ceiling down if it wanted to be sure of keeping the Capper in place, but she didn't have enough power.

She had one bone left. I had more. I didn't know exactly how many, but the Caretaker had saved our lives. I would be proud to share some of my precious bones with her. I ripped the bracelet from my wrist and tore teeth from it. I thrust my hand through the fire that surrounded the Caretaker's face, wincing as the flames licked at my flesh.

The Caretaker jerked her head back in surprise, but my questing fingers found her lips. She must have recognised the familiar texture of bone against her skin because she opened her mouth and reeled the fire back from my hand. I thrust the teeth into her mouth and whipped my fingers back just before she bit down. She swallowed, and I saw her smile before the fire returned to cover her skin once again.

With a growl of concentration, the Caretaker poured her new power through her hands and into the tunnel roof. The scorching javelin of power grew first in size, then brightness. Cracks echoed around us. Dust and debris showed down on us. My clan-sister didn't relent. I could feel the power she was forcing into the cave roof. She was working through bones that would provide me hours of light in only seconds.

The boulder that should have crushed the Capper cracked and then shattered. Underneath, the Capper stood, apparently unhurt, although the balloon heads it had carried were gone. It took a step towards us, then another. The Caretaker hissed in pain. The fire around her face flickered.

CRACK

The ceiling of the tunnel collapsed entirely, directly on top of the Capper. One moment it was there, implacably walking towards us. The next, it was swallowed whole, first by rubble, then by rocks the size of buildings. I turned to run but the Caretaker only swayed, hazily. The fire at her face flickered, then died. Her gaze wwas unfocused. her eyelids drooping. We didn't have time to bring her back to herself. I grabbed her arms and hauled her up onto my back, then into a piggyback. My legs howled in protest at the Caretaker's meagre weight, but I pushed through the pain.

A billowing cloud of dust engulfed me. I spun on the spot until I saw the light from Teya's glow globe breaking through the haze. It was far brighter than I'd expected. A hand grabbed mine and pulled me clear as a massive slab of rock crashed down on the spot where I'd been standing.

I burst, coughing, out of the cloud of dust and found it was Teya who had pulled me to safety. The Caretaker's weight made me stagger, but Teya grabbed my shoulder as we ran, and she steadied me.

An apocalypse of falling rocks smothered all other sound. The floor shook under my boots and dust swirled, threatening to swallow me. Fear had sunk its teeth into me. I'd never met anyone from my clan before. If I didn't escape this rockslide, the Caretaker would be taken from this world. I'd be taken as well, and I was surprised to find myself caring about that. Something had shifted during my time down in the dark.

I repositioned the Caretaker on my back and forced my legs to move faster. Teya matched my pace and, together, we escaped the tunnel. We reached Jaeson, and the three of us ran through the cavern, through vermillion gate, and reached the tunnel entrance beyond, just as the rumbling behind us died away.

"Well," said Jaeson, as the dust started to settle. "We're not going back that way."

Teya nodded. "Ay."

I repositioned the Caretaker on my back. "Our friend here had a plan. We have to assume she knew a way out. Shall we see where this passageway leads?"

Teya nodded in agreement. "Are you okay carrying the Caretaker?"

My legs said no. My heart said yes. "All day."

Teya grinned at me before holding her glow globe high and walking into the darkness. Jaeson followed and I brought up the rear.

The passageway was large and coiled downwards in a gentle curve. It was oval in shape and had a strange, distorted quality to it. The walls undulated in and out, peaking about every ten centimetres and dipping ten centimetres later. The peaks and troughs were perfectly smooth, and gave me the impression I was walking down a creature's throat. I'd been somewhere like this before...

"We're heading down," Jaeson said, after two turns of the enormous corkscrew tunnel.

Teya made an 'mmm' sound of acknowledgement.

"We're probably entering a new level of Tenebro."

"Seems likely."

"So, do you think there'll be another trap?" Jaeson's voice was casual but there was a distinct note of tension lurking within.

"Good question," Teya said. "This tunnel feels new to me – look at the weird way the walls ripple. Earth moving machinery couldn't have built a tunnel like this. If it's a new tunnel it wouldn't have a security system set up inside it. So, the question is, do the traps activate when people enter specific locations, or whenever unauthorised people reach a certain depth? It might be both."

Jaeson stopped moving. Teya didn't.

"Shouldn't we talk about which is more likely?" Jaeson asked, as I drew level with him.

"There's no point," Teya said, without slowing. "You don't know you're in a trap when it snags you. We can't prepare for it. Just remember why you're here. We're not trying to rob the place. As long as it's not like the last trap we fell into, we should be fine."

"And if it *is* like the last trap?"

"Then we'll be in trouble, but we can't go back, and we can't stay here."

We trudged along in silence for a few minutes. The Caretaker made a sort of groaning noise on my back but didn't otherwise stir.

"What was it like in Ekzilo?"

"What?" I said, "Why? What are you planning?"

"Nothing! It's just that we're all risking our lives to find means to defend it. I wondered what it was like to live there."

"Hm. That's fair enough. Look, the people of Ekzilo took me in when no-one else would. The people there are the kindest, gentlest people I've ever met."

Jaeson frowned. "You didn't actually answer the question."

"Teya liked living there, right Teya?"

"Right," said Teya, although the sharp syllable sounded more sad than affirming.

Jaeson looked from Teya to me and then back to Teya again. "Okay, then, how about this. What was your wife like, Teya?"

Teya sighed. "I think if you met her you'd think she was... complicated. She was driven. She became a cave raider when she could barely speak the language of this bizarre country because she needed to look after us and she had magic, even if it was barely controlled."

"Right."

I bumped my shoulder against Teya's. "Kyrene was nice. Not everyone fits in well in our village at first. We all arrive with a certain amount of stuff we need to deal with, but Kyrene really tried. She was a bit intense at times."

"Mm," said Teya.

"How long has she been missing for?" asked Jaeson.

"Two years," I said.

"Two years, five days," said Teya.

"Can she have survived down here that long?"

"Maybe."

We trudged along in silence for a few minutes before the chatty little human spoke up again. "So, I've been thinking about... what we talked about in the inn."

"Okay."

"And I've been thinking about what the peace trap showed me."

"Okay."

"The thing is... it was pretty bad for us in our village. We struggled to get enough food, there were barely any jobs..."

"Okay."

"And nothing seemed to change. We'd elect a different mayor and things might improve a bit, but never that much. And we'd know that everything would be fine if only we could get back to a time before... well, you know."

"Okay."

"I'm wondering if we might have been better off focusing our anger elsewhere."

"Okay."

We trudged along in silence for a little while longer. After another full spiral, I had to stop and give my back a rest by propping the Caretaker up against a wall.

"Do you want me to take her for a bit?" Teya asked, after drinking from her water flask.

I smiled down at the Caretaker's sleeping form. "No, it's okay."

We started walking again. Had it not been for the ridges in the floor of the tunnel, our steep descent would have been tricky. Our footsteps echoed around us, creating an arrhythmic beat of couplets. Jaeson's footsteps were light and quick. Teya walked with purpose but her footfalls were soft and careful. My feet thumped against the rock floor because of the extra weight of the Caretaker on my back. They were a booming bass rhythm to accompany my friend's lighter notes.

Teya's glow globe couldn't last. When it began to fade, she rolled it ahead of us and ignited a new one. The discarded globe skittered down the ridged tunnel floor, revealing nothing but empty tunnel before it was swallowed by the Hungry Dark. Teya made a satisfied 'mm' noise, took one more step, then froze in her tracks. Jaeson was only a meter behind her and didn't stop in time. He started turning back, but froze halfway.

If I had to guess, I'd say there was a trap where Teya and Jaeson were standing. I thought about bringing my light to life as well, in case we were trapped for a long time, but I couldn't risk dropping the Caretaker and leaving her on the far side of the trap from us.

I stepped forward.

There was a woman standing next to me. I was sure she hadn't been there a second ago, but I couldn't deny the evidence of my eyes. She was a little taller than me, with black hair and a weary expression. She wore good boots, a battered leather coat and trousers with pockets sewn into the outside to supplement the usual ones. A wicked pistol hung at her belt.

I recognised her. An old friend, maybe? No... My stomach clenched as her dead gaze bored into me. My chest tightened at her rictus smile. No. This woman wasn't my friend. I knew who this person was now – this was the person I hated the most in the world.

"Hello again," said Melita Eklumigi.

Chapter Fifteen

I clung to the roof of a temple. The fifty-degree slope made maintaining my grip difficult, and I couldn't move too quickly, or I risked smashing my glow globe on the roof. The globe was currently hanging from a piece of netting attached to my belt. It'd be better to hold it, but I needed both hands free to work on the roof.

In an ideal world I'd have a full team collaborating with me. Together, we'd have stripped the tiles from this entire section of roof and restored the whole thing. I didn't have anything like the time to take that approach. Back when I'd first entered the dark, I'd been meticulous and fully devoted myself to every task. That led to several buildings in Tenebro decaying beyond hope of repair, so now I patched what needed patching and moved on to the next task.

I knelt on flowing tiles next to a hole in the temple roof. The wooden frame that supported the tiles had started to rot, which had caused a minor collapse inside the temple. I'd already repaired the frame from the inside, now all I needed to do was replace the tiles.

I unclipped a line of string from my belt – the far end disappeared into the dark, off the edge of the temple roof, but I'd coated it in wax which the Hungry Dark wasn't interested in eating. I pulled up the string until I reached the knot which tied the string to a waxed rope. Then, I pulled up the rope. My shoulders complained bitterly as the bucket at the end of the rope dragged at them. Finally, the bucket rose out of the dark. I hauled it onto the tiles next to me, then began the laborious process of scooping clay from my bucket onto the roof's wooden frame.

Once done, I wiped sweat from my brow and rested on the tiles for a couple of minutes. I couldn't stay up here too long. My light was a beacon for any fallen that might happen to be about. I was also on bad terms with one of the local Collectors, and I didn't want to get caught by her up on this roof with only my creaking ladder as a safe way down.

Once I'd rested, I smoothed the clay out to a nice, even layer which covered all necessary beams. This little task represented about a week's worth of effort. Taking care of the frame had been easy – simple sanding and woodwork which anyone could do if they put their mind to it. Taking care of the tiles had been harder.

I'd needed to track down an interesting piece of arcano-tech to trade for currency as I'd run out. Then, I'd needed to buy a new ladder as I didn't have time to build one as a replacement for the one which wound up broken after a fallen ambushed me. Then, I'd needed to find a craftswoman who could make roof tiles of the sort I needed, because that was a specialist job I couldn't do myself. Then, I'd needed to find a craftswoman who could make roof tiles of the sort I needed and was happy to make temple roof tiles for outsiders, given the tiles weren't exactly sacred, but they weren't *not* sacred either. This proved tricky given how deep into the countryside the nearest entrance to Tenebro was. Once I had the three tiles (the two I needed plus a spare), I'd needed to find ingredients for the clay, mix it up and bring everything to the temple. All that work to replace two tiles.

I unslung my backpack and drew out the first tile. I checked it for damage before slotting it into place so that it sat above its sister, then I smacked and stamped it firmly into the clay. I did the same with the second tile, wiped the stray clay off and re-slung my backpack. I had the spare tile I hadn't needed in there, but I could store that inside the temple in case I needed it in future.

I nodded at a job well done and returned to my ladder. Melita was sitting on the edge of the roof. She nodded to me as I saw her and said: "I don't think you have many years left down here, Caretaker."

Light dazzled me – I was back on the surface. I was in a room, walls lined with shelves, each shelf packed with unfamiliar objects. A shop.

I traded a mechanical bird the size of my fist to the shopkeeper in exchange for a netted bag filled with glow globes. Next to me, Melita said: "That tree spirit nearly got you last week. That's five close calls in two weeks. You're slowing down. Your luck is running out."

Darkness. Rushing water nearby. I was back in the Hungry Dark, sitting on something hard and uncomfortable. I knew it was a bucket without looking because I was the Caretaker. I didn't understand why that thought was significant. I couldn't think about it now. I was staring at a bridge, and I was crying.

The bridge arched over a stream in a symmetrical curve. Six pillars, three on each side, had been drilled into the bedrock of the stream. Wooden railings ran along its length, arching with the bridge. The handrail was smooth, but the supports had been cut into an intricate pattern of squares and rectangles that ran the length of the railings. It was red. Two tones of red, one rich, warm, and beautiful, one washed out, thin and ugly.

The bridge was beautiful – it was *supposed* to be beautiful. Now, it was an eyesore. Corrupted. Because of what I did to it. One of the support pillars had started to rot. I'd taken the pillar out, put a new one in, prepped the wood and painted it. Now, I was staring at a bridge that was a work of art, apart from one pillar, which was an abomination.

I'd done everything right. I'd bought the same paint from the same trader I'd been buying from for the last three years. Something must have changed recently, or maybe this batch of paint had been mixed badly, because when it dried the paint was a completely different shade of red from the rest of the bridge. I had to decide whether I was going to leave the bridge like this, try to find some new paint that *did* match the rest of the bridge and repaint the pillar, or sand down the rest of the bridge and paint the whole thing with this terrible paint.

My head fell into my hands and I groaned. Melita sat next to me. She said: "Is this really worth it? We've been having these little chats for years. What have you really accomplished in all that time? You're caring for a dead city. Is there really anything more futile you could be doing? Maybe salting the sea. You should try that next."

Movement. I was standing in the same stream, next to the bridge I had painstakingly rebuilt. A small section of the cave roof had collapsed, blocking the stream. Biting cold water engulfed me up to my waist. I reached into the water, grabbed a rock, heaved it out and placed it onto the bank.

Melita sat on the bank of the stream, kicking her legs. She said: "I have a purpose. I'm here to take your pain away. This is your life you're seeing, Caretaker. Look at it."

I reached into the stream, grabbed a rock, and lifted it. It slipped from my hands and crashed back into the water. My fingers had gone numb. My breath felt ragged.

Up on the bank, Melita was eating a rice ball. I could smell the flaked salmon inside from here. Melita said: "Don't get me wrong, I want to kill you, Caretaker, it's my reason for being, you know? It's my whole thing. We all need a thing. You have this dead city you're caring for. I have killing people who aren't supposed to be here. That being said, I really do care about you, Caretaker. I know how unhappy you are. I can see it. It's all around us."

The next rock cracked down onto the pile I was building on the bank of the stream. The rock after that had a wickedly sharp edge on one side. I only noticed this after I picked it up, gashing my hand in the process. I hissed and clutched at my hand. Up on the bank, Melita said: "Oooh, that looks painful."

Sudden sunlight blinded me. Something soft under my feet – grass. The heady smell of earth after rain filled me. Trees lined the horizon, nestling around a snow-capped mountain crowned by cloud. A burly woman faced me, holding out a bag. She looked disgusted to be standing this close to me. I was trading a map of the caves to an outsider-hating raider in exchange for bones.

Behind me, Melita said: "I don't actually get any pleasure out of showing you your life like this. It doesn't give me a vicarious thrill to reflect people's misery back at them. Still, we each have things that we're good at. I mean, I don't have to be particularly good at my job to reflect the tedious things in your life back at you. There's a lot to choose from. For example, if I remember correctly, that cave raider is about to draw a knife on you."

I handed over the map. The woman took it in her left hand and drew a knife with her right. She slashed at me once, twice. I jumped back, nearly slipping on the wet ground. The woman leapt at me. I caught her knife arm, but couldn't stop her forcing me to the floor. As I struggled to get hold of the knife, Melita said: "Where was I? No, what I mean is, if your life was halfway decent, Caretaker, I couldn't show you all this stuff. Do you follow me? I'm flush with material here. Honestly, I'm drowning in choices at this point. For example, I could be showing you this:"

I was soaking in the hot spring, my eyes locked on the benches in the changing chamber. The paint on one bench had started to flake. I needed to sand and repaint it as soon as possible. Soaking in the spring next to me, Melita said: "Or this:"

I was repairing a paving slab, one amongst hundreds. Next to me, Melita said: "Or this:"

I was bandaging my crimson-stained fingers. Next to me, Melita said: "Spirits, this is so boring! How do you even do this every. Single. Day? I want to kill myself and I'm only watching it. Come on. Let me take your life, Caretaker. Come on. Do it. Do it. Do it. Do it. Do it."

Darkness. My feet pounded against stone. Only a tiny amount of ground in front of me was lit by a flickering flame wreathed around my head. I was sprinting down a stone-lined ramp designed for mechanical earthmovers. The ceremonial shroud I'd been carrying to the temple of Dusk had slipped from my grasp and tumbled into the darkness. I was chasing after it, praying that it wouldn't get torn or stained.

Running next to me, Melita said: "But you're not going to let a little thing like the utter futility of your work get in your way, are you? The thing is, Caretaker - and this is why it's a good thing we're able to have this little chat - someone has found you. Someone with this face I'm wearing, Caretaker. She's from your clan. She's your clan-sister."

The world suddenly stilled. I wasn't running anymore; I was standing completely still. Towering over me was an enormous dark serpent. Vakua. She wanted me to take her mask, but I'd seen through her traps too many times. I offered to lead the next cave raider I met into her trap and in return she promised to clear out a spinney of tree spirits that had sprung up on the first level of Tenebro. In my ear, Melita said: "Are you going to confess what it's really like down here? Or are you going to let her find out the hard way?"

I woke up in the restaurant, scrambling for my pack, terrified that I'd slept past sundown, and Melita said: "Are you really going to make her suffer all this?"

I was sanding down a gate, and Melita said: "She wants to live down here, like you."

I was sprinting to the surface, out of both bones and glow globes, and Melita said: "She wants to hide from the world, in the dark, like you. She wants to shine like the brightest star. In the dark. Where no-one will see her. It's quite poetic actually, like you salting the sea. Sorry, I mean, like you maintaining parts of a city that literally no-one can possibly live in."

I was bandaging my fingers, and Melita said: "Can you remember the last time you smiled?"

I was lying on a futon, crying as the lining of my uterus ripped itself free and Melita said: "I know you feel trapped down here. You think admitting to yourself that your work is slowly killing you will make you a failure. You're a lost cause. Poor little you. However, and this is my main point, this is the thing I'm driving at, Caretaker: Is your refusal to face reality a good enough reason to let someone else make the same mistakes you've made?"

Light bloomed – the light was a trap. A trap I'd set. A fallen was howling, sprinting towards the glow globe I'd left hanging from a lamp post outside a shop that used to sell carved wooden figurines of creatures from the surface. The fallen didn't see the second part of the trap I'd set for it until it was too late. It stepped into a loop of rope. I pulled the other end, hauling the fallen up by its trapped ankle. It dangled as I approached, a machete in my hand.

Leaning up against a lamp post, Melita said: "It really would be much easier if you let me take your life. No messy death for you. You wouldn't lead your clan-sister astray if you let me take you. She'd thank you for that, you know. There wouldn't ne any pain, I promise."

I approached the fallen. I repositioned my fingers on the handle of the machete once, then again. I couldn't get a comfortable grip for some reason. In that moment, I felt two distinct sensations. One was anticipation. I was going to take a femur from this creature and swallow it before blood loss caused it to die. I was going to fill myself with so much power I would burn for the rest of the week. I was going to shine like the sun, and I was going to feel better than I had in years.

The second feeling was fear, and that surprised me. Something inside me was squirming. I had memories that weren't my own – of stalking through the dark school alongside a caring woman who I didn't recognise.

No, that wasn't right. It was Teya. How could I have forgotten Teya? We'd discovered something. Something important. The fallen there, she'd done something to do with cat ears.

As I raised the machete, Melita said: "I'll always be here for you."

My stomach flipped as my arm moved all by itself. The machete bit into the fallen's flesh – the fallen who was alive. The fallen who might be more of a person than I'd always assumed. That was what we'd discovered. Teya and I had conducted experiments. We knew the fallen retained some fragment of their personalities, even whilst possessed by the Hungry Dark. It might, *might* be possible to return the fallen to themselves, and here the Caretaker was killing one of them.

My train of thought fractured. I was the Caretaker. But that was wrong. I had a name. I called myself the Caretaker because that was who I was. It was everything I was. There was a name as well, and that name was a problem. My name was Melita, but that was also the name the Trap was using. "Melita," I said.

"She speaks," Melita said. "I do feel privileged. One moment."

I was lying in the bamboo glade. The sun shone down on me, and Melita said: "Did you want to say something?"

"Melita," I said. I was in a trap. I was trapped. I had been in here for years, but if I concentrated, I knew it had been less time than that. It couldn't have been more than an hour, or my body would have been consumed by the darkness. "My name is Melita."

"No, *my* name is Melita," said the Trap. "Keep up." She nudged me, playfully.

"We're both Melita."

"Is this some sort of game?" Melita asked. "Because I don't get it."

"I think you meant to trap the Caretaker in this dream. You missed. You got Melita instead."

Melita's face fell. "You're kidding."

"No. Let me out."

"I can't have trapped the wrong person in the wrong dream. You're sure you're not the Caretaker?"

I gave Melita a look.

"No. No, no, no!" Melita said, her expression shifting from complacency to alarm. "If I've lost control over who I bring in, then my structure must be falling apart. Quick. You've got to let me kill you. If you're Melita, you have magic. Maybe I can absorb some of it. It'll keep me alive. Please!"

Melita reached out her hand towards me. I didn't take it.

"What are you doing?" Melita said. "I've seen how you live; I'm showing it to… someone as we speak."

"Why are you showing them that?"

"I wasn't supposed to be showing *them* that, I was supposed to be showing *you* how you live, and why you shouldn't be carrying on. I'm going to have to do the quick version. Melita, hello, pleased to meet you. Have you noticed how nothing you do ever seems to make your life better? You dive into the dark again and again and your Kaskado Disorder only seems to get worse? You've noticed that? Great. Now let me end your life so someone more useful can make use of your life force."

The hungry, desperate creature leaned towards me. Part of me wanted to take her hand, but the rest of me was cold. This trap was begging for her life. She was alive. She was a person. But what sort of person would see someone in pain and use it to enrich themselves?

"No."

"Come on, Melita, I'm losing my grip on you. Please!"

"No."

"You'll never be happy. You know that? As long as you try to find purpose by sacrificing parts of yourself to the dark you'll never, ever be happy. You don't have the strength to make a life for yourself in the light with Teya. If I kill you, you'll never have to even try. Come on, what are you waiting for?"

I turned and walked away from those ravenous eyes. A howl of despair only echoed in my ears for a second before I found myself in a heap on the floor of the tunnel, next to the Caretaker, Teya and the brave little human. The Caretaker was moaning in pain. I stood, picked her up and carried her a little further down the tunnel, away from the trap, then put her back down and stretched my arms.

Magic pulsed in the air, but it was fading fast. Previous traps had been able to hide from me. It felt as if this trap was losing even that ability as its magic faded. Good. I moved to a safe distance away but stayed close to Teya. I needed to be able to catch her glow globe in case she dropped it on the way out of the trap.

I felt numb. Not because of leaving the trap to die in the dark. I wasn't glad about that, but I wouldn't lose sleep over it. The hunger in its eyes. It would have killed every one of my friends if it had meant five more minutes of life. I had vague memories of conversations with other traps on the first and second levels. They hadn't seemed as dreadful as the one I'd just met. Or maybe I hadn't seen them as clearly.

I didn't understand what the trap had shown me of the Caretaker's life. There had to be more I hadn't seen. Maybe the futility trap had been like the peace trap – showing me only a selectively edited version of the Caretaker's life. The futility trap might have concealed every moment of triumph, of secret satisfaction. It might have done that, but it also might have been entirely truthful.

I stared down at the Caretaker's face. I hadn't really seen her features before. They'd either been obscured by fire or pressed into my back. There were bags under her eyes. She was covered in tiny scars. Looking at her forearms, I saw some scars that mirrored those that lurked on my arms. The ones I'd put there myself.

It was tempting to think that the reason the trap had mixed us up was because we were clan-sisters, but it looked a lot like the connection ran deeper than that. It was very cold in the tunnel. Very quiet, with the others still trapped. Just for a moment, when I looked down at the Caretaker, I was sure I saw Melita Eklumigi staring back at me.

Chapter Sixteen

Teya gasped. The glow globe slipped from her hand, but I caught it before it hit the ground. She staggered, and had to lean against the tunnel wall. "Well, that was weird," she said. She let out one long, slow breath before standing up straight, stretching and jumping up and down on the spot a few times.

"Did the trap beg you to give your life force to it?" I asked.

Teya shook her head. Next to her, Jaeson collapsed. His face was grey, his eyes staring from Teya to me and back to Teya again.

I patted him on the shoulder. "Come on, little human. Let's get going."

My back wasn't happy at the idea of carrying the Caretaker again, but I wasn't going to entrust my twin to anyone else. I lifted her up onto my back, made a few undignified 'Nnnnrg' noises, and resumed my descent.

"What happened to you in the trap, Meli?" Teya asked, falling into step next to me.

I filled her in on the Caretaker's nightmare, although I left out the parts about recognising my life in the fragments of hers. I still needed to do some thinking about that.

"Now that's interesting," Teya said, "because I didn't get a nightmare."

"You didn't?"

"No. I was living with some Talvik people. Occasionally I'd go to some university or something and get lectured at by some old women. I knew I was in a trap the whole time, so I was always waiting for some nightmare to come crawling out of the walls, but nothing happened."

"Nothing?"

"No."

"The place wasn't secretly full of hornets or something?"

"No, it was all fine. There was more variety in food. Meat was more common, that was nice. There was more tech – we had mechanised vehicles which worked the fields with us. If anything, it was a nice little holiday."

"So how did you get out?"

"I didn't. The trap faded and I was back here."

"How about you, Jaeson?"

Jaeson was chewing his fingernails. "Oh yeah, same. The trap faded."

"What was your nightmare?"

"I really don't want to talk about it."

I made an amused 'humph' noise, but Teya said: "That's fair enough, we won't push you."

Jaeson wrung his hands together. Tears brimmed at the corners of his eyes. He was quiet for a short while, before saying: "Have you two really not worked out what's up with Teya's nightmare?"

Teya scrunched her nose and stared up at the ceiling for half a revolution of our spiralling tunnel. "I was wondering if the Trap could only run one nightmare at once. so it ran the Caretaker's, then it ran yours, Jaeson. It never got round to mine, so it just kept me in a sort of holding pattern. Maybe the Caretaker experienced the same thing."

"Mm," said Jaeson. "Teya, the house you lived in during your nightmare. Tell me about the kitchen."

"Stone stove in the middle, wooden shelves around the outside, wood floors. It was pretty swish. Why?"

"And where did you sleep?"

"Large-ish room. Exposed rafters that made the place smell nicely of old wood. A nice red banner thing decorated with moons and stars over a shrine."

"Right."

"What is it, Jaeson?"

"My house."

"Sorry?"

"You saw my house. Your nightmare and mine got swapped. I recognised your village from the attack. In my nightmare, I was living there, and I was you, and it was just *so* hard and..." He looked as if he were about to burst into tears again.

Teya took pity on him. "Come on, lad," she said, ushering him a little further ahead of me. "Let's have a chat."

Their voices lowered as they walked away. I dropped back to give them some space.

"Mmmmm," said my twin, stirring on my back.

"Hello," I said. "Are you awake?"

"What happened?" She sounded disorientated, or mildly concussed.

"You saved us."

"Good. That's good. Stage one complete. Tick. What was stage two?"

"What are you talking about?"

"Nothing. Sorry. The Caretaker is a little woozy. Where are we now?"

I repositioned her on my back. "Heading down through the tunnels to the fourth level of Tenebro. Do you want us to drop you off somewhere?"

"No. Listen..." The Caretaker was quiet for a moment before she said: "Did you feed me teeth while I was trying to collapse the tunnel on the Capper?"

"It seemed like the only way we'd get out of there alive. I didn't want any of us to get 'capped.'"

"Thank you."

"You saved our lives; I should thank you."

She was silent for a moment too long before replying: "I was just doing a job. I will be paid well."

"Who paid you?"

"I can't tell you, not yet."

"What *can* you tell me?"

She was silent for another half-spiral before replying: "My name is Kinta."

"It's lovely to meet you, Kinta."

Ahead of us, the tunnel levelled out, an archway framing the passage to the next chamber. Teya turned as she reached the arch. "Can you go back to taking the lead, Meli?"

My twin shifted on my back. I met Teya's eyes and tried to work out how to say what I wanted to say.

She smiled and hefted her sonic cannon. "Don't worry, I'm sure I can manage. Hey, Jaeson. Can you use a compass?"

The chamber we entered was too large to fully take in, much like the main chambers from the first three levels. The floor was noticeably rougher, however. Buildings loomed on one side of the street – all hacked together from metal sheeting and rusted girders. Earth movers sat in a tangle on the other side. A metallic tang saturated the air, making my breath feel scratchy, and I couldn't clear the phantom taste from my mouth, no matter how many times I swallowed.

Something moved to the west – something white. It was only there for a moment before it vanished into the dark, but that moment was all I needed. Vakua was following us. She couldn't have come down the tunnel we'd used. She'd known where we were going, and how we were going to get there. That was interesting.

"Melita!" Teya hissed. "Are you coming?"

"Mm? Yes, yes. Sorry." I strode to catch up with Teya and Jaeson, Kinta grumbling uncomfortably on my back.

"Kinta," I said, before I caught up with my friends. "Did Vakua ask you to save us from the Capper?"

"I can't tell you," Kinta said, sounding on the edge of dropping off to sleep again. "She made me promise not to tell you."

"Okay. Don't worry. Go back to sleep."

So, Vakua wanted us alive. That was good. She still had plans for us. I needed to have a think about those plans. In the wake of that last trap, my life felt a little more... in focus than it had been. What did it say about my life that it took a glimpse at Kinta's to make it clearer? Still, I wasn't sure what I should actually *do*.

I finally caught up with my friends. Teya scanned the area, her cannon held ready, whilst Jaeson looked from Teya's compass to Kyrene's notebook and back again.

"How's it looking, Jaeson?" Teya asked.

"I think... I think Kyrene's third stash is just to the east of here."

Teya turned. "That way?"

"Yeah."

"Great. How are you doing for teeth, Melita?"

Even supporting Kinta, my wrist felt dreadfully light. "I've been better."

"Then we don't have time to waste. Come on, let's hurry."

We power-walked down a stone path, lined on one side by hulking industrial buildings, and on the other side by the jagged cavern wall. The people of Tenebro clearly hadn't treated this cave like the work of art it was. They'd cut the space they needed for their machines and then called it a day. I felt bad for the people who'd once worked down here.

Teya led us past jutting spurs of rock and through a gaping tunnel. Rough earth scuffed under our feet. The earth moving machines of Tenebro slept in side tunnels, Teya's glow globe only illuminating fractions of the once proud machines – rusting jaws and decayed wheels. The hush was only broken by our footsteps. Phantom sounds rose from echoes - drips of fluid, creaking, shifting metal.

"Uh-oh..." said Jaeson, staring at the ground. He'd spotted a bone - a femur. My stomach rumbled at the sight of it, but the owner was long dead, rendering it useless.

Teya forged ahead. The light of her glow globe fell on a second bone lying in our path. Then a third. Then a fourth.

"Something really bad happened here," Jaeson whispered. "Are you sure this stash is worth it?"

Teya nodded, grimly. "It'll be worth it. The first stash had a trap. I wouldn't put it past Ky to hide another stash in the lair of some particularly nasty monster."

Jaeson tugged nervously at his earlobe. "Should we see if it's home before we blunder into its lair?"

"Fair point." Teya bent down and scooped up a rib which lay in her path. She hefted it experimentally before hurling it ahead of us into the darkness. I lowered Kinta from my back and lay her flat. I drew my pistol as the echoes of Teya's ballistic bone faded, then died altogether. Silence reigned.

A gulping, groaning noise to my left made me spin, point my gun, feel the trigger under my finger... Kinta. Kinta was struggling to her feet. She swayed a little but steadied herself on my outstretched hand. Considering how long I'd been out after I'd drained my magic, I was impressed to see her able to move, let alone stand.

"Looks like we're clear," Teya said, turning back to the dark tunnel of bones. "Are you okay to continue, Jaeson? Or would you like to stay here with the Caretaker?"

Jaeson shook his head. "I can help."

"That's the spirit."

Teya strode forward. Jaeson followed.

"Would you like to join us?" I asked Kinta. She looked unsure as to what to do with herself. Her gaze darted from point to point to point.

"What?" she asked, then seemed to see me, and the wall of darkness that was approaching as Teya moved away from us. "Sorry, let's go. I was just thinking of... something. Do you live on the surface? Above a restaurant?"

"Yeah. You saw that, did you?"

"Yes. Did you see..."

"I saw you taking care of Tenebro. It didn't look easy."

"It wasn't. It isn't."

"Do you need any more bones?" I asked. "Your necklace is nearly empty."

Kinta shook her head. "Don't worry about that, the Caretaker will have bones aplenty soon."

I nodded, reluctantly, and strode ahead to catch up with Teya. Every step there were more bones. We had to either walk on them or discover we had the ability to defy gravity. They cracked, screeched, and skittered under our boots. Carpals, ribs, and clavicles by the hundred. The noise was like sinister, shifting rain. The air was stale and thick with a cloying scent I didn't recognise.

The corridor opened up into a rough, square cavern. Drifts of ivory had formed against the walls, maybe fifteen metres away from where we stood. In the middle of the cave stood a squat, metal-walled building. It lacked the elegance of the houses from the level above. It looked like a storage room of some sort. If Kyrene's stash was still here, it would probably be in that building.

We crept closer, Teya covering the shed with her canon. The grip of my pistol dug into my hands. Feeling the shifting bones through the soles of my boots was starting to get to me. This was the sort of perilous scenario I would have delighted in only days ago. In that moment, I felt tension throb in a band across my forehead. I was gritting my teeth. I wanted to find Sirmo and get into the sunlight.

That thought made me lose myself in thoughts of the surface world. I wanted to sit in the noodle shop near Teya's house. I wanted to drink rice wine with her, bathing in the setting sun. We'd be heroes after rebuilding Ekzilo using tech from Sirmo. We'd toast Kyrene's memory with a quiet 'cheers' and a long, cool drink. It would be sad, but Teya would finally have closure. We'd sip our wine in the evening breeze, and –

Click.

I'd stepped on something more mechanical than a bone.

With a howl of fury, a dark shape lurched out of the morass just ahead of us. A shadow cloak hung from white hot iron bars. It twisted in the air, moaning, before it hurtled towards me. I couldn't move. I'd been lost in the sensation of phantom breeze on my cheek. To be wrenched back into the dark was cruel. Too cruel.

The wraith lunged for me just as I wrenched my pistol up and pulled the trigger. Pressurised air cracked from my gun. Teya's sonic cannon bellowed at the same time. The wraith was struck three times, first by a diamond-hard projectile from my pistol, then the wall of sound from Teya's cannon, then the drift of ballistic bones that had been caught up in Teya's shockwave. It tumbled back and struck a corner of the shed. It struggled, howling, before it collapsed in on itself, leaving behind only its cloak of shadows.

The cloak hissed, then boiled under Teya's glow globe. In seconds, it burst into streams of screaming darkness that fled the light. Bones rattled and skittered on top of each other. With a pathetic rasp of metal on metal. one wall of shed collapsed.

The ringing in my ears started to fade as Teya passed her glow globe to Jaeson and pointed her weapon at the new door she'd inadvertently made in the shed. Jaeson held the globe high, forcing the darkness from inside the building. Inside, tools were pinned to the walls, and a futon lay wrapped up in one corner, along with a canteen and a metal storage crate.

"Do you think Kyrene could bind wraiths into traps?" I asked, as Teya entered the room.

"Looks like it. She made some notes about it in the second notebook we found but I can't understand much of it."

Kinta and I moved forward as Teya stepped into the building. Jaeson followed, causing the light in the cavern to shrink to a thin stream around us. "Keep an eye out please, Meli!" Teya called. "Whatever lives here might yet come back."

That prompted an idea. I turned to Kinta. "Have you been here before?"

Kinta shook her head. "I don't come down to the fourth level that much. It's dead down here. Nothing to maintain. No beauty, only industry."

"Hm. Because there's something bothering me about the bones."

Kinta looked down at her feet. "Have you wondered what the bones mean?"

"Yes. Something's wrong about them." I shifted my foot in the drift of tarsals, arm bones and pelvises at my feet.

"You nearly have it," said Kinta.

"It's..."

Crunch, crunch, crunch.

My eyes widened. The bottom of my stomach fell away. "Oh no..."

"Yes."

"The bones... there aren't any skulls."

Crunch, crunch, crunch.

"If there aren't any skulls..."

Crunch, crunch, crunch.

"Whatever lives here must have another use for the heads."

"That's right," said Kinta. She snatched the last bone free from her necklace and I twisted one free from my bracelet. We slammed the bones into our mouths and swallowed. Fire roared into life around Kinta's head. A golden glow shone from my skin. We stepped away from the metal building and both saw, walking towards us with deliberate purpose, the Capper.

"I am sorry, my sister," said Kinta, "but you have fallen into the Caretaker's trap."

Chapter Seventeen

The Capper's tunic was dirty but not torn. Otherwise, it didn't look particularly the worse for wear for having a tunnel dropped on it.

"Teya!" I called. "Jaeson! Get out of there! The Capper's back!"

"The Caretaker was sent to rescue you from the Capper, but only once," said Kinta. "The Caretaker was then asked to make you an offer."

"What? What sort of offer."

"The Caretaker will save you again. The Caretaker will get all of you to Sirmo, safe from the Capper. You, Melita Eklumigi, looked the Capper in the eyes. It's following you. It will never stop. It dug itself out of a tunnel to pursue you."

"Great! So, help us!"

"Ah, now that's the part you might not be happy with. In order for the Caretaker to help, either Melita Eklumigi or Jaeson Eyler must agree to wear the Benefactor's mask."

I rounded on Kinta. "You won't help us unless we take on the cursed mask?" My stomach clenched. My fingernails bit into the palms of my hands. "I gave you my teeth so that we could all escape the Capper together!"

"What's the problem?" Teya asked, scrambling out of the shed. She carried a pack – obviously Kyrene's. Teya's face greyed as she saw the Capper. Jaeson followed close behind.

"Your friends have a choice to make," said Kinta, impassively.

The Capper strode towards us – towards *me*. I felt unsure and off-balance, trying to maintain my footing on the unstable mass of body parts. The Capper walked across the shifting bones with the effortless grace of a dancer. Teya dropped Kyrene's pack, raised her canon and fired. A thunderous wall of sound slammed into the Capper. Bones and dust were blasted out of the way. The Capper stopped. The fabric of its tunic flapped furiously in the wind. Then it started walking towards us once again.

I raised my gun and shot twice. Projectiles glanced harmlessly off the Capper's skull.

"You're wasting resources," said Kinta. "You must accept the Benefactor's bargain or perish."

I shook my head. I didn't see another way out. "All right! I accept!"

Kinta nodded. "The Benefactor will be nearby. I will protect you for as long as it takes to reach her. If you do not fulfil your part of the bargain, I will withdraw my protection."

"Melita, what did you just agree to?" Teya asked, fear flooding her voice.

Kinta stepped forward and unleashed a torrent of flame from her hands. The Capper didn't even slow down, although parts of it did appear to catch fire.

Teya raised her canon and fired once, then twice. Three times the Capper was struck, first by two shockwaves, then by a hail of bones. Kinta's flames were driven back by the wall of sound. For a moment, the bone creature was wreathed by a halo of flames.

"We're dead," Jaeson said.

"Patience," said Kinta. "The Capper moves slowly. Simply move back behind the building. We'll lure the Capper around the building and then continue in a circle. We'll wind up with the building in between it and us, with our backs to the passageway. We can escape from it then and find the Benefactor."

"Who's the Benefactor?" Jaeson asked.

"Oh no…" Teya moaned. "Vakua? You're working for Vakua?"

"Temporarily," said Kinta. She didn't wait for us to follow her plan. She ducked out of sight behind the shed and crept around to the far side. Lacking any other coherent plan, the rest of us followed. We retreated carefully until the Capper reached the corner of the shed we'd just left. We then moved around to the next corner. The Capper followed us, impassive and unstoppable. As soon as the shed was between it and the cavern entrance, leaving us with a clear exit route, we ran.

Kinta led the way back into the main cavern. We kept up a decent sprint for maybe five minutes before dropping down into a jog. I didn't know where we were going and in that moment I didn't care. We turned corners seemingly at random, down streets lined with long dead factories, their windows staring out at us, dark and uncaring.

Kinta skidded to a halt on a wide street just outside an enormous warehouse, whose nearest wall had collapsed. She looked around. "This will do," she said.

"What will do?" Teya panted. "What deal did Melita strike?"

"She is to take the Benefactor's mask, and you will not stop her, Teya Teresi."

"The hell I won't."

"Teya, that thing dug itself out of a tunnel to come after us," Jaeson panted.

I took Teya's hand and squeezed. "Teya, we still don't know where Sirmo is. There might be info in Kyrene's pack, but we don't have time to examine it, not if…"

Click. Click. Click.

Inevitability echoed between impassive walls, faint but unmistakable.

"Not if that thing is going to keep following and following!" I said.

Teya held up her hands. "Don't panic, Meli, it's slow, we can just keep running."

Jaeson was visibly shaking. "Yes, but for how long? Does it need to eat or sleep? Trapping it in a collapsing tunnel didn't stop it. Are we ever going to be safe from that thing?"

Click. Click. Click.

Jaeson was right. The Capper was relentless. It would never slow or stop. It wouldn't rest until all three of our heads were bobbing above it, wires wrapped around the shredded remains of our necks.

"Kinta," I said. "I re-affirm my commitment to our deal. Where is Vakua?"

Kinta nodded. "Yes. She should hear us from here," She lifted her head and bellowed: "Benefactor! The deal is struck!"

Kinta's voice hung in the air long after her mouth had closed. It ricocheted between buildings, each echo trapping me in place. My light... my light was fading already. I reached to my wrist and found only one tooth left.

How was my supply that low? I'd had ten hours' worth! But... I'd fed around half my supply to my twin. I'd had to rescue Jaeson from a wraith. I shook my head, slipped my last tooth into my mouth and concentrated. A timid cyan glow illuminated the ground around us, as well as the Capper stalking towards us out of the dark.

I felt as if I was looking at the impassive monster from an awfully long way away. I felt as if my world was shrinking down to a tiny sphere of light. I'd used the last of my bones. I wanted to go home.

"Kinta," I said, my mouth dry, my voice faint, "why are you doing this? I was looking in a mirror whilst in the trap meant for you. I'm your twin. I gave you bones that were precious to me. Why not just help us?"

"There is no helping against the Capper, The Caretaker is giving you a way out," said Kinta.

I rounded on her. "Oh, drop this 'Caretaker' thing, Kinta! I've seen your life. I know you think you're preserving beauty, but did it occur to you that you could care for historic buildings on the surface? You're not a caretaker, some great preserver of art and culture, you're hiding down in the dark because it's better than facing life on the surface. I know you, Kinta, you can't hide from me! We're the same! Help us!"

Kinta couldn't meet my eyes. "I can't. I can't! There's so much to do. I need light. If I don't complete this deal…"

Click. Click. Click.

"Do we run?" Jaeson asked.

"We're going to have to," said Teya.

"The Benefactor will be here soon," Kinta said, although she didn't sound as certain as she had a few moments ago.

We backed away from the Capper. Teya adjusted and re-adjusted her grip on her sonic weapon. Sweat beaded on her forehead, and her hands shook, rattling a loose fitting on the flank of her canon. A rumbling noise rose in the distance.

"In another life, I would have preferred not to have things end this way," said Kinta.

"It's not too late."

"It is for me."

The rumbling drew closer. It sounded like an earthquake tearing through the city towards us. The Capper took a step forward, and then Vakua exploded through the wall of a nearby building. She'd been traveling fast – so fast she shot straight past the Capper, and impacted against a wall on the other side of the street, causing it to crack and then half-collapse. She recovered quickly and shot towards the Capper.

The Capper completely ignored Vakua, at least until Vakua dove in between it and us. The Capper continued walking until only one pace separated it from Vakua. It stared up at the serpent for one, quiet moment.

The Capper flung out a hand, striking Vakua's flank. Vakua screamed as a hole twice my height opened in amongst the churning mass of pearlescent darkness that was her body. She slammed one enormous fist down onto the Capper, who didn't even flinch.

The Capper stared at me through the enormous hole in Vakua's body. It raised a claw but Vakua struck first. She lashed her tail out, striking the Capper in the arm. A thunderous crack echoed around us. The Capper turned its skull to gaze at its arm... where its arm had been. Half of it was now missing.

The Capper struck out at Vakua with its remaining arm. Vakua didn't dodge in time, another person-sized tear opened in her flank. Vakua screamed and flung herself forward, coiling her body around the Capper. She rolled and flung her tail away from us, hurling the capper deep into the dark. A seismic cracking sound shot out of the dark, then a rumble, then a series of crashes and bangs. If I had to guess, I'd say that the Capper had hit a building and the building had come off worse.

Vakua swung around to face us. "So, is it Jaeson Eyler or Melita Eklumigi who is to wear my mask?"

I felt a hand take mine and squeeze hard enough to cut the blood flow off. I didn't need to look down to know whose it was. "I'll take your mask, Vakua!" I called. My free hand shook.

Vakua nodded. She turned to Kinta. "Thank you for your assistance, Caretaker. Your bones are waiting for you in the factory bordered by the three fallen towers. You'd better hurry, it looks like your light won't last much longer."

Kinta bowed to me. "I'm sorry, my twin." She didn't look back as she fled into the darkness.

With the slow speed of a predator toying with its prey, Vakua lowered her mask down and down and down towards me.

"Melita," Teya said. "It doesn't have to be this way."

"We can't find Sirmo if we're headless, Teya."

"We can! We can stay ahead of the Capper for long enough, Meli, we're close. I know it. We're so close! We can't give up now!"

I squeezed her hand. "I'm not giving up, but I don't see another way out of this."

"I know you don't. I know. But... think of your magic. If you take on the mask, you'll never swallow another bone. You'll never bring light to the darkness again!"

Strange. That thought should have convinced me. Instead, it made me feel glad. "My magic's killing me, Teya. I'm not a shining star in the dark, I'm burning myself alive from the inside out."

Teya clutched her fists to her temples, her expression caught between horror and desperation.

"I know, Meli, and I'm so happy to hear you say that, but this isn't the solution to that problem! You already feel like you don't have a place on the surface. If you take that mask, you're effectively condemning yourself to living the rest of your life in Tenebro."

I nodded. It was strange how if I'd been presented with a way to stay indefinitely in Tenebro before the humans had attacked, I would have considered myself lucky. "I know. It's all right. If you're happy to visit me occasionally it won't be too bad."

"What?" Teya asked. Her hand loosened in my grip.

I closed my eyes. In the distance, I could hear rubble shifting. I could hear the screaming of metal. The Capper was digging itself free. I opened my eyes and turned to Teya, whose gaze burned.

"What are you talking about?" Teya said. "I'm not visiting you."

I nodded. Tears tracked down my cheeks. I'd risked Teya's life too many times by dragging her into the dark. If she wanted to make a safe life for herself on the surface, that was a good result. The best.

"Melita," Teya said, she reached up and drew me into a hug. "If you take on that mask, I'm not leaving you down here. If you stay down here, so do I."

I buried my face in her shoulder. "No. No, no. Not you too. We can't both –"

Teya's embrace tightened. "So, fight. Fight alongside me, Melita Eklumigi. Let's outrun the Capper together. Let's find Sirmo and bring help to Ekzilo together. You and me. Sisters forever."

I stepped out of the hug and dried my eyes. I shook my head. "No."

"Sorry?"

"We need Vakua. We can't risk having the Capper follow us whilst we search. If it doesn't get one of us it'll get Jaeson."

"I'll help you gladly if you take my mask," said Vakua.

Distant debris shifted. Less rumbling, less heavy. The capper was digging its way out of its shallow grave.

"We're not taking your mask, Vakua," Teya said.

Vakua shrugged. "Fair enough. I'll wait a few minutes. The Capper will focus your resolve. It's better to live than to lose your heads."

Teya took two steps forward, so she was nose to mask with Vakua. "What's wrong with you?" she bellowed. "Why can't you just help us? There must be something else you want that doesn't involve condemning Melita to a life in the dark?"

Vakua rose, waving a dismissive arm. "Calm down, Teya, this doesn't concern you. This is between me and Melita Eklumigi, or Jaeson if he would rather."

"Calm down? Calm down? Look around you, Vakua! Where do you think we are? This isn't a game. These are real lives you're toying with!"

Teya's anger burned brighter than my light. Philia poured out of her like fire. Her fury was sharp and desperate. She was doing everything she could to save me. To save us. Something about her, standing face to face with

Vakua, reminded me of an image. A scene I'd seen before. Years and years ago... but that thought was forced out of my head by another: we couldn't bully Vakua into doing what we wanted. She was determined, but we'd broken her determination before. For how long would she stay resolute in the face of a single question? A question born from twin questions.

I stepped forward to Teya's side. "Vakua," I said, quietly. "Teya asked you two questions the last time we met. She wanted to know why you wouldn't let her take your mask and why you wanted to help us find Sirmo."

"I remember. I didn't answer them, and I won't answer them now. The Capper has freed itself, by the way. It's approaching."

"That's fine. I don't pretend to understand you or why you won't answer those questions, but... If I take your mask here and now, I'll take on your form, yes?"

"Yes."

"And what will happen to you?"

Click. Click. Click.

I took another step forward. "You'll be a human."

Click. Click. Click

I pointed into the darkness. "The Capper is right over there."

Click. Click. Click.

"I wonder if Teya will help you when she looks into your eyes and sees the person who sacrificed me?"

Vakua reeled back as if struck.

"Help us, Vakua," said Teya. "Help us."

Slowly, Vakua reached up to cover the holes in her mask with her stygian hands. Her head drooped for a long moment. When she dropped her hands, I was sure she was looking at me. "Well argued, Melita Eklumigi," she said. "Very well. Teya, does that sonic cannon still work?"

"Like a charm," Teya said, hope blooming in her voice.

"Right. You're right. You're right. I'll help you. We don't have much time. I'll grab the Capper. Teya, when I do, unload everything that weapon has at the pelvis. Not the legs, not the torso, not the head, the pelvis. Got it?"

Teya nodded. "Pelvis. Got it." She started playing with the knobs and dials on the side of her cannon.

"Get ready to run once you've fired. Whatever happens, good or bad, we'll need to be fast."

At the edge of our light, the Capper stalked into view. Vakua coiled herself into a spring, although she groaned in pain as the two holes in her side flexed.

"Ready?" Vakua asked.

"Ready," said Teya.

Vakua leapt forward. I followed, shoulder to shoulder with Teya. Jaeson skittered along behind us. Vakua wrapped her tail around the legs of the Capper, before grabbing its remaining arm in one hand. Her other hand grabbed the Capper's torso. Vakua pulled, her tail stretched one way and her arms pulled the other.

The Capper found itself stretched between Vakua's tail and hands. Creaking and cracking noises filled the cavern, although I couldn't tell whether they were coming from Vakua or the Capper.

"Now!" shouted Vakua.

Teya dashed towards the Capper, who thrashed in Vakua's grip, trying to get at her. Teya aimed her cannon at the Capper but didn't fire. I took a step forward – I didn't understand what she was doing. Did the cannon have a malfunction? Was Teya seconds away from getting capped?

Grey spots flashed at the edges of my vision. I took another step towards the Capper, trying to think of something I could do to help – but then I saw the way Teya was standing- at 45 degrees to the Capper. Her cannon swayed in smooth arcs, following the Capper as it thrashed in Vakua's grip, twisting too much for Teya to get a clean shot off.

An idea. A desperate idea. I ran to stand next to Teya. The Capper had locked onto my gaze way back when it had claimed Yilin's head. It now wanted my head more than anyone else's.

I took another step, leaving me less than an arm's reach from the Capper. Its head snapped around, it's blazing gaze meeting mine. It reached out with its unbound half-arm, but didn't have quite enough reach.

Next to me, a mechanism clicked. Techno-arcana hummed. I had just enough time to smile. I'd distracted the Capper for long enough for Teya to get a clear shot.

Teya had clearly pushed her cannon far beyond safe limits, because the *BOOM* that followed caused her to fly backwards at some considerable speed. She crashed into Jaeson, and they both rolled into the dark. I sprinted after them, bringing them into my light just in time.

"Come on! We have to go!" cried Vakua. She held the top half of the Capper by the arm, its lower half had been blasted clear. Its head and torso swung about wildly but couldn't seem to do any damage to Vakua.

I pulled Teya and Jaeson to their feet. As one, we followed the giant serpent.

"Any idea where we're going?" panted Teya as we sprinted.

"Nope."

We ran through empty streets, only turning on major thoroughfares. Vakua moved fast but I'd seen her move much faster. She must have been holding herself back so we could keep up. We crossed over an enormous bridge that led into the cavern wall, leaving behind streets and factories, and entering wild, natural caverns.

We scrambled through twisting tunnels, dashed past caverns rich with bioluminescent lichen and eventually found an enormous oval chamber. Ekzilo could probably have fit inside, were it not for the lake which occupied most of the chamber. The lake was still, perfect and unbroken other than for a small island in the centre. A wooden rowing boat had been pulled up on the shore near to the cavern entrance.

Vakua skidded to a halt at the lake shore, spraying gravel around her. "If we gave the Capper enough time, its other parts would find ways to return to it," she said. "The key is to reduce it to such small pieces it cannot reconstitute itself."

"How are we going to do that?" Teya asked.

"Throw a pebble into the lake," said Vakua, staying remarkably still for someone holding a furious Capper in her grip.

I scrabbled around until I found a stone about the size of my fist. I heaved it into the lake, where it splashed, pleasingly.

"Do you see anything?" Vakua asked.

"No," Jaeson said.

"To be safe, you three had better get away from the edge of the lake," Vakua said. "About twenty metres should do it but be ready to get back further if trouble starts."

"Vakua," Teya said, her voice cold and dangerous. "What's in the lake?"

"Look," Vakua said. Her hands were busy, but her mask nodded at the lake.

I peered around the serpent and could just about see a hand and forearm poking above the surface of the lake, waving desperately.

"Someone's drowning!" I said. "We have to help them!"

Teya took a step away from the water. "Oh no... no, no, no. Is that..."

"A drowning woman?" asked Jaeson.

"No," replied Vakua, "it's not a drowning woman."

Vakua hurled the Capper into the lake. It splashed into the water next to the waving arm, which stopped waving, whipped around, grabbed the creature, and dragged it under the water.

"I think we'd better get a bit further away from the edge of the lake," Teya said, as the water churned violently.

"What was that?"

"A mermaid."

"Like Yilin?" I asked.

"You met Yilin, did you?" Vakua asked. "Well, she's young. There are other mermaids. They're dangerous, territorial, and they all hate Cappers, mainly because Cappers are one of the only things that can damage them."

"That hand and arm looked small, though, much smaller than Yilin's limbs."

"Not an arm, a lure. Not all mermaids have them. Others look like Yilin, human to the waist and piscine below that. Get ready to run. It can't get out of the lake, but it might be able to snatch us if we get too close."

We must have been more than fifty metres from the edge of the lake. I didn't understand why Vakua was worried. Still, a sinking sensation in my stomach combined with Vakua's warning made me take three large steps backward, just as the mermaid burst to the surface.

It was difficult to make out exactly what the mermaid looked like, because all I could see was a churning mess of flesh and blood. In the middle was the Capper, who didn't look happy to find itself in the mermaid's grip. The mermaid was enormous, around the same size as Vakua. Its flesh was a sickly white, and she had huge tentacular forelimbs which were tearing at the Capper. The Capper, for its part, was using its one remaining limb to punch and claw at the mermaid.

The mermaid finally managed to get its tentacles wrapped around the Capper. It then slammed the demi-skeleton repeatedly into the shore of the lake, fracturing the bedrock, before dragging it back under the surface.

The water of the lake churned, violently at first, then it slowly began to still.

"Good," Vakua said. "I don't think the Capper's going to bother anyone for some time after that."

I sighed and collapsed backwards onto the gravel shore. After a moment, Jaeson joined me. Teya stared out over the lake and chewed her lip. Vakua swayed on her tail. She didn't seem to know what to do next. She turned to Teya, who ignored her and pulled out one of Kyrene's notebooks.

"So," said Vakua. "I..."

I waited, but she didn't seem to know how to finish the thought she'd been having. It was strange. I'd never seen her hesitate like that. I'd been bracing myself for her to demand I take her mask as payment for dealing with the Capper. She wasn't demanding anything. She was just standing there. Why?

"We have a problem," Teya said. Her voice was flat and expressionless. We all turned to her. Her cheeks had greyed, and she was staring at the pages of Kyrene's notebook.

"Not another one," I groaned.

"Afraid so. I've been checking Kyrene's notes. Her last cache is located on that island in the middle of the lake."

Chapter Eighteen

The surface of the lake around where the mermaid had dragged the Capper into the depths churned gently. The island, impossibly far from our beach, was unmoved by our stares.

Teya folded her arms. "Obviously, it would be ideal if we didn't have to go out onto the lake, but if we find Kyrene's last stash, we find Sirmo. So, we've gotta get that boat and find some way to avoid the mermaid. Once we're on the island, we should finally know what happened."

I winced. "Haven't you learned anything new from that last stash? No notes on Sirmo, nothing?"

"No."

"Hang on..." said Vakua, who was still lurking nearby. "You're still looking for Kyrene? How? Why? You're at the very bottom of Tenebro. The entrance to Sirmo is practically round the corner! You're closer to finding it than you are to finding your wife."

Teya shook her head and turned her back on the serpent. "Thank you for your help, Vakua. I won't forget what you did for us, but this doesn't concern you. Now. Melita, Jaeson. How are we going to do this?"

Waves still played on the lake. The air around us was cold and humid. Thin streams of mist hung in the air in the wake of the mermaid's fight with the Capper. "I don't think we can, Teya."

"Why not?" My friend stared at me intently.

"Because we couldn't deal with a Capper. We needed Vakua's help, and even she wasn't enough. She needed to throw the Capper, something we had no chance against, to the mermaid. The mermaid is the one thing we know for sure is capable of dealing with a Capper... and that's what you want to go up against next?"

Teya's jaw tightened. "We're so close. I can't give up now. We've come so far and we're *so* close. There's just one more thing in our way."

Jaeson heaved a breath in and let it go. He looked out to the lake, then back at Teya. He turned to face her, drew in another breath, and then fell to his knees in front of my friend. "Teya... I'm sorry. I'm sorry we attacked you. I'm sorry we drove you to this. I'm sorry for everything we've done. I was wrong. I was wrong about you, and about Melita. You've treated me with more care and compassion than I would have treated you if our positions were reversed. You asked me, after the peace trap, if I would purge our country of outsiders if it would solve all our problems. My answer is no. No, no, no absolutely no. I was wrong. I was wrong. So please, listen to someone who has been so wrong about so many things: you are wrong about this. We cannot go out onto that lake. We need to find Sirmo some other way. If you ask us to go out onto that lake, you'll be asking us all to sacrifice our lives. Please, Teya, don't be as wrong as I was."

Teya pinched the bridge of her nose. "You don't... I can't... Look. Look. I didn't want to search for Ky. She was dead. I mourned her. But then *hope* wormed its way into my heart, and that hope has been growing inside me like a cancer and I know Ky is dead, but I don't know how she died or where she died, so there's the possibility, just the tiniest possibility that she's alive. That hope is burning me and the last flicker of it is *just* over there and if I turn away from it that'll be like leaving her for dead all over again. You're asking me to give up on my wife for the second time, just because it's completely *futile* and... and..."

She stared at Jaeson. The little human wasn't crying. His eyes were wide, and his fists were clenched tighter than tight. "Please get up, Jaeson," Teya said, her voice low and quiet. "Please don't kneel for me."

Slowly, cautiously, as if he were worried that if he moved too quickly, Teya would make a break for the boat resting on the beach, Jaeson rose to his feet. "You'll try to find another way? We can find Sirmo and regroup there?"

Teya nodded, slowly. "It's this darkness... I keep forgetting that our friends on the surface still need us. If Sirmo really is out there, we need to see if they can help. Once that's done, we can try to come up with a new plan. Maybe we end up back here eventually, but maybe not."

Jaeson chewed his lip but nodded when he saw Teya was still looking at him. Teya turned to me. "So, Melita, how many teeth have you got left?"

I held up my bare wrist. "Sorry. I used the last one when we were fleeing the Capper."

Teya nodded. "Don't worry, Meli. We've got plenty of glow globes. We're nearly through the stash we brought with us, but we've got plenty from Kyrene's packs."

"What?" said Vakua, who was still hovering nearby. Her voice was far louder than before and contained a note of rising panic. "You're not relying on those things, are you? They're years old!"

Teya's brow furrowed, and she turned to face the masked serpent, who noticeably shrunk back in the face of Teya's stare. "Vakua, why are you still here?"

Vakua seemed confused by this question at first, but she gave a nearly imperceptible shake of the head and shifted closer to Teya. "Two reasons. The first... well, forget about the first. But as for the second... would you believe me if I said I was lonely?"

Loneliness? Would that explain her strange behaviour since defeating the Capper? "Maybe," I said.

Teya rounded on me. She looked as if she was holding onto her temper with both hands. "No, Melita, no. She said it herself. All she wants is for us to take her mask."

"Sure, but she helped us, Teya. The least we can do is be civil to her."

"Melita, look at her! She's stuck like that and we are the only key to her salvation. Do you really want to keep her around so you can find out what she might decide to do in order to convince us to take her mask?"

I tapped my chin. "That does sound rather fun."

"No, you don't," said Teya, throwing her hands in the air. "The answer is you don't. Melita, I can't believe I have to explain this... Jaeson, can you talk to her? I can't deal with this right now."

Jaeson looked from Teya to Vakua and then to me. He swallowed, walked forward, and tugged at my sleeve. "Teya's right, Melita. I don't like saying this, because it feels like something I would have said before, but we can't trust Vakua."

"You can't stay down here with nothing but Kyrene's glow globes!" Vakua said, her voice rising from her usual low moan into something altogether more tense.

"We'll find a way," Teya said. "Thank you for your help, Vakua. I really mean that, but I hope you won't take offense now, because I'm going to ask you to leave."

Vakua still didn't say anything. She swayed on the spot before turning away. She slithered towards the nearest passageway, before stopping... then she resumed her exit. When she was nearly out of sight, she turned once more.

"Teya," she called, her voice shook, "stay safe, gorgeous grebe."

Teya's head snapped around. She sprinted towards the serpent, forcing Jaeson and me to follow with the light.

"What did you say?" Teya asked. "Say that again."

Vakua shrunk under her glare. "I said... I... I said stay safe, gorgeous grebe."

"Only Kyrene ever called me that," Teya said, through gritted teeth. "What... how did you..."

"Well..." Vakua said, coiling in on herself. "Here's the thing..."

"Well?"

"I... I..."

"What?"

"I am Kyrene."

Silence dropped like a guillotine blade.

A vein pulsed at the side of Teya's neck. "Absolutely fuck off. You're not Ky."

Vakua dipped her mask. "Yes I am."

"You don't sound anything like her."

"Well, I'm sorry that being possessed by an ancient bio-technological parasite has changed my voice a little."

Teya narrowed her eyes. "Where did we get married?"

"Slayer's plaza in Shai."

"Where did you ask me to marry you?"

"*You* asked *me*, and it was whilst we were on holiday, at that little hotel overlooking the Crystal Falls."

"Why did we come to Talvik?"

"I had some power which none of us ever really understood. It would leak out at unexpected moments and break things. We heard that witches here had expertise that had been lost from Akoma and wondered if they'd be able to help."

"What's my favourite book?"

"I don't... Oh, that thing about the train heist?"

"Try again."

"I don't know, Teya, you always had your nose in some book or other, I couldn't keep track of them. How about the witch who can awaken powers in other people, but she has to make sure she gets consent first?"

Teya stared. "Oh, no," she said. She clutched at her head.

"Is she okay?" Jaeson whispered to me.

Slowly, without wishing to draw anyone's attention to me, I shook my head.

Teya burst into tears. She threw her arms around Kyrene, who coiled tenderly around her wife.

"Why didn't you tell me sooner?" Teya asked, in between sobs.

"You've seen what I look like. I couldn't. I didn't want you to see me like this."

Teya hugged Ky even tighter. "I came for you. I came."

My light flared. Warmth grew within me as I thought about how hard we'd worked to make this moment happen. My power strained, trying to push out further and brighter, but I kept it under control. Still, I marvelled as the light changed from blue to yellow to orange and then, finally, a triumphant crimson. Tiny animals tumbled and played at the light's edge, right where the crimson ended, and the Hungry Dark began.

"I'm sorry you have to see me like this," Kyrene said. "You have no idea just how sorry I am, but we need to get you out of Tenebro and down to Sirmo. The longer you're here, the more danger you're in."

"Great," Teya said, "absolutely. Once we're there we can restock and get back up to Ekzilo, and you can come with us."

Kyrene chuckled softly. "I can't, gorgeous grebe. You know how people react when they see me. It'll be chaos."

Teya exposed her teeth in a glassy grin. "I'm not leaving you, Ky. I've only just found you.

Kyrene froze. "You can't stay here, Teya. You'll die."

"We'll see about that."

"No, we won't. Come on, be realistic. You're going to need to go to Sirmo."

Teya released her wife and looked up at her. "Okay, okay. Look, I'm not keen on spending the rest of my life in Tenebro. If you really don't want to come to Sirmo with me, give me the mask and I'll come with you to Sirmo."

Lightning flashed through me, and judging by how Jaeson reacted, a similar jolt of energy had struck him. Only moments ago, Teya had told me we couldn't trust the serpent because all she wanted was for us to take her mask.

"Teya, hold on," Jaeson said, but his objection was smothered by a cry of alarm from Kyrene.

"Absolutely not! No! It's bad enough that I'm stuck like this, I'm not going to let you suffer this curse."

Teya folded her arms, lowered her eyebrows, and rolled her shoulders. "You're not?"

Kyrene uncoiled. Slowly at first, her face rose so that it loomed over Teya, then towered over her. Kyrene drew herself up to her full thirty-meter height. Her roiling dark body held perfectly still in front of us. Slowly and deliberately, she folded her arms. "No."

Teya folded her arms. "Is that supposed to be impressive?"

Kyrene shifted on her tail. "A bit, yeah."

Teya shifted into her first language from when she'd lived in Akoma. The vowel shapes were strange, and her pitch rose and fell seemingly at random. She sounded furious, but other than that, I couldn't understand a word. Kyrene replied in the same language. I watched this back and forth, fascinated, until I realised Jaeson had been trying to get my attention for a little while. I turned to him. "Sorry, Jaeson, what's up?"

"Do you think we could do this somewhere that isn't next to a lake containing one of the deadliest creatures in the dark?"

The surface of the lake was deceptively still. I nodded. "That'd probably be wise."

I sidled up to where the couple were still having their row. I hovered, waiting for a break in the conversation that steadfastly refused to emerge. Eventually, I got bored. I coughed. This didn't get anyone's attention. I said, "Excuse me," which didn't work either. I flared up the light around my eyes. This caused Teya to wheel around to face me, still ranting in her first language. She switched, seemingly without effort, after only a second: "For the love of the spirits, Melita, what do you want?"

"Now we've found Kyrene, Jaeson and I were wondering if we could do this on the way to Sirmo? We're not entirely safe here."

Teya nodded. "Okay. You know the way, Ky?"

"Yes, but I wasn't kidding about not relying on those glow globes."

"Why not? You left them for us to use!"

"I didn't leave them for *you* to use. Last time I saw you, you were happily working in a bakery. I left those glow globes for my own use, and I left them there two years ago. I haven't needed light since then. This body isn't made from the Hungry Dark, exactly, but it's *of* the dark. It drinks it in. I'm like those enormous deer on the third level. I haven't needed light in two years. Those globes are decaying or decayed. We can't rely on them."

Teya nodded. "Okay. Well, let's check to see how much light we actually have. We might not be completely safe here, but we could be ambushed at any minute when we head back into Tenebro. Don't worry, Jaeson. I'll be quick."

Teya knelt on the beach, opened her pack and drew out the packets of glow globes she'd looted. She inspected one. Her brow furrowed. "Cracked seal," she muttered, and slipped it into an outer pocket of her pack. She inspected the next globe. "Unreactive elements." The third globe had another cracked seal.

Not knowing how to help, I wandered over to Kyrene. "Have you been to Sirmo?"

"Yes, before I took on this shape."

"What's it like?"

"Amazing. The cliff that Tenebro was built into ends abruptly, leaving Sirmo in a natural valley. There's sunlight and water from a river that runs through the valley. That's the good news. The bad news is that the entrance is guarded by a massive cluster of wraiths."

"How massive?"

"Last time I checked there were about thirty of them. The Hungry Dark seems to want them to be there. I think they're supposed to be guarding Sirmo, but I'm not sure. Working out what the Hungry Dark wants is a bit tricky."

Teya shouted something very loud and extremely angry in the Akoman language. She looked up at us, her face a storm cloud. "They're dead. All the glow globes from your packs, Ky. None of them work."

The glow from my hands was less bright than I would have liked. The glow globe Teya had been using had long since faded to uselessness.

"We have whatever fuel Melita has left in her pipes and a few emergency flares," Teya said.

"How far is it to Sirmo?" I asked Kyrene.

"It depends on how fast you can run," she said, "but I'd be amazed if we could do it in under an hour."

Teya shouldered her pack and rolled her head from left to right, then right back to left. "We have to get moving. We'll figure out a solution as we move."

My friend nodded to her wife, who coiled down so she could fit into the exit passageway. Teya followed, as did Jaeson. I sighed at the sight. I felt as if some of my muscles were slowly relaxing.

A watery noise from behind me made me turn as I was leaving, but the lake was too distant for me to illuminate whatever had caused it. I thought of nipping back to check, but we no longer had the luxury of time. I hurried after my friends.

CHAPTER NINETEEN

Kyrene led us through a warren of tunnels, and back into Tenebro. As we crossed the bridge which led into the city itself, Jaeson dropped back to walk alongside me.

"Melita, aren't we missing a rather obvious solution to our light problem?" he said, after we rounded a corner and walked down a side street to avoid a collapsed wall. The street was packed in between two huge buildings that loomed up on each side. The smooth concrete walls weren't perfectly straight, and they closed in on us from both sides as we walked.

"A solution? That's great. What is it?"

Jaeson's expression didn't change, and it didn't change in a very careful manner. "Huh. Give me a second." He jogged ahead, to where Teya was busy arguing with her wife. They held a quick, hushed conversation. Teya looked around at me. I waved. Teya and Jaeson put their heads back together.

The side street constricted so much that Kyrene could barely squeeze through, but when we emerged on the other side, we found ourselves in a wider avenue, lined by long-dead lanterns. Kyrene led the way, Jaeson followed, whilst Teya dropped back to match her pace with mine, running her hands through her hair.

"How are you doing, Melita?" she asked.

"Oh, I'm okay. Jaeson seemed to think I had a solution to the light problem. He wouldn't go into details, so I'm curious as to what it is that you and he are being so coy about."

"You're going to take some bones from me and Jaeson."

"Ha, good one."

Teya was silent. She waited, completely calm, completely composed. Her eyebrows raised just the tiniest fraction.

"What?" I asked.

"I'm serious, Melita. You're going to need to take our bones."

"No."

"What do you mean 'no'?"

I couldn't tell her. She'd think it was stupid. I shrugged and looked down at my boots. They were more battered and scuffed than I could ever remember seeing them. The air was still around me, scents of rust and decay filling my head.

"Melita, you know this is the only way we'll survive for long enough to get to Sirmo."

I shook my head, my hair flicking in front of my face, hiding my frown. "You'll find another way."

"What other way? We're stuck down here. We might be able to get a fire going and create some flaming torches, but they wouldn't drive the darkness back well enough to keep three of us safe. This is the solution, now stop complaining and eat my bones."

I shook my head. "No."

"Why not?"

I turned my head away. I'd never been scared of crying in front of Teya before.

"Melita?" Teya asked.

Our footsteps echoed between the factory walls for a few minutes more, then I heard her increase her pace. A couple of minutes later, I heard the argument between Teya and Kyrene restart, although it had less enthusiasm in it this time.

"Hi, Meli," Jaeson said. I hadn't heard him drop back to walk next to me. "How's it going?"

I moaned.

"So, here's the thing, if you really don't want to take bones from Teya or me, I'm sure we can find another way. Maybe we have to run all the way to Sirmo, or maybe Kyrene can find something for us. It's okay. I do have just one question... Why does the idea upset you so much?"

I was silent. I stared at the floor. We were on cobblestones here. They were grey and curved in rows around some central point which was lost somewhere in the darkness ahead of us.

"I've seen you face down a Capper. I've seen you be constantly courteous and polite to Kyrene, even when she was just a thirty-meter monster who wanted to eat us. I'm curious as to why this is a problem for you. You don't have to tell me, but I'd like to know."

I couldn't tell Teya, but Jaeson might understand.

"I've never had to remove a bone from someone before," I said, quietly. The tips of my fingers circled gently against my palms.

"If that's the problem I know Teya would be happy to cut one of her fingers off. And that's a sentence I never thought I'd say."

I shook my head. My cheeks felt hot, and I was struggling to get the overwhelming sensation of *NO* I was feeling into words. "That's not it. The teeth I've consumed, they're all baby teeth. Whenever I've been given some other type of bone, I've always, always made sure that it was lost as part of an accident.

"The humans – your friends – one of the reasons they hate witches is because they see us as predators. I thought if I stopped consuming bones that had been taken and only ate bones that no one else was using, then that might make your people hate Ekzilo less and some of us might get to go home."

I heard Jaeson breathe in but I held up a hand. "And I know that's stupid and childish and at least part of it is my Kaskado Disorder talking... but another part of the same thought is – that's how I want to live. I don't want to be a predator. I want to be me, and I want to use my power to make people happy but only if no one else has to suffer along the way. My power won't be the same if it's tinged by your pain or Teya's.

"My bones aren't meals, Jaeson. I can remember the names of every person who has donated a bone to me."

"You're kidding."

"Erica Sheh, Stephanie Mendez, Rachelle Posit, Thadeus Noyer, Laura Heger, Marin Alyx, Jennifer Miler, Alexis Dodge, Lucien Nichols – "

"Okay, okay, I get the idea. I'd no idea it meant that much to you."

I shrugged; my fingers drummed a disjointed beat on the palms of my hands. "This power is all I am. The bones I take in are what activate my power. It follows that the bones I've swallowed are all that I am."

"You're more than your power, Melita."

"It's all I'm good for."

"That's also extremely untrue. You've been absolutely relentless in your search for Sirmo. I think Teya and I would have given in to despair long ago were it not for you."

I rolled my eyes. The weight in my chest had felt like it was crushing my ribs for hours now. "Oh, Sirmo. That's just a lie I told Teya in order to get her to come on an adventure with me down in the dark. I never thought we'd actually find the place."

Jaeson frowned. "So you had no interest in helping Ekzilo."

I let out a frustrated hiss. "Not *no* interest. I just didn't think it was possible, and I knew Teya would like the idea."

"Hm," said Jaeson. "No. Sorry, I don't believe you."

I shrugged. That sounded very much like his problem. Still, the confession hadn't lessened the crushing sensation in my chest anywhere near as much as I'd have liked.

Jaeson tapped a finger against his chin. "I'm trying to understand here. Let's say you suggested looking for Sirmo in order to help Ekzilo, and Teya said 'nah, let's just go on an adventure instead', what would you have said? What would you have said, as the lives of the people of Ekzilo hung in the balance?"

I groaned. "I probably would have said we could have an adventure and look for Sirmo at the same time."

"So you *did* want to help Ekzilo?"

"Yes. No. Look, the Peace Trap said–"

"The *Peace Trap*?" Jaeson's voice was a sudden rasp.

"Yes…"

"You're tying yourself in knots, convincing yourself you're a selfish monster who doesn't care about anything except adventure, because of something the Peace Trap said to you? The malevolent creature who would have said literally anything in order to take your life?"

"Not *anything*. I think she wasn't technically allowed to lie."

"Sure, she might not have lied. I'm sure a part of you wanted to go on an adventure, but to take that tiny part of you and assume that's everything there is… I think you're doing that same thing right now when it comes to taking our bones. You're worried that if you use power born from us, it'll make you a bad person. It'll make you what my people think you are. It'll make you human. It won't, Melita. I want you to take my little finger."

I shook my head. My fingers drummed against my palms faster and faster until I was sure Jaeson was going to notice. I clenched my hands into fists to halt the relentless drumming.

If Jaeson noticed, he didn't say anything. "Teya said we have some ointment that takes pain away. I won't feel a thing."

I couldn't look at Jaeson. I shook my head.

"It's a gift. You're not taking anything. I'm offering it to you. I would be honoured to have a part of myself inside you."

I shook my head.

"But not in *that* way," said Jaeson.

I couldn't stop myself laughing.

"I want to see your light, shining like a beacon, and I want to be able to look at it and turn to Teya and say, 'we made that together. Me and Melita. It's our light.' Would you like that?"

It was an idea I'd never even considered. Someone being happy to share such a moment with me sounded impossible. I couldn't answer, I couldn't even think about what such a moment would be like. Was it something I wanted? I'd no idea. I repeated Jaeson's question to myself. I repeated it and repeated and repeated in the hope that I'd be able to come up with an answer. All I got back was white noise, thick and impenetrable. I was locked up. I was useless.

I rubbed my face, trying to let the question go. No luck. I shook my hands out, away from me, sending the question off into the darkness. I tried to focus on the place beyond the question, and beyond the answer to the question. What world did I want to live in? The world where we all died down in the dark or the world Jaeson had described? The world that sounded unbelievably beautiful...

Put like that, there was only one answer. I nodded to Jaeson.

Jaeson patted me on the shoulder. His touch was light and gentle, like a falling petal of plum blossom. "I'll be right back." He jogged to catch up with Teya and Vakua. They stopped at an intersection surrounded by factories on all sides and let me catch up.

Teya drew a jar of black ointment from her bag and handed it to Jaeson before throwing her arm around his shoulders and walking him away from the intersection, far enough to have a little privacy but not so far as to be out of my light. Kyrene stayed with me.

She lowered herself down to nearly my height. "They don't want you with them for this next bit. Teya said to tell you this was between her and Jaeson."

"Okay."

"They'll be fine, don't worry. We all have to make sacrifices down here."

I stuck my hands into my pockets. The interior cloth felt crusted and stiff. Dried sweat. I took my hands out of my pockets and wiped them on my jacket. "Can we talk about something else?"

"Of course."

"I've been meaning to ask about Kinta. Did you really persuade her to do a deal with us to take your mask if she'd save us from the Capper?"

"Who's Kinta?"

"The Caretaker."

"Oh, yes. After Teya worked out I was trying to trick you or Jaeson into taking my mask, I saw the Capper was catching up with you. I knew Teya wouldn't accept help from me, given what had just happened so I went to find help. I found the Caretaker."

"I'm surprised she agreed to help. Had you tried to get her to take your mask?"

"Yes, years ago. She's one of the divers I tried to threaten into taking it. She doesn't hold it against me because she's a pragmatic sort. I'm surprised you're not angrier with me about trying to get you cursed in my place, to be honest."

"How could I be angry with you? You're Teya's wife. You're taking us to Sirmo.'

"Melita... I don't want you to be under any illusions here. If it weren't for Teya, I'd have tricked you into being cursed in my place. I would have refused to help with the Capper in the hope that you'd take my mask."

"What would you have told Teya if I'd have taken your mask up at the castle or the shrine of peace?"

"In the shrine I'd have asked you to go somewhere quiet with me and a couple of glow globes. I'd have got you to take the mask somewhere Teya wouldn't see, then I'd have slipped off with the globes, waited a few hours whilst trailing Teya and then 'accidentally' stumbled across her. That way she'd still see me as her swashbuckling wife, not the monster I'd become."

"I don't think you're a monster, Kyrene. I think the dark brings out the worst in people. My twin, for example..."

"You have a twin?"

"Kinta. The Caretaker."

"I'm sorry, I'd no idea she was family to you. I hope you won't think too harshly of her for bargaining with me. She was desperate. She needed light and I had bones. She didn't have much of a choice."

"Where did you get the bones from?"

"The fallen. There are plenty of them around at this time of year, I just have to hang about in the first level of Tenebro and wait for cave raiders who are overconfident in their own abilities and underprepared." I must have visibly winced, because Kyrene waved her enormous hands at me. "Don't worry, the fallen don't feel pain. It's like pruning a furious tree."

"That might be true... but Teya and I did a little experimenting earlier. A fallen who was following us managed to hold onto some part of herself from before she fell. It's possible the fallen can be brought back to themselves."

Kyrene swayed back. "You're kidding."

"Nope."

A low rumbling noise groaned out of Kyrene's mask. "Do you know how many fallen I've killed?"

I shook my head. Kyrene was as still as the rock under my feet but her voice sounded as if it was fighting past a lump in the throat she didn't have.

After a while, she shrugged, helplessly. "Neither do I. I haven't been counting. The number must be in the dozens by now. It would be wonderful if they could be brought back to themselves, but I hope for my sake that's impossible."

"And for their sake?"

"Let's just say I'll be a little less cavalier about them until we've had a chance to test your idea, shall we?"

A grunt of pain from the near distance made my head whip around. Kyrene's hand flashed out at head height to block my view. "Don't look at them, look at me. They're fine."

I looked up at Kyrene's mask. I felt lost and alone amongst my best friends in the world. Questions lined up and fired soundlessly in my head. I picked one of them. "Before you admitted you were Kyrene, you said you were lonely. Was that true?"

Kyrene hesitated before answering. Her mask dipped slightly, and I heard a low mournful hum that might have been the closest Kyrene was able to get to a sigh without breath. "You have no idea how true."

"I don't understand why."

"You have no idea how much it hurts to see the fear in people's faces when they look at you. It didn't bother me at first, but it happened every. Single. Time."

"But Teya would have seen past that!"

"She might have, yes. She might have. Or she might not have given me the chance. She might have just seen a monster. I tried to tell her, I really did, but every time I climbed up to Ekzilo, I found myself picturing the look on her face when she saw me for the first time."

"She was grieving for you, Kyrene. It was tearing her up. You could have put an end to her grief at any moment just by telling her!"

Kyrene sighed, the sound causing the ground under me to shake. "Look. I was in shock for days after I put the mask on. I couldn't believe what had happened to me, but then I got myself together. I made my way to the surface, but I happened across a cave raider. She was from one of the other villages but I'd encountered her before. We'd traded a few bits and pieces, betrayed each other a couple of times, the usual. I called her name, and she turned and... she saw me and... she ran. I followed, calling after her. I told her who I was. I pleaded with her to stop, but there were wraiths. A whole cluster of them. She saw the wraiths, and turned to see me closing the gap between us. She tried to fight her way through the wraiths. She was more scared of me than creatures who wanted to carry her into the dark. They tore her apart before I could get to her. Every time I tried to tell Teya, I saw that cave raider being torn to shreds merely because of how I looked."

"Ah."

"Yeah."

I heard a sharp intake of breath from where my friends were sacrificing themselves for the safety of all. I wanted to cry, but this moment wasn't for me. I focused on Kyrene. I needed to hear something positive, so I didn't lose myself in the pain my friends were experiencing. "What's it like seeing Teya again?"

"It feels... it feels like everything is going to be okay. She's amazing. She's grown so much in the time we've been apart."

I nodded and wiped my eyes. "I couldn't ask for a better friend."

"How do you ever get her to do something she doesn't want to do?" Kyrene asked.

"You should know," I said.

Kyrene nodded to my two friends. "I used to know. Now, I'm not so sure."

"I see. Well, you have to either appeal to her logic or send her on a guilt trip. That's what I usually do. More of the guilt trip than the logic, but sometimes..."

"Mm. Maybe I'll try the logic side because I've been getting nowhere with the guilt trip. Can you believe she wants to stay here with me?"

"Yes."

I heard footsteps. I spun to face the returning heroes. Their left hands were bandaged. I felt sick, but then I saw their faces. They weren't screwed up in pain. They were determined. The jar of black ointment was gone, but Teya still held the knife she'd used, and the back of the knife was still stained with ointment. If I touched that black elixir, I'd feel some of the pain my friends had felt. I'd truly understand their sacrifice.

I shook my head. I was being selfish. I was concentrating on the sacrifice my friends had made, rather than trying to recognise the beauty in their actions. Teya strode, unstoppable. Little Jaeson had spent most of the time I'd known him cowering in fear. He wasn't cowering now. He was walking tall.

I smiled, and sparks danced in my light. "Thank you."

Teya nodded to me. "Thank you for getting us this far."

We set off, following Kyrene once again. We walked for twenty minutes before the light from my last tooth faded to the point where it was no longer useful. I hugged Jaeson and thanked him for the bones he had gifted me. I brought my power into life for the first time in hours.

Our light bathed us in amber, whilst cherry blossom streams danced around Jaeson. It was the first time I'd been able to share the light with the person who'd helped me create it.

"Teya," Jaeson said.

"Yes?"

"See this," Jaeson said, spreading his arms.

Teya nodded, smiling.

"We made this," Jaeson said. "Me and Melita. Isn't it beautiful?"

"I'm not sure if I've ever seen anything quite so beautiful," Teya said.

"Hey..." said Kyrene.

I would have liked to reply, but I couldn't get any words out past the lump in my throat. The tears streaming down my face helped catch the beautiful light Jaeson and I had made, and reflect it back at the Hungry Dark.

We were making good progress when the screams of a fallen cut through the dark towards us. Kyrene whirled around, trying to pinpoint the direction from which the scream came.

"Don't hurt it!" I shouted. "We're near Sirmo! We can take it into the light and see if that burns the darkness out of it!"

Teya unslung her sonic cannon. "That might not be possible, Meli."

Kyrene's mask was turning slowly from left to right. Her movement was smooth and controlled but every time she turned, she moved a little quicker. "I can't see it. I think it's coming from the street due east, but the screams are echoing so much it's hard to tell."

"Can I have a weapon?" Jaeson asked. The little human was swaying on his feet. He looked scared, but he wasn't actually hiding behind one of us.

I unclipped the collapsible spear from my pack, extended it and tossed it to him - gently so he had a chance to catch. He looked as if I'd just thrown him a dead fish, but he gripped it in both hands, the left of which was blessed by bandages.

A scream turned into a growl. This fallen wasn't charging straight at us. The lower throaty noise sounded as if it was coming more from the south. I unslung my pack and drew out a length of rope.

"Melita, we don't have time for this," Teya said, fear creeping into her voice. "Ky, how far is Sirmo?"

"Ten minutes."

I grinned, "My light will last way longer than that!"

"Not if we have to use it to fight. Your light is one of our best weapons against shadow creatures. You have one bone in the tank and another as backup. We can't waste it."

"I won't waste what you gave me, but I won't abandon someone who might need our help, not without trying."

I turned on the spot, tracking the fallen's footsteps as best I could. They were staying clear of my light – either cautious or cunning.

"Where is it?" Jaeson asked – staring into the darkness, his gaze wide and wild.

Kyrene lowered herself down and coiled around us so that her body was blocking us from any angle the fallen could approach from. "It's circling around, trying to ambush us."

Teya lowered her cannon and looked up at her wife's mask. "Ky, we can't defend ourselves if you're blocking our line of sight."

"Yes, but the fallen can't get at you either."

"It can attack you."

"It can't damage me."

"But we're wasting time! We don't have time for this! Our light is dying, we need to—"

Kyrene's body was blocking my view of the street, but a flash of tan high in my eyeline made me look up. A furious, bedraggled figure was hurtling down at me. Must have leapt from a rooftop.

She struck me in the chest and drove me to the floor. Instinctively I dropped my rope and slapped my arms against the ground as I landed, breaking my fall. My hands stung at the impact, but I managed to keep my head from hitting the ground. The fallen clawed at me, her unkempt hair thrashing in front of her face. She was focused on my light. She wanted to extinguish me.

I flung my arms up to cover my face and felt her bite down on my forearm. Teya dashed in and tried to lift her off me – no good.

"Teya! Duck!" called Jaeson. He swung the shaft of the spear like a bat into the fallen's head. He looked like a wasp attacking a bear, but the monster rasped at the impact. Jaeson let out a cry of nervous triumph before raising the spear again. The creature thrashed, hair flying in every direction, spittle raining down on me. For a moment, my determination wavered, but then Jaeson struck her again. Jaeson was staying strong in trying to save this fallen. I could too. I reached up and snatched at the fallen's hands, trying to grab them and hold them still.

Kyrene loomed over us, unstoppable as the tides. She reached down and plucked the fallen from on top of me. It thrashed – Ky dropped it – grabbed it again, by an ankle this time. She yanked the fallen up into the air as if she weighed nothing at all. The fallen twisted and nearly fell, but Kyrene's other hand reached up and encircled the creature's body gently, yet with unstoppable force. The creature struggled but couldn't break free.

Teya ran to her pack and snatched out a rag, which she forced into the fallen's mouth. The screams died away behind the gag, and my sigh of relief was echoed by one from Jaeson.

"Oh, no..." Teya said.

"What?" I asked. "What is it?"

"Come and look at this, Melita."

Teya's gaze was locked on the fallen's face, her bandaged hand covering her mouth. I looked closer. Recognition sucked the air from my lungs. The fallen was Kinta.

Chapter Twenty

My twin's neck, where her bone necklace had been, was bare. She'd tried to trap me. She'd tried to force me into taking Kyrene's mask... but I'd seen why. She hadn't been malicious or cruel by forcing me into the serpent's bargain, she'd been trying to live down in the harshness of the Hungry Dark. I couldn't hate her, but I'd be a fool to trust her if what I wanted stood between her and her life down here. Still, she'd fallen to the dark. Some part of her was still alive in there. Life and hope stood hand in hand. I wanted to break her free of the dark. If I managed that...

Teya sighed. "The Caretaker. Well, we can just go ahead and leave her here. No point in sticking our necks out for someone who tried to sell us to a cursed snake. No offence, Ky."

"Teya," I said, my tone so serious it caused my friend's head to snap round. "I've seen what her life was like. She was desperate, living a nightmare of her own making. Yes, what she did was awful, but I want to break her free of her cage, in the same way you've been breaking me free of mine."

Teya winced. "Really?"

"Really."

Our gazes locked together. Whatever she saw in my expression caused her to nod, slowly but deeply. "All right. You trusted me when the Capper was chasing us. I can't very well not trust you about this, Meli."

I gave Teya the quickest, tightest hug I could, before turning to her wife. "Kyrene, do you have her?"

"I have her."

"Then let's move. We have to get her into the light."

"Meli, how are we going to fight a cluster of wraiths if Vakua is busy stopping the Caretaker from killing us?" Teya asked.

"Good point... I swear I had something for that... Ah, yes!" I snapped my fingers and grabbed my coil of rope from where I'd dropped it earlier. Teya helped me bind my snapping, thrashing twin and, before long, Kyrene could hold Kinta securely with only one hand.

Teya tested my knots before nodding, satisfied. "Okay, Ky. Just drop her if we need to fight." She glanced at me, before adding, "As gently as possible, please."

Kyrene nodded. "How many rounds have you got left in that gun, Melita?"

I checked the cylinder. "Three."

Teya unslung her crossbow, which hadn't seen much use since she'd acquired her sonic cannon. "Here you go, Meli. You know how to use this?"

I nodded, took the crossbow, and slipped my arm through the sling. It dragged at my left shoulder, but I didn't want to face this final challenge without being fully armed. Some familiar noise sneered at me from the dark. "Let's move," I said. "I don't think we're alone."

"The Wraiths by the door to Sirmo will try to drag you into the darkness," said Kyrene, as we set off. "They don't have many weapons of their own, although their claws can cause some damage. When they see us, they're going to charge, then try to get in close and grab you. Don't let them."

Kinta rasped from behind her gag.

"If anyone gets grabbed, I'll get them back," I said.

Teya nodded. "Melita, you stick with Jaeson. I'll hold fast near Ky."

"Will you be safe from the darkness?" I asked.

"I'll get her back to you in one piece, Melita. Don't worry," said Kyrene.

Kinta made a gagging, gurgling noise.

"How are you doing, Jaeson?" Teya asked.

"I'm ready to be back in the open."

"Can you fight?"

"I don't know, but I'm not going to let the Wraiths get me. I've been rescued by you too many times already."

"Good lad."

Kyrene held up a hand. "We're here." She placed Kinta on the ground with more care than I'd given her credit for. Kinta, for her part, thrashed about like a fish on the riverbank, but was unable to shake free of her bonds.

"We'll come back for you, sister," I said.

Teya checked the charge on her sonic canon. She looked like her normal determined self, but a small smile twitched at the corners of her mouth and hope glowed in her eyes. She nodded to Kyrene, then Jaeson and finally me. "We're nearly there, everyone. One more push."

I nodded. "One more." I met Teya's gaze and slipped the bone she'd given me into my mouth. "Thank you."

"You're entirely welcome, Melita."

I closed my eyes, trying to tune out Kinta's thrashing. Jaeson's breathing was fast and barely controlled, whilst Teya's was more measured. A slight breeze tickled my cheeks. I grinned, and opened my eyes. "Let's go."

Teya raised her sonic cannon and strode into the final passageway. I followed her and raised my light, notes of persimmon and red plum joined my amber glow at the edges.

The passageway was wide, maybe five metres across. At first, I thought it was so long that my light was struggling to reach the end, but as my eyes focused, I saw that my light was only reaching ten metres deep into the passageway. There, it was blocked by a throng of Wraiths. The seething darkness chilled me for a moment, but not to the bone. I was going to fight my way into the light. I wouldn't let them keep me here. The wraiths turned to face us as my light fell on them. Then, as one, they charged.

I raised my pistol in both hands and squeezed the trigger three times. My gun spat three metal shards - one Wraith reeled back, then shattered into scraps of fading darkness. I jammed my pistol into my belt and unslung Teya's crossbow.

The wraiths howled closer and closer - I managed to squeeze a shot off, which hit another Wraith in the chest. It reeled, but two more figures flowed past it, reaching out to me. I took a step back, just as Teya stepped forward. She exhaled, and fired her cannon. The nearest wraiths shattered, but the ones behind didn't slow. Before I could reload, they were on us.

I ducked under a swinging claw - a Wraith's night robe snatched at my face. My skin stung at the touch. I snarled and lashed out, forcing light out of my hand as my fist rammed into the wraith. The creature crumpled under the blow.

Wraiths streamed past me. I slotted a new quarrel into the crossbow, and nailed a Wraith in the back. Another night-clad figure flew towards Jaeson. I dashed to intercept and punched its cowl with a burst of golden light. I grinned as it shattered, but three more Wraiths took its place.

"Duck!" shouted Teya.

I turned just in time to see Teya aiming her canon at the wraiths bearing down on me. Jaeson ducked. I dropped too, but not fast enough – I was still falling when Teya fired. The bulk of her blast sailed over my head, but a fraction still hit me, hurling me through shards of shattered Wraiths.

The cave flipped upside down, then right-side up again. My head hit something hard, and my vision swam. My ears were filled with a throbbing, a shrieking. I rolled over, found grit in my mouth, and rolled over again, unsure of which way was up.

Hands grabbed at me. I panicked and tried to fend off my attacker, but a face swam into focus – Jaeson. He helped me to my feet. My head pounded and I nearly collapsed back down. He threw my arm over his shoulder and held me up.

Off in the distance, Teya fought next to Kyrene. The couple were fighting like angels. One leapt over to fend off a Wraith that was searing towards her wife's back whilst the other lashed out at the creature in front of her. Around the couple, the world was hazy and unclear. The ringing in my ears made it dreadfully hard to concentrate, but I couldn't look away from the pair. It was one of the most beautiful sights I'd ever seen.

I felt helpless, draped over Jaeson like damp linen. My golden light stretched out far father than I'd intended. How much power did I have left? I couldn't tell. How many wraiths were left? Too many but... a metal door in the distance set into a sheer wall... That door was our way out of Tenebro.

I could end this even if I held back enough power to not immediately fall unconscious. I just had to concentrate. I'd rescued Jaeson at the hot spring - I just needed to do the same thing again, albeit on a significantly larger scale.

Focussing on the largest cluster of wraiths, I forced my light into my palms. My power grew, fighting to slip free. The power jumped and bucked, but I held it, breathed, let it flow. I rose a hand, pointing at the monsters. I breathed. I let my power flow.

A golden beam fell on the monsters. One – the nearest – burned. The others rounded on me, furious at my impudence. My fingers burned – I'd gathered too much power and couldn't let it flow fast enough. No – that was wrong. I breathed. I focussed, and the beam of power tightened. Three more wraiths burned under my light, whilst the others charged at me and Jaeson.

Rents opened in my fingertips and my power writhed. I gritted my teeth, fought past the pain, focused, and exhaled. I released my power as the air left me. My breathing grew ragged as my vision swirled, but I concentrated on the sensation of power flowing up from within me, the power that Teya had gifted to me.

Teya's power contracted into a humming, fizzing steam of light, thin as a cotton thread but so bright it illuminated the entire tunnel. With a minute flick of my finger, my light cut through the wraiths. My light bisected them, shattering their frames, burning their cowls. They were nothing but shadows, helpless in the face of the dawn.

As the last one fell, I reeled my power back in – or tried to. The power momentarily slowed, but it was like trying to dam a river with my bare hands. I was draining myself dry.

Having no luck with stopping the outflow of power, I focussed instead on diffusing it. My skin lit up like the sky on the night of a festival. I shaped my power into a sphere around me and looked about the place for more monsters. My vision swirled and Jaeson faltered under my weight. I concentrated. Were there any more wraiths? No. No more.

I collapsed to my hands and knees; my eyes locked on the floor. I breathed in and out, reeling my power back in, making sure that my light didn't falter. Sweat ran down my back. My fingertips felt searing hot and freezing cold concurrently.

A rhythmic thumping boomed in the distance. Metal screamed, then a catastrophic wrenching howl filled the tunnel. One of the Wraiths must have survived. I raised my head, focussing in the direction of the calamity, ready to focus my light and destroy it. Instead, light mingled with my golden glow. One of the siblings had opened the metal door, and outside...

Outside was daylight.

Jaeson helped me to my feet. I couldn't let my light die just yet, not until I was sure. Together, we stumbled past fragments of darkness. A wall of darkness hurtled past me - Kyrene bearing Kinta towards the light.

Jaeson swayed under my weight – my right arm a millstone over his shoulders – but then Teya appeared. Her soft hands slipped my left arm over her shoulders. My two friends drew me through the door and onto the moss on the far side.

My friends sat me down with my back against the rock wall and ran to Kinta's side. She was thrashing, thrashing, thrashing. I couldn't focus on her. She seemed an awfully long way away. My head lolled back, and I searched for the source of the daylight. It came from a massive crack in the roof of the cave.

No. The walls of this place climbed up and up and up, but they didn't curl over at the top to form a ceiling. This wasn't a cave. We were at the bottom of a valley. We were out. We were free.

Scents of grass and earth soothed me. Cicadas and birds sang, making my heart soar. I hadn't realised how much I'd missed the sounds of life.

Click.

Click.

Click.

The noise meant something but, in that moment, I couldn't tell what. A ghastly screech pierced the air nearby. Kinta lay still. Darkness was pouring from her mouth, her nose, and her eyes.

Click.

Click.

Click.

My head felt heavy. I rolled my head to face the clicking sound – back down the passageway through which we'd just escaped. Two red lights glared at me. A skeletal hand reached out, struck the floor of the passageway with a *click*, dragged itself forward. A knot of jumbled, broken bones, pulling itself out of the dark, out of the tunnel towards me. Staring intently at me, its gaze cold and knowing.

It was what remained of the Capper. It had come for me. I opened my mouth to cry for help, but I couldn't make a sound. I wanted to get to my feet, but my legs wouldn't obey me. All I could do was watch as the Capper dragged itself closer and closer to the door out of Tenebro. Would it stop with me? Would it turn its gaze on my friends once it was done? Would my head restore it to its former power?

Click.

...

The Capper stopped. Its gaze bore into me, but it didn't move any further. Its skeletal fingers had stopped mere centimetres from where the sunlight struck the ground. Around it, the dark was weak but resolute.

Tendrils of darkness churned through the air from my left, tiny filaments of hissing, spitting shadow that rushed to rejoin the darkness inside Tenebro. I rolled my head to the left and saw the ribbons of darkness leading back to Kinta.

The Capper remained in the dark, staring at me. It couldn't reach me as long as I stayed in the light. I was safe from it. I'd won.

Except we still needed to get back to the surface, to bring help to Ekzilo. If we were going to go back into the dark, the Capper would come for me again, and if I left to take shelter in Sirmo, the Capper might find a way to reconstruct itself. It had managed to get away from Yilin's grumpy mum. If it could do that, it could do anything, except maybe survive in the light.

I tipped sideways, slumping to the ground. My cheek thudded against grass, and my vision darkened momentarily. I forced my arms to move. I reached out first one, then the other and dragged myself a little closer to the Capper. It wanted my head. I had to trust that it wanted my head more than it wanted to kill me. It was unbelievably strong. If I got this wrong, it would whip me into the dark and my friends would never see me again.

I rolled onto my side and grabbed onto the valley wall with both hands. Gingerly, I moved my foot closer to the Capper. It didn't move. I moved my foot closer. Scant centimetres separated the bone fingers from my boot. Still the Capper didn't move. I groaned, then moved my foot just a little bit closer.

The Capper's hand twitched. With all my remaining strength, I hauled my foot back just as it reached forward. It grabbed at my boot - clamped down onto the leather, but it didn't have time to reel me into the dark before I pulled my leg back towards the light.

The Capper's bone body juddered against the ground, its clawed hand gripping my boot tighter and tighter. Its grip crushed down on my toes, causing pain to sear up through my leg, but I threw my weight behind the kick, turning my body so as to drag the Capper fully into the sun.

My foot came to rest on the ground, and the Capper clattered to a stop just behind it. Bright, warm light seared down onto bleach-white bone. For a moment, the monster didn't react. Its eyes stared at me, dreadfully close. Then, the darkness inside its skull burst out through its eye sockets.

The Capper collapsed. Its chest crumbled into individual shreds of bone. Its single arm disintegrated. Its strange, bird-like skull rolled towards me, jawbone falling away. It bumped into my chest before crumbling into dust.

I slumped, my head resting on fresh grass, its rich, vital scents intoxicating. I shifted from side to side until I found a position that wasn't painful. It was over. I exhaled, raggedly, and felt my light die.

Wings fluttered overhead. Birds. I hadn't realised how much I'd missed birds, either. One landed on a bush just in my eyeline. It looked at me. It looked right at me, first with the eye on the left side of its head, then the one on its right. It must have been satisfied with what it saw because after a few moments it vented steam from under its wings and took off again. I lay still for quite a long time, puzzling over the steam bird. I'd never seen a steam bird before. I'd seen a steam engine and I'd seen a steam pipe and I'd seen steam cleaning, but I'd never seen a steam bird. I drifted off to sleep, questions about the strange, mechanical bird flapping around in my head.

"Melita?" Teya called my name, gently. I lay in her shadow – her head haloed by the sun. She was drenched with sweat, and her smile was triumphant. "How are you doing?"

I thought about this. I frowned. How was I doing? I wasn't sure. Everything felt very distant. I must have used more power than I'd meant to. I was definitely a little woozy. How could I express that?

"We need to move on, down to Sirmo if we can," she said. "We don't know how long the light is going to last here and we're still really close to Tenebro,"

That made sense. I nodded.

"Can you walk?"

That was an interesting question. I blinked a few times and kicked my legs to test things out. My body didn't co-operate.

"Kyrene says she's happy to carry you if you can't walk. Would that be okay?"

I thought about it. It did sound okay. I nodded. Teya grinned at me. She rested a hand on my head briefly. "You'll be all right. Rest up." I smiled up at her, and then she was gone, leaving me smiling to myself.

Words sailed in the distance, and then Kyrene slithered towards me. She lifted me with her tail, depositing me into the palms of her hands. Her fingers were longer than I was. I rested where I'd been placed, a doll in Kyrene's palm. Kinta lay next to me. She seemed to be sleeping peacefully. I hoped she was okay.

The landscape moved around me. A waterfall drifted past. The valley around us slowly widened out and became greener. Trees – cypress and cedar – in a huge blanket tucked up against a settlement at the far end of the valley. I couldn't tell from here how big the settlement was, but it couldn't be anything except Sirmo. The relief at feeling safe was teaming up with the fuzziness in my head to smother any sense of wonder or joy at the magnificent sight of the valley lying before us. All I wanted to do was rest. I snuggled down into Kyrene's hands and went back to sleep.

I woke to movement. I was being lowered tenderly to the ground. And it was ground - actual ground. There was grass and everything.

"Oh hey," I said, surprised to find myself both awake and slightly alert. "What did I miss?"

"Nothing much, sleepy grebe," Teya said. "Look over there."

She might have been pointing at one particular tree – we were in a copse of the things. Beyond were some fields – a farmer giving the ground a good seeing to with some sort of hoe. Teya might have been talking about the farmer, or maybe the cottage behind her. Or the town beyond that – traditional wooden houses, taller civic buildings, towering temples and glass monuments...

"Sirmo..." I said.

"You made it," Kyrene said.

"Okay," Teya said, her voice soft. "This is where we part."

"I thought you wanted to stay with Kyrene?" Jaeson said.

Teya nodded. There was something wrong about the way she was standing – she looked as if she was being slowly crushed. "I do, I do." She looked up at Kyrene. "Do you want to tell them?"

Kyrene jerked slightly. "About what?" she asked.

"About how you're not actually Kyrene," Teya said, flatly.

"What?" I asked.

"What?" Jaeson echoed.

"Teya…" Kyrene swayed on her tail for one long, terrible moment, before lowering herself a little, so she was more at our level. She stilled. Some aspect of her, some energy that had been present since the first time I'd met her seemed to have fallen away. "How did you know?" she asked.

Tears ran down Teya's face. She nodded. "You first. How did you know all those things about my wife?"

Kyrene pulled herself together in a miserable little coil. "Kyrene…." She hesitated before going on, her voice sounding more certain. "She'd been ambushed by the Capper. She escaped, but not without cost. One of the things about this mask is… it can absorb peoples' memories. I think one of the things it was originally for, was to pass on perfect information from one generation to another. Everything your wife was, is in here with me. Along with a dozen other people. I found the mask, abandoned in the castle. I put it on, and Kyrene's memories were mine."

"That's how you knew about our past…" Teya said.

"I wanted to tell you, Teya," Kyrene said, "but I couldn't. I'm sorry. I'm too much of a coward. I knew you'd only send me away again. All I wanted was for you to take my mask, but every time you tried to take it, memories from Kyrene would flood to the surface and I couldn't go through with it. So, I told you about my mask and since then I just wanted to spend time with you all, and… I gave you false hope just so I could be less alone for a little while. I'm really sorry."

"Don't worry about it," Teya said, her voice tight and controlled. "Between you and me, you did a terrible job of pretending to be my wife."

Kyrene's head jerked to the side. "Sorry? I just did what I saw Kyrene doing in her memories."

"Which memories?"

"Memories of you and her, that was pretty much the point."

Teya nodded. "Did you look at how Ky interacted with people who weren't me? Did you look at the memories where she encountered other cave raiders?"

"I didn't really have time."

"That's okay. Here's the thing: Ky was kind and loving, but she was also impulsive and reckless. She was tough. She needed to be. When we were roaming from town to town, searching for answers to her condition, she was battling bandits and magical creatures every thirty seconds, but she couldn't *enjoy* it because she was always worrying about me. So, when Ekzilo took us in, she found a place where she could leave me without worrying I'd get myself killed if she took her eyes off me for two minutes.

"I saw the relief in her face. She could use her magic to explore Tenebro without worrying about collateral damage. She was a conquering hero and would return to find me waiting to hear her stories. I wasn't a burden then. I was an adoring audience. Your mistake was that you were being too nice, too nurturing. You were behaving like the wife I wanted, not the wife I actually had. The wife I wanted would always be there for me. The wife I had could only stay with me for a few days at a time without getting bored. She thought understanding her magic took second place to being a swashbuckling heroine in the Hungry Dark."

"I thought you'd be angrier when you found out."

"You got us to Sirmo. How could I be angry? Just don't... don't..."

"I won't see you ever again," Kyrene said, dipping her mask. There was deep sadness behind the words. I found the fingers of my right hand drumming against my left wrist in a quick staccato rhythm. My toes tapped against the ground.

"Thank you," Teya said. She turned towards Sirmo and hauled Kinta up and onto her shoulders in a firefighter's lift. "Let's go!"

Jaeson looked between Teya and Kyrene before following. I got to my feet and dusted myself down. "Thank you for everything, Kyrene," I said, giving her a hug.

"I'll miss you, Melita," Kyrene said.

"Stay close, I'll come and see you," I said.

"That's not a good idea."

"Why not?"

"I'll try to get you to take my mask."

I nodded, thoughtfully. "Well, see you soon!" I said, then scuttled off after my team.

CHAPTER TWENTY-ONE

Teya was still carrying Kinta when I caught up to her, whilst Jaeson scouted ahead. We followed a track which wound languidly through the trees. A flock of birds lazily circled overhead, although they seemed to be literally circling – describing a perfect O over our heads.

I was busy staring up at the birds when I suddenly bumped into Jaeson, who had stopped in the middle of the track.

I nudged him. "What are you doing?"

He pointed out, past the last of the trees, to the farmsteads beyond. Our winding track turned into a road, and that road led down through stepped rows of rice paddies. Only one farmer seemed to be working today. She looked relatively unsinister - thigh-high boots to keep the water out, a plain grey robe, and a wide brimmed, sun-defeating hat.

"That farmer look normal to you?" Teya whispered.

I watched the farmer intently. "Maybe."

Teya shifted Kinta about on her back, but didn't move.

"Let's go," I said. Want me to take Kinta?"

"Nah, I got her. Let's get this over with."

"Get what over with?" Jaeson said.

"We're about to find out what sort of people live in Sirmo. How friendly they are."

"Ah, yes, that," said Jaeson.

"Yes," said Teya. "That."

The farmer looked up and nodded to us as we passed. I bowed in return, doing my best to look harmless.

"Hopefully a good sign," muttered Teya once we were out of earshot.

Approaching Sirmo from our road, the place looked ordinary enough. Houses which could have been lifted straight from Ekzilo or Tenebro. The road turned sharply just before we entered the town itself, and, after turning this corner, all three of us stopped dead in our tracks.

Hundreds of people lined the road ahead. Four long rows, two on either side of the road, leaving a cavernous gap in the middle. They stood. Patient. Waiting. I couldn't tell if they were being respectful, or were about to sacrifice us to some sort of blood god.

Teya glanced at me. I shrugged. We turned to Jaeson. He shrugged. Together, we strode on. I felt as if I were leading a particularly half-hearted parade. As we walked past the lines of people, they bowed and murmured messages of welcome.

We passed young people and old people. We passed witches with marks of clans that weren't my own. We passed people with visible disabilities. I kept an eye out for people who weren't obviously from Talvik, of which there weren't many, but other than that the place looked like a haven.

I tried to keep my breathing under control. I hadn't dreamed there would be other witches in Sirmo. I was deeply suspicious that everyone watching was going to suddenly draw knives, or maybe I never made it out of the dark and was just hallucinating Sirmo. I concentrated on putting one foot in front of the other. There was no way I could fight if things turned ugly. My muscles were spent. My head was nothing but a bank of fog. I'd given all I could give.

The street opened into a square, dominated by an enormous temple complex at the far end. Standing in front of the splayed temple doors stood several women in formal dress. One, who looked as if she might be concealing a firearm inside her canary yellow robe, stepped forward, bowed, and held out a small cloth-bound box. After only a moment of hesitation, I stepped forward, bowed, and accepted the gift with both hands.

The official straightened and smiled. "Welcome!"

I tensed. If everyone was going to don sacrificial robes and attack us, they'd probably take that as their cue to start. The lines of people on either side of us dissolved into chaos, with people walking every which way. Smells of frying meat and vegetables filled the air. Several people did pull out knives, but they used the blades to chop vegetables which, after getting myself all worked up, was a little disappointing.

Behind us, sharp snaps split the air. Drums. Not gunfire. Drums. A whole band joined the drums moments later. The song was fast paced, vibrant and seemed to be a protracted argument about whether rice was a side dish or not.

The canary-robed official relaxed out of her formal upright pose and waved behind her. Two young women in black fought their way out of the crowd, carrying a stretcher. Teya lowered Kinta onto the stretcher, gratefully. Around us, the gradual chatter of voices rose to a persistent babble. There was excitement in the air.

"Sorry for being so formal," said the official. "My name's Ikia, I'm arbiter of Sirmo. One of our automata saw you leave Tenebro, so we prepped this little festival. We don't have many excuses to celebrate down here, and the arrival of visitors is a better excuse than most. Our doctor is waiting in her clinic to take a look at your friend."

"Did you say automata?" I asked.

Ikia nodded. She reached into her robes, drew out a silver whistle and blew it, her cheeks puffing out alarmingly. The same mechanical bird I'd seen just after I'd killed the Capper flapped down and landed on her shoulder.

"Wow," I said, surprised but still feeling at a distance from everything.

Ikia smiled at my surprise. She nodded to the stretcher bearers, who picked up Kinta in the stretcher. "Cassandra and Shelby here will take your friend to our doctor. You can go with her if you like, or you can stay and enjoy the festival. We've also arranged lodgings for you." Ikia handed me a folded piece of paper. "That's a map to a house. You're welcome to stay there for as long as you like. You must be very tired. Please, don't feel you need to take part in the festival if you don't want to. Take care of yourselves, you've clearly been through a lot."

Teya, Jaeson and I shook Ikia's hand. The stretcher bearers took this as a cue and carried Kinta away from the crowd, down a side street. We didn't need to discuss what to do next – as one, we followed Kinta.

The stretcher bearers carried my twin up into a glass-fronted building where a doctor – a serious, fat woman who introduced herself as Crista, ushered us through to a waiting room. I wanted to stay with Kinta while she was examined, but the doctor politely refused. I took a seat next to Teya and Jaeson in the waiting room. My leg jiggled. I stared about, waiting for the next... the next... something.

When nothing happened for ten minutes, I unwrapped the present Ikia had given us. A grey object – rectangular. The size of a clenched fist. I poked it. It remained motionless, but its texture was familiar. I turned it over in my hands, and gave it an experimental sniff. Scented soap. Jasmine – fruity and sensual. I couldn't help but close my eyes as the scent drained the tension from my limbs. I passed it to Teya so she could have a smell as well.

After a few minutes more, Crista emerged from the exam room, drying her hands. "Your friend looks like she's been through the wringer. She's got multiple fractures and one of her eyes has suffered some recent trauma. What happened to her?"

I closed my eyes, shutting out the enormity of the question. "She was possessed by the Hungry Dark. When we got her into the light, the darkness fled through her eyes, ears, nose and mouth. She hasn't woken up since. Will she be okay?"

"I don't know about the eye, but everything else should heal, given time. I want to keep her in for a while. Can one of you stay with her? She'll want to see a friendly face when she wakes up."

I opened my mouth, but Teya rested her hand on my arm. Her touch – casual and reassuring - made me feel strange – as if we were home. "I'll stay," she said.

"I should stay with my twin," I whispered to her.

Teya shook her head, a small gesture that would have seemed casual were it not for the tension in her shoulders. "Melita, please. I just learned some pretty devastating news. I need some time to process that. Spending time here, in peace and quiet, will be perfect. Will you be okay leaving her in my hands?"

I smiled, "There are none safer."

"Thanks, Meli."

I stood, stretched and nodded to Jaeson. "Come on, lad. Let's take a look at this house they're letting us stay in."

Jaeson nodded, stood, and followed me out of the doctor's office. We studied the arbiter's map, worked out a rough direction and set off through the festival. Families bustled past, herding kids ahead of them. We turned into a street lined with brightly coloured stalls. Banners hung above them, boasting of their wares. Homely smells floated across to us – grilled chicken, frying cabbage, soy sauce and fish broth.

My stomach rumbled, and I found myself joining a queue at a stall producing savoury pancakes. Jaeson joined me after only dithering for a moment. The people ahead of us in the queue didn't pay for their pancakes. They simply walked up to the chef, said how many they wanted and were presented with that many plates.

"Next!" cried the chef.

I stepped forward - "Two please – I'm new. Do you want trade for these?"

The chef looked up at me, beamed in delight and cried: "Welcome! Thank you for visiting my stall. No payment required, we don't do that sort of thing here. Please, enjoy yourself!" She handed over two plates, bowed to me and Jaeson and then turned to the person behind us in the queue. Jaeson and I took our plates, bowed, and walked away from the stall.

"What did she mean, they don't pay for things here?" said Jaeson.

I shrugged. "Some places don't use money or trade or whatever. They don't have money in Teya's home country. Took her a while to get used to Talvik because of that."

We found a quiet place to eat as, above us, the sky darkened. I kept having to remind myself that I didn't have anything to fear from the darkness out here.

"You know something," I said, after I finished my pancake. "I think that chef might have been human."

Jaeson looked at me, his eyebrows raised. "Yes, probably. Most people are human. Teya is human. I'm human."

"No, I mean…" I frowned, and scratched the side of my head. "I've never been around this many people who might be human without someone yelling at me."

Jaeson nodded. "Well, that's desperately sad."

"That's life as a witch, little Jaeson."

"That might not be the case down here. Sirmo seems lovely."

"It looks that way now, yes. Let's hold off on deciding that before we have all the facts, eh?"

We resumed our walk, keeping our plates with us to wash up when we found the house. We passed under an enormous gate, painted brown rather than the traditional red. Two rows of paper lanterns hung from the top crossbeam, illuminating the street below in the fading light.

"Just... I just want you to give them a chance," Jaeson said, after a few minutes of silence. "Not all humans are like the ones from my town."

"Hey, if they're all like the people we've met so far, me and these humans are going to get along just fine, but you've got to remember they're only half of the problem."

"What do you mean?"

I clicked my fingers. "Sorry, Jaeson, I was forgetting. I've got a cluster of mental problems. I don't really understand them, because they're part of the framework I use to try and understand them if you follow me. Anyway, they lead to me slipping into dark moods and being unable to engage in this whole thing." I waved my hands around at the crowds, the shrines, the houses, and the stalls selling buns stuffed with red bean paste.

Jaeson followed my gesture. "Do you mean life, Melita?"

"That's it. So even if these people are lovely and welcoming and open, I'm still going to run up against my own problems. They shut down any chance I had of a healthy life in Ekzilo, and they'll probably do the same here."

"Spirits, Melita. Is there anything I can do?"

"Being here helps, but it's not enough. If I had access to a doctor who knew about mental health or medication then sure, but I've only ever heard of those things being found in the big cities. We found answers about Kyrene, that's something. What are you going to do, little Jaeson?"

"I don't know. I've still got a lot of thinking to do. I'm glad to be somewhere like this – somewhere like home but no-one knows me."

"Take your time, lad."

"Thanks. I can do that. How about you? I've been keeping an eye out for things that might be able to help Ekzilo..."

I nodded. "Me too. Some advanced tech down here. Nothing immediately obvious that would protect Ekzilo without the need for violence so far." I scratched my chin. There was the shape of an idea at the back of my head, but I needed somewhere quiet to think about it.

"Say, Melita?"

"Mm?" We turned down a darker street lined with houses, the comparative silence wrapping around us like a blanket.

"Your light."

"What about it?"

Jaeson checked the map, looked up at the houses on our side of the street and then back down to the map. "It changes colour a lot. Is there a reason for that?"

I shrugged, rather pointlessly as he hadn't looked at me since he'd started this odd line of questioning. "I have no idea. I've never really thought about it – it's just one of those things that happens, you know? Why?"

"Huh. See, I had this idea that it changed colour depending on what your mood was. It seemed to shift into warmer colours when you were feeling happier."

I opened my mouth to object – I'd been feeling perfectly happy when I'd first met Jaeson... but then I remembered that was wrong. I'd stepped off the temple of peace less than twenty-four hours after we'd met. What had Teya called that state of mine? Ecstasy. Happiness's sinister sister. Since I'd saved Teya's life at the temple, things had changed, and then changed some more... "You might be onto something there," I said.

"Something to think about, maybe," Jaeson said. "I think this is us." He'd stopped outside a two storey wooden house, identical to its neighbours but for the brass number plate in the door, and the wisteria lining its windows.

I checked the map as well, just to be sure. "Looks like it."

"Shall we check it out?"

"Can't think of a reason not to."

I slipped off my shoes off before stepping inside. It seemed like a perfectly ordinary house: wooden floors that filled the entire place with the homely smell of cedar. Woven straw mats lined the sitting room floor, and I thought I saw one of those fancy heated tables people use in the winter stashed in a corner. I went around checking all the cupboards and hidey holes for assassins or lurking monsters.

Once I was done, I found Jaeson in the kitchen, washing up our plates from the festival.

"You alright?" he asked.

"Not sure yet, but it seems like we might be okay. We might be safe."

"You're swaying on your feet, Melita. Why don't you go and have a lie down?"

I wanted to object to this suggestion, but aches in my limbs and my back chose that moment to remind me of their presence. I nodded, climbed the stairs, and collapsed onto a futon.

A *crack* woke me up. I shot bolt upright. It was dark. That noise – had it been the Capper? Had it come back again? I couldn't kill it again. I was so tired. There was a figure in the room with me, looming. Its small silhouette somehow familiar...

It was Jaeson. He was standing at the window, looking out over the village. He turned as I stirred. "There are fireworks, Melita. Sorry if they woke you, I can only see them from this room. Don't worry. We're safe. Go back to sleep."

Relieved, I rolled over.

The next morning, I woke up and was only slightly surprised to find my-self alone in my room, as opposed to being surrounded by robed figures preparing to sacrifice me to a fertility spirit.

I lay on my futon and took stock of how I felt. My muscles were solid steel cables which ached at the smallest movement. My legs were particu-larly unhappy. My wrist felt light – I didn't want to think about how much work it would be to replace the bones I'd used in the dark. I could feel my mood dropping. The sense of triumph at finally making it out of the dark yesterday had fled, leaving behind the empty feeling that had followed me around for most of my life. My chest felt so heavy. My head was locked up tight, making it hard to follow any one thought for more than a sentence or two.

I'd made it into the light. I needed to rest. I needed to live here, find a place here, stop living only to die. But… no. Ekzilo still needed me. I needed to push through the pain one last time to find their help. Then, and only then, could I rest.

It took well over an hour for me to be able to get out of bed. During that time, my head cleared a little, and the scale of the task ahead loomed over me. When I'd suggested finding Sirmo, I'd thought the actual 'getting help for Ekzilo' part would more or less take care of itself. Now I was here, it was pretty clear I'd managed to complete the first part of a many staged process. I wasn't sure how much more I'd be able to do. Still, I had to try, and I had to try *now*, before things got even worse on the surface.

I pulled on my trusty battered leather coat, which smelled unpleasantly ripe but I couldn't afford the time to clean it, or myself come to that. I staggered downstairs and out into Sirmo.

Ideas swirled in my head for how to proceed, but by far the simplest involved finding someone important and simply asking for help. My head was too foggy to tease apart any more complicated plans, so I asked the first person I encountered where I'd find the arbiter.

After a few wrong turns, I found Ikia the arbiter sweeping the street, alongside several other people doing the same. Behind her, dozens of people were hard at work deconstructing stalls and generally clearing up after last night's festivities. Ikia stopped industrially sweeping as I approached. "Hiya," she said. "Should you really be out of bed? You look... very tired."

"Y-," I said, then cleared my throat and tried again. "Yeah. Tired. Yeah. I just need to find something out first. My friends and I came to Sirmo because our home on the surface was attacked." I paused, finding the next part of what I'd been going to say had slipped away from me.

Ikia's eyebrows rose and her eyes widened in concern. "Oh no! Is there anything I can do to help?"

I snapped my fingers. "Yes, that's it. Thank you. I was supposed to be asking for help. We need help."

"Great, we'll do whatever we can. What sort of help do you need?"

I closed my eyes as the world spun around me. "Is there any technology, anything you have that can stop... rioters without causing injury or loss of life?"

Ikia's face fell. "I'm sorry, no. We have plenty of technology but the Hungry Dark has meant we haven't needed anything for self defence for centuries. We don't really need any peacekeeping apparatus. In fact, you're currently looking at one hundred percent of our law enforcement system."

I sagged. "What sort of technology do you have down here?"

"Oh, all sorts. We have machines that work the fields, they've increased crop yields tenfold. We have calculating engines that can solve logistical problems. You've seen our clutch of recognisance birds. That sort of thing."

I nodded, slightly surprised that this terrible news hadn't caused the weight in my chest to grow any heavier. "That's a shame. Can you think of anything that will help retake our village from... invaders? Anything at all?"

"How many of them were there?"

I tried to remember, but gave up. "A lot."

Ikia frowned, and shook her head. "If I think of anything, I'll come and find you immediately," she said. "I promise."

I nodded, shook her hand again, and left her to her sweeping. I was crushed. Empty. My quest had been pointless.

I shouldn't have been surprised. Sirmo didn't even have walls. They'd let us walk into the centre of the place and had thrown us a festival. The Hungry Dark, awful as it was, had kept this oasis peaceful. And *that* thought, allowed me to put words to an idea that had been slowly forming within me for the past few days. I was feeling a little more myself after chatting with Ikia, but running the idea past someone felt like a smart plan.

Teya wasn't in the doctor's office when I arrived. Crista, the doctor, reported that she'd spent the night there but had left early in the morning once Kinta's condition had stabilised.

At least Teya had left a note. It read: 'Meli – I've gone to look for some tech that will help Ekzilo. Meet me back at the lodgings they set us up with for lunch.'

"Thanks," I said to Christa, "by the way, and this is a bit of a long shot, but do you have the facilities down in Sirmo to manufacture drugs that can counter the effects of Kaskado Disorder?"

Crista shook her head.

"Figures. Okay, take me to my twin."

Crista raised an eyebrow. "You're sororal twins?"

"I'm sorry but I'm far too tired to explain."

Christa ushered me into the examination room before leaving me and my sister alone. Relief washed over me at the sight of her alive, causing me to rock back on her heels. She looked thinner than I remembered, and a gauze patch was taped over her right eye

"How are you doing?" I asked.

"I've lost the use of this eye," my sister said, tapping her cheek near the patch.

"A parting gift from the dark?"

"Something like that. The sun ripped the dark free from my system. Eyes don't like things being ripped from them."

"What happened to you, Kinta? Last I saw of you, you were heading off to get your payment for trapping me."

Kinta's shoulders slumped. "I couldn't find the bones in time. I ran out of light. I ran out of time. I was lost and alone in the dark. I didn't want to die."

I nodded. "When the trap in the tunnel leading down to level four showed me flashes of your life it looked... difficult."

"Mostly maintenance, scavenging for tech and running for my life, was it?"

I nodded, my teeth grinding together as memories the trap had shown me rose unbidden within me.

"Well, there were good parts. Seeing the gates painted a brilliant vermillion and knowing that without me, they'd be nothing but rotten wood? That made me feel so proud... But then I lured you into a trap so I could get enough bones to properly sand and repaint the workshops around the shrine on level two..."

"You don't have to do any of that work in the dark, Kinta."

"I know. I wanted to use my magic and... back when I first came to Tenebro it made perfect sense. I think I got lost along the way somehow."

"Me too. What are you going to do if you don't go back into the dark?"

"I have no idea. How about you?"

I shook my head self-consciously. "I'm feeling pretty rough. I've gone from being absolutely essential for my friends' survival to being just... me. In Tenebro I dreamt of entertaining people with my magic. I wanted to try that here before I headed back up to Ekzilo, but then I remembered I'd used all my bones in the dark. I need to find new bones, but they need to be powerful ones and... I don't know if it would be worth it. Do you know what I mean?"

Kinta shook her head. "Sorry, Melita, my magic isn't like that. I don't really get the impulse."

"Don't worry. I just... I felt useful in the dark. But I saw you and you reflected me and I think... I think I might have been self-destructing."

Kinta nodded; the movement slow as if she were trying to delay saying something out loud for fear of what admitting it would mean. She raised her head, she opened her mouth, then closed it again. She made a tiny, defeated noise in her throat that sounded almost like a cough. She looked up at me. "Self-destructing? Yes. Me too."

"So, what do we do if we don't want to self-destruct?"

"Well, I want to stay in the light for a bit. I've been alone in the dark for so long I need to just... Focus on real things. Try to work on whatever part of myself was willing to trade in other peoples' misery as long as it got me what I wanted. What about you? You have Teya and Jaeson, they'll help."

"Yes. The thing is, I need to get back up to Ekzilo, to drive back the humans, gather our people together and rebuild the town. I wonder if I could run an idea past you?"

Kinta's jaw dropped as I explained my idea. Once I'd finished talking her through the details, her brow furrowed, and she didn't say anything for five long minutes. We talked about this and that, then she made a suggestion that she said would make things go a lot smoother.

Chapter Twenty-Two

It was lunch time by the time I'd worked out a plan with my twin, so I returned to my lodgings to meet with Teya. Jaeson gasped when he saw me come in, rushed me into a chair and fed me cooked fish and rice until I stopped swaying.

Teya let herself in just as I finished my second bowl, strode through to the kitchen and dropped an enormous, lightly singed book onto the table, making the chopsticks jump.

"How are you doing?" I asked.

Teya shrugged. "I've been better. Not too bad, all things considered. I'm alive and so are you two. I'll take the win. The bad news is I haven't been able to find anything that'll help Ekzilo. There's plenty of tech down here but most of it's geared towards farming and crafts. Quality of life stuff. Technically they can access the sea but there's a load of tricky currents and rocks in the bay that stop all but small fishing boats getting out."

"That's what I found, yeah," I said.

"So we're stuck?" Teya asked. "Sirmo can't help reunite Ekzilo?"

"Still working on that," I said.

At that point, Jaeson bustled up and practically dragged Teya to a chair and wouldn't let her say anything until she agreed to eat something.

"So, what's in the book?" I asked, once Teya had finished her first bowl.

"Ah, now that's the one interesting thing I managed to find. So, there was this tech research station on the edge of town. Something particularly experimental burned the place down, and one of the researchers rescued some of their archive, including this book - part of the station's cataloguing system.

"There's an item listed in here that can absorb the Hungry Dark. Maybe. There's no description and it's listed as experimental. Sirmo's archivist reckons if they ever actually developed a prototype it was lost in the fire, or maybe in Tenebro during testing. Still, if we could find that, we might be able to establish a new Ekzilo down in Tenebro or something."

"Huh," I said, not trusting myself to say anything more without giving away my schemes. Teya's artefact might be nothing. It was probably nothing. It would have to wait. I had schemes to enact.

Twenty minutes later, I went to find Kyrene. She was lurking in the forest, pretty much where I'd left her on the previous day. She'd coiled up around herself tightly, leaving herself little more than a mask and a jumble of darkness.

"Hiya!" I said, as I approached her. Behind me, the bushes stilled, and the wind died down.

"Hello, Melita," said Kyrene, misery saturating her voice.

"So, I've been meaning to have a little chat with you about your identity. Obviously, I can't keep calling you Kyrene. Is your name really Vakua?"

"Vakua is a pseudonym. I've been trapped inside this body for so long I can't remember my birth name."

"You can't remember it at all? Not a hint? Not a glimmer?"

Kyrene shifted about, her mask rocking from side to side, almost imperceptibly. "What's this about, Melita?"

"I'm just here to talk, but if you'd rather I left you alone, I can always just..."

"No, no, sorry. I'm happy to talk. What did you want to talk about?"

"You told Teya that your mask contains the memories of those that died wearing it. I'm interested in that. Kyrene's memories came through so clearly, you're able to speak fluently in Akoman - you even have a bit of an accent. What other people are in that mask with you? What are their names?"

"Ariadne Gazis... Luci Lauda... Danae Regas... do you want me to recite the whole list?"

"Two more, maybe."

"Ida Kyrkos and Khloe Sarri."

"Tell me about Khloe."

"Oh, she was nice. Could be a bit spiky but had a good heart."

"Born in Talvik, was she?"

"Born and raised."

"Great. Can I hear what her voice sounds like please? Because I noticed you're still speaking with a bit of an accent. Honestly, it's barely noticeable but every once in a while, your pitch intonation isn't exactly right for someone born in Talvik. You sometimes forget to drop your pitch at the end of a word or drop it a syllable too early. I wouldn't bring it up, but sometimes Teya does the same thing."

In the still air behind me, I heard a bush stir, rustle, and settle back down. Kyrene didn't say anything. The idea that had been fizzing about in my head for the last day solidified.

I shrugged, the picture of a witch defeated by a robust and thorough counterargument. "Well, never mind about that. Let's talk about the time you persuaded my sister to trap me in your mask."

"Do we have to?"

"I think it would be a promising line of conversation. The first time you tried to trap me, with your bizarre purification ritual... by the way, I've been meaning to ask. Did that ritual do anything or was it all just a way of trying to get me to take the mask?"

"I was trying to get you to put the mask on. I talked wistfully about how powerful it was. It was in your hands. Honestly, I'm still astonished that didn't work."

"I think your time in the dark might have made you cynical. Anyway, that trap was pretty straightforward. Then you offered the mask up freely, having claimed a change of heart. You panicked when Teya tried to take the mask. This would make sense if Kyrene's memories were particularly strong in your head, so I'll let that one pass without comment. Then we get to the really curious scheme, where you refused to help us with the Capper unless I took the mask."

"Nothing curious about it. You pointed out that I'd be vulnerable to the Capper if you took my mask. That's why I helped you."

"Well, that was the point I was making, yes, but I don't think that's why you helped us. I think you helped us because of something else I said. I can't remember exactly the words I used, but I think they had something to do with Teya refusing to help you if she looked into your freshly human eyes and saw the person who just sacrificed me to save themselves.

"Now, you could have still refused to help. If I'd taken your mask, Teya would have been furious with you, but she wouldn't have knocked you out and left you for the Capper. If you have Kyrene's memories, you would have known that. She might have refused to help you, but she wouldn't have killed you. Besides, I would have had your power. I would have dealt with the Capper, or at least slowed it down long enough for you to get away. You could have held Jaeson hostage or just stolen a glow globe from Teya and fled."

Kyrene didn't reply. I knelt on the grass in front of her and let my hands rest in the long stalks. They felt cool on my skin, with the faintest hint of dew left over from the morning.

"The only way I can make sense of your last trap is if I assume there was something about you that you didn't want Teya to see. Maybe your face.

The face of Teya's wife. Her wife who, if her plan had worked, would have just sacrificed an innocent to free herself from a curse."

I waited for a moment to see whether Kyrene wanted to say anything, breathing in the fresh, herbal smell of the grass. She stayed quiet, so I carried on. "I might have believed you when you said you weren't Kyrene, but then I remembered seeing you and Teya fighting alongside each other in Tenebro. You moved as one. You were perfectly in sync. Are you really telling me that one set of memories out of a dozen allowed you to act as Teya's wife?

"I think you have only one person's memories in your head. There aren't any other personalities in there with you, either. I think you, Kyrene, found the mask in the dark. You put the mask on, and it transformed you into this serpentine form. You've been desperate for me to take your mask, but Teya has been with me the whole time. You couldn't reveal yourself to Teya, because you were terrified she'd reject you. Or maybe you were scared she'd insist on taking your mask. Rightfully so, as it turned out. As soon as you revealed you were Kyrene, she demanded the mask from you.

"I think you lied to Teya when we made it out of the dark. You knew she'd never let you go. She wanted to take your mask, to save you from this fate. If you tried to run and hide to save her, she'd never stop looking for you. So, you lied. You let her believe her false assumption that you weren't Kyrene. You told her that her wife was dead. You told her this so she wouldn't demand your mask, to take on your burden so you could be free. You didn't want wonderful Teya to turn into a monster at any cost, even if it meant your freedom."

Kyrene didn't reply. I shrugged, stood and stretched. "No? Nothing. Okay, well, if you're not going to tell me, then I'll just—"

"Don't tell her," said Kyrene. "Please. She's been trapped by my disappearance for two years."

"Mm. What really happened, Kyrene? How did you come to wear that mask?"

Kyrene grumbled quietly to herself, her voice sounding like a distant earthquake that was deeply unhappy but didn't want to come across as rude. "I'd heard rumours of a piece of arcano-tech that had been designed to destroy the Hungry Dark. I traded some information with Yilin, which led me to the mask. Teya told you I have some magic? Well, I could feel the mask's power. I thought it was the artefact that would destroy the dark, or at least it would help me become a better cave raider. I was right, in a way."

"And *does* the mask destroy the Hungry Dark?"

"I don't know. It turned me into this creature, and my body now draws power from the dark, but whenever it does, I grow. I didn't start off this huge, I was only about ten metres tall at first. The more I tried to draw on the dark's power, the more I grew. I had to stop eventually and spend more time in the open, near Ekzilo, to slow the growth. As a matter of fact, I was heading to the surface to do that when we first met."

"And check on Teya?"

"I may have looked in on her from time to time. I had to enlarge the tunnel, but this mask can bore through rock like butter."

I nodded, but Kyrene jerked forward, wringing her enormous hands together, making a sound like a whetstone grinding against steel. "Look, Melita, please don't tell Teya. Don't prolong her misery. She might be able to move on if she thinks I'm dead."

"What if you could return to her?"

Kyrene's hands froze. The tip of her tail twitched. "Well, yes, Melita, that would be wonderful, but I can't. Someone would need to take this mask on willingly, and no one is going to do that."

"Well, no, I suppose they wouldn't. To take that mask on, someone would need to feel lost and powerless. They'd need to have spent most of their life wishing their existence would end because they don't feel they have a place in the world. They'd have to see your mask as an opportunity to do some good in the world rather than a burden. They'd have to want to get back to the surface, to protect their home; to take on a form that was truly terrifying to the superstitious and the short-sighted humans who had recently attacked, so that they could defend their village without violence."

Kyrene didn't reply.

"Give me the mask, Kyrene. Please."

"Melita, no!" Teya rocketed out from the undergrowth.

Birds fluttered up into the air from the nearby trees. They circled over us as I rounded on Teya: "I told you to stay in that bush no matter what you heard!"

"You didn't say you were going to sacrifice yourself!"

I rolled my eyes. "Weren't you listening to anything I said? It's not a sacrifice! Kyrene thinks it is because she has some weird social anxiety thing. Whatever, I'm not one to judge other people's mental health problems. The point is she hasn't thought about what that mask can do. Think about it, Teya! In that serpent form I'd be able to drive the humans away from Ekzilo without hurting anyone. I'd be able to protect everyone in the village. We could even connect Tenebro and Sirmo for the first time in generations because the creatures of the dark wouldn't be a threat anymore! Think of the benefits for Ekzilo and Sirmo!"

My friend gripped my shoulders with both hands. "Melita, listen to me. I know you have problems. I know you don't feel useful a lot of the time, and I get that, but you are a person and you are wonderful. I don't care that you're not productive by capitalist standards. Your worth is not decided by your ability to be productive. You're my friend and I love you and you don't need to become a monster so you can help Ekzilo!"

I blinked, long and slow, feeling tears forming in the wake of Teya's words. The Peace Trap had been wrong when she'd said Teya would choose Kyrene over me. "Teya... my disability has been hounding me for decades.

I don't want to go back to risking my life in the Hungry Dark every time I feel that life isn't worth living. I know you love me, and I love you, but what you're asking me to do is live in a state of just... endless misery, endless pain."

Teya's hands released my shoulders, slowly, slowly. She looked as if she was having a nightmare and didn't know how to wake up. "You don't know that'll change if you put on the mask. We can get you medication, we can—"

I shook my head. "I checked with the doctor. They don't have meds or therapy down here. There's no hope of getting medication if I can't get back to the surface and we can't get back to the surface without that mask.

"I can't live like this anymore, Teya. I'm done. I'm done with hurting myself and trying to end my own life, but something has to change. Even if wearing the mask doesn't lead to the change I want, at least you'll have Kyrene back. At least I'll be able to keep Ekzilo safe. The worst-case scenario here, the *worst case* is I'll have freed someone from a life they find intolerable."

"Meli... Meli you need to *rest*. We've been through so much and you were exhausted even before the humans attacked and you need, you *need* to take care of yourself."

I smiled. "I know, Teya. I will. I promise I will. I just need to do this one thing first."

Teya was crying, the tears leaving trails that glistened in the sunlight. She looked very small in that moment. "It doesn't have to be you, Meli."

"I know it doesn't have to be me. I want it to be me."

Teya fell silent, reached a hand up and wiped away a tear. She stared out into the distance for a long moment. Then she shook her head. "I'm not going to be able to talk you out of this, am I?"

I gave my best friend a hug. Somewhere nearby, a bird sung happily to the cicadas, who sang right back. The air around us was still and filled with the scent of baking earth and cypress trees. Teya rested her cheek on my shoulder.

"I love you," I said, "and that's never going to change. We're going to do some amazing work together, Teya."

Teya hugged me back for a long time. Her arms were tight around me at first, but her breathing slowed as we stood together, her arms relaxing around my waist. In that moment I knew that she was going to be okay. Eventually, she let me go, and stared up into my face without stepping back. Her eyes shone. "Thank you, Meli."

I rested my forehead against hers. "Thank you, Teya."

After a moment of pure peace, where my mind was quiet and the world around me was still, I drew back and turned to Kyrene. "I'm going to take your mask off now."

"Are you sure?"

By way of confirmation, I reached up to her mask. I released one catch, then the next, then the next, and then the last. I lifted the mask from Kyrene's face. It was light in my hands, just as it had been when I'd held it back at the castle. The mask shrank down until it was the same size as my face. It was small and harmless. It was a festival mask.

I held the mask to my face, and power flooded into me. My body shifted. It felt *right*. I rose without moving, first to the height of the trees and then beyond. I stretched out my arms and saw my flesh darken further into a beautiful shade of shifting onyx.

Kyrene looked very much as I remembered her. I smiled, although I knew the twitch of my lips was now hidden behind the great mask. Still, I could feel the memory of muscles moving. I still felt the warmth of that smile fill me, and I sighed as Teya threw her arms around her newly returned wife. They kissed, and Teya's eyes closed. She looked at peace for the first time in two years.

"Look after each other," I said, "I promise I'll be back."

Teya broke away from Kyrene and ran over to me. She wrapped her arms around my tail and hugged tight. I coiled around her, gently. I felt her breath against my skin, then the patter of falling tears. After a long moment, Teya released me and stepped back, her eyes glistening, the corners of her mouth lifting into a smile. "Good luck, little grebe."

"I'll see you soon," I said.

Chapter Twenty-Three

The metal door which protected the surface world from the Hungry Dark jammed when I first tried to open it. I pulled with a fraction more of my strength, and the door gave way, its wheels screaming in their tracks.

Outside, blazing sunlight played on my skin as I slithered up the hill towards Ekzilo. The exterior fence was charred, and a gaping wound had been torn in it towards the north gate. My mask tightened as I tried to clench a jaw I no longer had. If the humans had chased my friends away, and had tried to take their place...

I cracked my knuckles, but tried to stay calm. If the humans had left, and my friends had returned home, I couldn't just storm the village and give everyone inside a heart attack. I needed to be a little more subtle.

My chest ached as I slowed my approach. I slinked up to the exterior fence, trying to concentrate on the surrounding soundscape and not worry about the exact mechanics of how I was moving. I'd tried to critically observe the way I was slithering, rather than walking, on the way up, and had ended up falling over and crushing a factory.

I focussed, trying to shut out everything except sound. Birdsong, crickets, the crackle of a fire and... what was that. Crying? The tip of my tail twitched. I lost my patience and raised my head fractionally, so I could peer over the fence.

Burned out skeletons that had once been homes. Our beautiful vermillion bridge charred black. Glittering shards of glass lined the roads. Figures I didn't recognise stalked back and forth. Mostly women, some men, all human. An area had been cleared near the middle of the village. Cages. Wooden cages, twisted together in a knot. People huddling inside. Tiny at this distance, but if I concentrated...

Selia, our long suffering doctor, her face tear-tracked and stony. Thadeus Noyer, holding his head in his hands. Dozens, dozens, dozens of others. A growl built deep in my throat. I didn't know what the humans had planned, but I knew how their plans would end.

Lifting my head a little further over the fence, I scanned the streets. Just below me, a human stepped out of the house that had once belonged to the Tolis family. She was whistling, but didn't look up.

"Hey," I said, my voice deep, and humming with barely suppressed fury. The human looked up. The human saw me. The human froze.

I allowed myself a long, long moment of watching the terror track across the human's face. Her mouth moved, silently. She rocked on her heels, causing ripples in the newly formed puddle at her feet. Her breath shuddered in and out of her throat.

I glided ever so slightly closer, "Run," I said, "and never come back."

Her nerve cracked, and broke. She turned and ran, her screams soaring across the village. A murder of crows startled, burst into the air, spotted me, and bolted for the horizon. More screams harmonised with the first.

Slowly, gently, not wanting to damage my village, I eased myself over the fence. Along the street, doors opened and faces I didn't recognise emerged to see what the fuss was about. I ignored them and made for the centre of town, where the cages lay.

Their occupants were yelling and rattling the bars. I kept my distance, and didn't look closely at their faces, not wanting to see the expressions Kyrene had warned me about. Not yet, at least. I turned and saw cowering figures peeking out from behind walls. I rose to my full height, wobbled a little, held out my hands, wobbled some more, then found my balance. "Invaders!" I bellowed, my voice a fog horn in the still air, "This village is under my protection! Leave now, and keep your lives. If you remain here, I cannot guarantee your safety."

Thirty seconds later, every last human was fleeing for the gates. Some had stopped to grab valuables but most had been wise – or as wise as humans can be. I turned, watching them stampede, and only when the last had skittered through the gates, did I lower myself back to the ground. I turned to the cages, and made the mistake of looking at Selia's face.

Fear. Revulsion. Disgust. I'd expected them all, but they still made my vision fuzz and my fists clench. I'd known Selia for years. The last time I'd seen her, she'd been so proud of me. If I fled back into the dark, I'd never have to see people look at me like that again.

I shook my head. That thought was a reflex. I reached down and felt the rough stone paving of Ekzilo's street under my fingertips. I was home. The familiar heavy weight in my chest dragged at me. I wanted to close my eyes, to run and hide. No, I wanted to get better. I wanted to see Teya, Jaeson, Kinta, and Kyrene. I wanted Ekzilo to be safe. I wanted to rest.

I nodded, slowly so as not to startle anyone. I looked again at Selia's twisted, terrified face. I could just let her and the other captives out of the cages, but they'd probably flee, and tell the other survivors of the monster that had nearly feasted on their bones. I needed to calm them down a little first.

I lowered myself to the ground, and backed up a little so there was a comfortable space between me and the cages. "Hi Selia," I sad. "Hi Thadeus. Hi Mamie. Hi Rio and Helena. Hi Savesti and Ritsa. Are any of you hurt?"

Stunned silence, then a torrent of whispers. I waved a hand, slowly but in as friendly a manner as possible. "My name is Melita Eklumigi. I live in Ekzilo. Teya and I fled into the dark when the humans attacked. Long story but… I found this mask and, well, you can see the results. I thought I might be able to drive the humans away."

More whispering. The pace picked up, as did the volume until I could catch snatches as they flew past. "She saved us…" "monster…" "It can't be Melita!" "Ask her!" "Better off with the humans!" "Have you lost it? They were going to throw us in one of their prisons! She drove them off!" "She drove them off?" "She drove them off!"

Eventually, Selia staggered forward. It looked a lot like someone had given her a shove. "Er, will you let us out of the cages? Thank you for driving the humans away, but we'd like to be out now. We'd like that."

I thought about keeping them in the cages so I could explain that I meant them no harm, but I had to trust them. Besides, I had no idea how long they'd been in the cages. I wouldn't keep them inside any longer than I had to.

I nodded to Selia, and plucked the bars from the cages as if they were strands of silk. I then backed up, giving my friends space to emerge. One by one, they stepped out, clearly worried that I was about to snatch them from their feet and drink their souls. I had to focus their attention.

"Somewhere near here, the citizens of Ekzilo who weren't caught are probably hiding. They might be hoping the humans get bored and leave their village, but they might not wait long. It'll be autumn soon. They might go their separate ways, or try to start a new village elsewhere. Who knows how many will make it through the coming winter with such a desperate start?

"Thadeus, your wife's lungs struggle with the cold. Rio, you have a sweetheart, but she might not find another village willing to harbour one of the Stolen. Please, I beg you, go and find those that fled on the night the humans attacked. Tell them that the village is safe. I can protect you. I'd love to protect you, but I know I look a little… intimidating. If you'd rather I not stay, then I can leave."

No-one moved until Selia took a step towards me. "Are you really Melita?"

"I am."

"Prove it. When did I last see you?"

"You patched me up when a trio of humans attacked me. Attacked us."

Thadeus stepped forwards. "Where do you live?"

"Above your wife's restaurant."

Rio stepped forward, then Mamie. They asked question after question. I couldn't answer all of them, and after one particularly difficult question, I found that even though the mask had replaced my face, I was still able to cry.

I'd faced down Cappers and fallen. I'd taken bones from my friends and been through magically crafted hell down in the dark. As I honestly answered every question, trying to fight the suspicion on my friends' faces, my heart beat harder, my throat clenched tighter and my chest twisted tauter than at any moment in the dark.

When the questions dried up, my friends looked at each other, clearly still unsure. There was only one way to convince them I meant them no harm. I had to give them space. I wouldn't return to the dark, not until the village was safe enough for me to risk visiting Teya, but I could wait outside the walls for them to make their decision.

Turning to go, I wondered if I'd made a terrible mistake in taking on the mask. The feeling only lasted a moment. I'd broken those cages and chased away the humans. I'd need to remember that in the nights to come, because I suspected the sight of my terrified friends would haunt me.

"Melita?" said Selia.

I froze, not wanting to turn around. "Yes?

"Can you really stop the humans from coming back? Can you?"

I turned back to my friends, and was only a little sad that they couldn't see my smile. "Selia, look at me. They wouldn't dare come within a kilometre of our walls."

The air was still. Even the crickets seemed to hold their breath. Then, Selia's expression hardened. She turned back to our friends. "You heard Melita. Every moment we delay, the more we risk those who got away getting attacked by predators or striking out by themselves. Rio, take Mamie and Helena. Search the western hills. The rest of us will check likely spots in the forest."

My friends raised their fists and cried acknowledgement. They formed their groups and strode out of the village gates in record time, all except Selia, who hung back. "Sorry, Melita," she said, shifting from foot to foot, "but could you hide a little way from the village? I'll need to explain about you. It may take some time."

I knew it had been too good to be true. Still, I had to trust them. "I'll wait by the entrance to the caves."

Selia bowed, and then ran off after her search party. I waved after them, but none saw. A sigh fell in my wake as I slithered out through the northern gate, and down the thirteen slippery steps to the caves.

I wanted to curl up in the dark and sleep for a couple of years. I let the weight in my chest bear me to the floor. I curled up around myself, and I breathed.

Could I have said something that would have made Selia truly trust me? Tension flicked in my tail, and that made me pause. I wasn't resting - I was dragging myself back into the dark. I uncoiled and rolled onto my back. I stared back at the sky, a soul-invigorating indigo. I sighed, then I sighed again, and then again, each time feeling the tension flow out of me and into the ground.

My magic was gone. With no mouth I had no way to consume bones. I'd performed my final light show. Still, what a show it had been. Dazzling javelins of power crushing Wraiths down in the dark. A dazzling symphony created by me, Teya, and Jaeson.

I'd given up my magic for the mask. Selia and the others would find and re-unite the splinters of Ekzilo because of the mask. The mask was giving me this moment to myself, where I could simply be.

I'd done everything I could. Given everything I had to give. What remained was simply Melita Eklumigi. Not a witch, not a friend, and not a saviour. Just me. Simply me. I sighed once again, and I felt the weight in my chest lift, ever so slightly.

If I let myself rest, I might recover some of my old energy. If I recovered some of my old energy, the mask could forge expeditions between Ekzilo and Tenebro, connecting the two villages for the first time in centuries. Then, once the mask had done its work, it could do something for me. It would take me to one of the great cities, where I would find a doctor. That doctor would be able to help me tackle my Kaskado Disorder.

I'd probably never be entirely free of Kaskado, but if we worked together, we might be able to lift the weight in my chest a little more each day. I may never have the life the Peace Trap had shown me, but that was okay. At least my friends were safe. At least Teya had Kyrene back. Put next to those results, giving up my magic wasn't even a sacrifice. It was the greatest opportunity I'd ever had.

Still, the opportunity would mean nothing if I kept pushing, kept killing myself by centimetres every day. I needed to lie here and accept what remained of myself. I could still shine like the brightest star, even without my magic, but only if I took the time to just *slow down*.

If my friends returned and asked for my help in protecting Ekzilo, I would answer the call, but until that moment, I had to heal. Teya and Kyrene were re-united. Jaeson was safe. Ekzilo was healing. There was nothing more for me to do, except live. I closed my eyes, feeling the soft, soft grass under my hands.

I'd thought the moment the Peace Trap had shown me, where I'd wowed people with my magic had been perfect. It was wonderful to discover just how wrong that was. It turned out perfection was a good deal quieter. And the truly wonderful thing was moments of perfection like this could happen over, and over, and over again.

www.ingramcontent.com/pod-product-compliance
Lightning Source LLC
Chambersburg PA
CBHW050808190726
48285CB00005B/1843